THE BUTCHERS' BLESSING

Published by Tin House, Portland, Oregon

Distributed by W. W. Norton & Company

Library of Congress Cataloging-in-Publication Data

Names: Gilligan, Ruth, author.
Title: The butchers' blessing / Ruth Gilligan.
Description: Portland, Oregon : Tin House, [2020]
Identifiers: LCCN 2020013302 | ISBN 9781947793781 (hardcover) | ISBN 9781947793880 (ebook)
Classification: LCC PR6107.I467 B88 2020 | DDC 823/.92--dc23
LC record available at https://lccn.loc.gov/2020013302

First US Edition 2020
Printed in the USA
Interior design by Jakob Vala

www.tinhouse.com

The Butchers' Blessing

RUTH GILLIGAN

 TIN HOUSE / Portland, Oregon

For my father with his warm heart and his great hat.

And since the war had claimed all eight of her men
She decreed, henceforth, no man could slaughter alone;
Instead, seven others had to be by his side
To stop the memory of her grief from dying too.

—from "The Curse of the Farmer's Widow"

PROLOGUE

New York, January 2018

Even now, twenty-two years since he took the photograph, he still cannot quite believe the lack of blood.

The cold store isn't a big room, maybe twenty by twenty at a push, the wall-tiles riddled with cracks and greenish buds of mould. Below, the floor is a dismal skim of concrete; above, the bulbs' glare is a merciless white; in between, the metal brackets traverse the ceiling, the meat hooks laned empty in their rows.

The lack of windows means it is impossible to tell whether it is night or day outside. It also means the walls are bare, save where a portrait of the Virgin Mary has, inexplicably, been nailed. And apart from Our Blessed Mother, there is only one other person in that dilapidated room.

There is a man, hanging from the ceiling, upside down.

The Butcher is still fully clothed, minus his socks and boots. His overalls are fastened. His pale shirt is neatly tucked. Only the wounds confirm the worst—that he isn't just unconscious; isn't just sleeping the wrong way up like a bat—only the holes in the bridge of his feet where the rusty hook has been pierced through, taking the weight of his body and holding it aloft.

Leaving aside the wounds, there is something almost languid to the flow of the Butcher's limbs. The flesh has been drained of any trace of violence—any trace of how he possibly found himself up there—while the eyes betray no pain as they stare out from beyond death towards the cold-store doorway, where they meet the blinding flash of the camera.

"Jesus Christ."

Ronan steps back from the photograph and trips on a roll of bubble wrap by his feet. Usually his apartment is pristine; today it is a chaos of boxes and gaffer tape. He glances at the clock on the wall. The delivery men will be arriving any minute. He is leaving this one unwrapped until the last possible moment.

Two decades on, there is still no denying the impact *The Butcher* has on him. He has started to accept that, maybe, he will never produce a finer shot; that maybe, despite the awards and the international shows, his peak was right back at the very beginning when he was only a young eejit wandering the Irish borderlands with a second-hand Canon and a baggie full of pills; a determination to find the perfect image that would get his career off the ground at last.

So he supposes it is ego, more than anything, that has finally persuaded him to put this photo on public display. It is good—very good. It deserves to be seen. In the past he always concluded, reluctantly, that showing it just wasn't worth the hassle. There had been rumours around the body—suspicious circumstances and all that—which meant the image would have been treated more like a piece of evidence than a piece of art. But by now the dust has long settled—no one even mentions it any more, the ancient group they called "The

Butchers"—especially not over here in some small museum on the outskirts of Manhattan where every curator looks about half his age and every photograph is accompanied by a brief wall text that reduces the image to its biographical minimum:

The Butcher
by Ronan Monks
(County Monaghan, 1996)

> The man in the photograph is thought to have belonged to a group of ritual cattle slaughterers known as "The Butchers." Composed of eight men, the group travelled the length and breadth of Ireland practising their folkloric customs. However, around the time of the photograph, "The Butchers" disbanded after hundreds of years of service. Today, very little record remains of their ancient, unorthodox traditions.

The buzzer sounds and Ronan startles. He presses the button by the intercom, then hears the delivery men coming up the stairs, their heavy footsteps and easy drawl. It won't take them long to move the pictures; the museum is only a twenty-minute drive across the river. Some of them will probably be half-Irish just like him. All of them will probably expect a tip. But for these final moments the only man that matters is the one in the photograph, his shadow pooled black, his toenails curved white in ten tiny crescent moons.

Ronan slides the metal chain and undoes the latch. This could be a mistake, he thinks; could mean giving up a secret buried safe for twenty-two years.

"Jesus Christ."

He turns the handle and the light comes blinding in.

CHAPTER ONE
Úna

County Cavan, January 1996

Úna had no idea it would be their last farewell dinner. And anyway, she was far too distracted that night by the prospect of a mouse.

Outside, the barren fields lay flattened by the January cold, the kind of chill that got into your bones and under your gums. Frosty vapours rolled in to lend the borderlands a haunted disposition, as if they needed any help in that regard. Beneath the beech trees, a flock of sheep huddled close for warmth, their wool crystallising degree by falling degree, until eventually their fleeces had frozen together to form a single, shivering mass—a terrified creature that might not last the night.

Inside the house it wasn't much better, the cold working its way in quickly through chinks and gaps, and more slowly through the seep of plasterwork damp. But down in the kitchen, the air had been roused to such a glorious swelter it would stave off the worst of the freeze for another hour or two yet.

The feast was almost ready, the pots thuddering on the boil, the oven fan sucking up delicious vapours of its own. In the middle, Úna was setting the table—not just the usual cutlery and plates, but all the fancy accoutrements given the occasion.

There were coasters and placemats, napkins dug up from where they lay buried deep for the rest of the year, their pretty scalloped edges creased and slightly frayed. In the corner of one she spotted a bloom of mould so she tried a rub of spit. It wouldn't budge. She folded the napkin and put it in her place.

On the sideboard, the radio was wavering somewhere between static and the final bars of a Simply Red croon— apparently Mick Hucknall was pure delighted by the very idea of *coming home to you.*

Hearing the words, Úna almost laughed at the irony. Then she thought of the bleating frozen mass outside and this time she laughed outright.

Coming home to ewe.

She was about to share the joke with her mam, who was over by the sink looking dolled up, gorgeous in her earrings and heels. Even though the whole point of the dinner was to celebrate the fact that, for one last night, none of them would be going anywhere.

Her mam, though, seemed too frazzled for jokes, so Úna tucked her mousy hair behind her ears and concentrated on double-checking her arrangement. Or maybe triple-checking was more appropriate since the three place settings were lined up precisely where they belonged. After tomorrow, dinnertimes would only be set for two, the pair of them chattering and chewing away, swapping jokes and silly stories from the day, while secretly both were half thinking of him; half wondering what he had managed to get for his own tea; half hoping he and the other Butchers had found a wayhouse where they could spend the night.

Right now her father was upstairs finishing his packing. He would set out tomorrow at the snap of dawn. If the freeze kept up its belligerence it was bound to be a slippery sort of farewell. He always told her that, apart from the knives, of course, the most important thing was a decent pair of boots. Their feet got annihilated on the road, blisters and bunions and pus weeping in between toes. So this afternoon, Úna had offered to take his pair and buff them up to a conker sheen; had said she could even re-wind his laces. But after he thanked her very much, he explained such tasks were a Butcher's prerogative. Úna had felt a swell of pride and jealousy all at once.

"Right, you can call him—I think we're ready."

Úna looked at her mam. "Don't you mean *Simply Reddy*?" She thought she caught a glimpse of a smile. She sprinted out to the hall—"Dad! Dinner!"—and her voice carried up through the bones of the house. On the way back to the kitchen, she glanced around her before opening the boiler cupboard quickly, just to check. The knuckle of cheese on the mousetrap had frozen a solid white.

Once in place, they closed their eyes and reached out to clasp hands. Úna felt her father's calloused skin, thick and hard like leather. By comparison, hers was still baby-soft. First they gave thanks for their meal and the beautiful bit of meat that sat resting before them. Next they acknowledged the lovely month they had enjoyed the three of them together. Then they prayed for her father's travels tomorrow and the safety of his return; prayed all eight men would make it through another year. They were the usual entreaties, though Úna thought her mam's voice sounded just a bit thinner on them tonight, a hairline crack when she whispered the final word, *Amen*.

The meal began. Plates passed. Wine poured. Spuds skewered. "Have you finished all your Christmas holiday homework?" and "What about New Year's resolutions? Mine's sit-ups every morning—need to stop the old middle-aged spread!" As ever, her father was the full whack of himself, trying to leave an imprint on the kitchen air, a compensation to ensure his presence would linger—as if, somehow, that would be enough.

Úna forced herself to eat slowly, savouring each salty chew in turn. Because on top of everything else, tonight was the last night before their meat-meals were rationed down to once a week. The freezer out in the shed stashed all the properly slaughtered beef which the Butchers carried back each December for Úna and her mam to eke eke eke eleven months. Úna scraped her knife as she pictured it—the flesh-Famine up ahead; her dad's absence at the table. She knew that missing a person could leave your stomach as hollow as hunger.

Plates licked and rinsed, she headed off to change into pyjamas. Outside the boiler cupboard she checked again, then produced the morsel of meat she had snuck into her pocket. As her Christmas gift this year, Úna had asked for a bit of money, then bought the trap down in the village shop on the sly. According to the label, it was one of the new "humane" varieties that worked mainly on balance—no spring loadings or metal decapitations; no poison or jam-thick layers of glue. Instead, the weight of the mouse tipped it over until a plastic door sliced shut behind—no chance of escape, but no blood to it either.

She cupped her hand now and waved it back and forth to help the steak smell waft into the cupboard. She hoped mice liked their beef rare, same as her. She would check the trap again tomorrow, right after her father had raised his leather hand to the morning sky and broken both of their poor hearts.

She was certain she wouldn't sleep, but she must have dozed a bit because a few hours later she awoke with a start. Was it her prey that had woken her, scuttling out for a midnight snack? She strained her ears. The sound wasn't squeaks, but hushed protests.

"Cúch, what if I can't face another year?" Through the darkness, the crack in her mother's voice had turned into a fissure. "You have no idea just how lonely—"

"Ah, Grá, don't be starting all that." Her father's sigh was so heavy, a draught underneath her bedroom door. His next words were woollier. "Grá, you know the rules. If I don't go then the others can't go and then—"

"What if I don't care about the rules any more?" The fissure became a chasm.

Úna shut her eyes as if that would make it stop.

According to the ancient Irish custom, there had to be eight men present at every cattle slaughter; eight different hands touching the animal's hide as it passed from this life to the next. So now eight Butchers spent eleven months of the year calling on the few families around the country who still believed, and killing their beasts in the traditional, curse-abiding way.

Úna's father had been a Butcher her entire life. In those twelve and a quarter years she had never known her gorgeous mother to complain.

"What if I came home?"

She had also never heard this question asked. She opened one eye.

"What do you mean?"

"Halfway round. We're usually over in Monaghan for June." Her father paused, letting the implication take. "I could pop back for a couple of nights. Spend a bit of time with you both."

The pause that followed was the longest yet. Úna opened her second eye and pictured her mother's, the emerald greens piercing the shadows to see if the offer was really true. But Úna had to figure out the answer for herself because no more words arrived, only giggles that eventually turned into moans. It made her tingle beneath her pyjamas in embarrassment, but it was nice, she told herself, natural. If anything, it was a bit like animals.

The dawn was barely cracked when the time came for departure. Her father would walk to a crossroads about a mile down the road where the others would be waiting with the horses and carts. Sometimes her mother, for a mess, suggested the Butchers should drive; should invest in a minivan. *They say Ireland's getting more "modern" by the day—why not keep up with the times?* Úna knew better than to laugh at that joke. Nothing about the old ritual was allowed to change.

Her mother hovered next to her now on the front step, the pair of them sheathed in their dressing-gown furs. The air outside was well below freezing, making white of their good-bye breaths.

"You're a gorgeous girl," her father croaked as he leaned down for a kiss.

It took all her strength not to beg him to stay. But she had to remember that at least this year it wouldn't be so bad, because this year there was a secret plan that meant she would see him again in June. Plus, she had been making her own secret plans for while he was away.

When she got inside, she would check the mousetrap again.

The Butcher embraced his wife one last time, then ambled slowly out the gate. He looked so giant as he moved—big enough to be a myth himself. The fields around were raw with silence, the hillsides stony-pocked and sparse. It was a wonder anything would ever grow again.

And Úna was so distracted she almost forgot.

"Love, your shoe?"

But as soon as her mother spoke, she took her slipper from her foot and flung it hard; watched it arc through the air, then land in the shimmering frost. It was another custom meant to wish him luck on his travels. Her father didn't turn, only removed his hand from the pocket of his overalls and raised it high in acknowledgement.

Úna stayed out on the doorstep watching, her left foot slowly going numb, until she saw the manshape blacken, then shrink, then disappear. Eventually her whitebreath faded too as the moon bowed out and the sun arrived instead, hurling itself cold and radiant into the morning sky.

They returned to bed for comfort, Úna tucking herself in next to her mam, but soon enough they were up again and dressed, counting down to ten o'clock when the next stage of the ritual could commence. They always visited Mrs. P on the morning of farewell—without any children of her own, the departure of her husband, Sol, meant she was left all alone.

Even though it wasn't long since breakfast, Úna knew the old lady would lay on some treats for the occasion, a bit of sugar to try to take the edge off the pain of the day. Sure enough, as soon as they arrived a tray of biscuits was produced, a full Jacob's selection pack left over from the festive period. Úna opted for a custard cream, her tongue licking ruts through the butter icing, and listened as the women launched into their annual natter, word for word the same if she wasn't mistaken.

"Did he get off all right?"

"Bitter enough, the weather."

"They'll be Leitrim-bound tonight."

As she watched the pair, she conceded they were a pretty un-likely match. With her grey hair and cardies, Mrs. P looked old enough to be her mother's mother, which Úna supposed made her the granddaughter down the line. She had asked before about the other Butchers and why they didn't have wives as well, but apparently some of them did—there were two over in Clifden, two not far from Donegal. Apparently they tended to be clustered in pairs for this very reason—so the women could keep one another company while they were left behind for the guts of the year.

"I don't know why, but I found this time so much harder."

Her mother's confession, though, wasn't part of the usual script. There was a weariness to the voice Úna barely recognised. And it didn't even make sense, given the promise that had been made last night.

I could pop back.

Spend a bit of time with you both.

The thought alone was sugar to Úna's teeth.

"Grá, I know it's difficult," Mrs. P assured. "I've been saying goodbye to Sol for almost fifty years . . ." Then she tried to help by changing the subject. "And what about all this stuff on the news about the BSE? I presume you've heard the latest—they're saying the mad cow disease might be back."

Úna swallowed her biscuit and chewed over the strange words. *Mad cow disease.* She hadn't heard the earliest, let alone the latest.

Her mother was silent. "I read something, all right," she eventually replied. "But they say it's only over in England. Irish cows are safe—it's got nothing to do with us."

"But what if it spreads?" Mrs. P persisted. "What if Ireland's farms get contaminated too? What if—"

"Just because we're feeling maudlin this morning, let's not go *looking* for things to fret about."

This time it was the sting in her mother's voice that Úna didn't recognise. She saw the old woman flinch, biscuit crumbs spilling from her lips to her lap. They soon moved on to discussing a new recipe for soda bread, the various superstitions around this being a leap year; but the goodbyes definitely came a little earlier than usual. On her way out, Úna slipped a pair of Bourbons into her pocket. She realised her mam hadn't eaten a thing.

That night, Úna waited in her own room before she crept out across the landing. When she showed up at her parents' bed, she found her mam lying there wide awake. The duvet was lifted without hesitation; Úna slipped in against the thin and anxious frame. Before they dropped off, they each placed eight fingertips on to one another's skin. It was a secret ritual they had whenever one of them wasn't feeling right; an ancient tradition to banish all worries and flinches and stings.

•

The following week, it was time to say goodbye to the Christmas holidays too, which meant that Úna was back to the early starts. The world was still black when she set out, the roads glazed silver with the aftermath of last night's freeze. She noticed wee prints divoted in the dirt and thought of the fox she sometimes saw in their back garden. Would there be a fresh litter of cubs this year? She considered the question as she buried her hands in her pockets and walked faster, trying to outrun the cold.

The school corridors, by contrast, were baking, the ancient radiators making the strangest noises, though the din from Úna's classmates was soon so loud it drowned out everything else. Details of festive feasts and present hauls were swapped back and forth all morning until a winner was officially declared—Peadar Noonan with a Super Nintendo! The younger ones boasted about stacks of Pogs and shiny Premier League stickers, while the older gang went in for strawberry lip-glosses and Michael Jackson CDs.

Úna wandered from class to class, yanking down the jumper that kept rising up over her midriff. She was going to need a new one soon. Though really, it was a waste of money since the uniform didn't even serve its purpose—she still stood out a mile. The weirdo. The first-year freak.

The Butcher's daughter.

Sometimes it was just funny looks she got, whispers wafting up through the class like a bad smell. Other times the girls would scream when she brushed against them, claiming she had cursed them under her breath. Once, the boys had circled around her, pawing at the tarmac with their shoes, their fingers horns on the side of their heads. Mrs. Donoghue had shown up just before they charged.

At first Úna had been confused—hadn't her father always told her how important the Butchers were? How integral a role they played in Ireland's history? So if anything, when her parents decided to stop her home schooling and send her to secondary school, she had thought her new classmates would all be dying to be her friend—angling for invites to Sunday tea to taste her family's meat and hear their stories. But when the reality had set in, Úna asked her mam why everyone seemed to hate her, and her mam could only garble some excuse about her being "special." "And 'special' isn't always easy to understand, love, so instead people just push it away."

"Howdy, cowgirl," someone called now from the end of the corridor. "What did Santa bring *you*?"

"Ugh, she probably still believes in him, too."

"Yeehaw!"

"Or maybe her lot would rather slit poor Rudolph's neck?"

Úna turned from the laughter—she was used to it by now; didn't let it upset her. Instead, she distracted herself by trying to guess what her mam might have put in her lunchbox today. She hoped it was tomato and mustard sandwiches, her favourite kind. Sometimes it was so spicy it hurt, and sometimes that was good.

•

After another week, though, Christmas was long forgotten and a fresh distraction had taken hold, because down in the village there had been a new arrival. It was a McDonald's—the very first in the county—and everyone seemed elated by the news; famished, yes, but also proud as punches that their little corner of countryside muck had been deemed worthy of such a place. The school corridors thrummed with chat about juicy "Big Macs" made out of giant American cows; about ice creams drizzled with caramel sauce. For only a couple of quid you could get a box called a "Happy Meal," although Úna doubted cheap American meat could make anyone particularly happy.

The teachers tried to remind the students they weren't actually *allowed* to leave the school grounds for lunch, but suddenly every afternoon the yard was strewn with wrappers bearing the gaudy yellow *M*s. One Tuesday, Úna was wandering behind the prefabs when she saw Mrs. Donoghue and Mr. Feary huddled together sharing a greasy hamburger and a cigarette.

Of course, Úna wasn't able to find out for herself what all the fuss was about. If you believed in the Butchers you weren't allowed to eat from places like that—shudder to think how their poor cattle had been killed. Instead, she sat in the corner of the playground and took a bite from her sandwich. Today it was cucumber and cheese—not her favourite combination, but it was better than the mashed-up turnip her mother sometimes tried when everything else was out of season.

As she swallowed, Úna thought of her father. The Butchers would be reaching Tobercurry some time this afternoon (she had learned the ancient route off by heart and back again; had pinned a knackered map on her bedroom wall). There they would visit a farmer named Francine Duff who always got them to slaughter half a dozen shorthorns, then skin and bleed them from half a dozen hooks. Afterwards, Francine Duff would divvy up the cuts of meat between the other families in the area who still believed. Sometimes he let the Butchers sleep in his barn. Sometimes he stood them a pint in the local pub. For whatever reason, in the last couple of years, neither offer had come.

There were about five hundred across the country who still followed the traditional ways; who still chose to heed the ancient curse of the Farmer's Widow. As for the rest, apparently it was just easier to let the thing die out, Ireland leaving the past behind and finally catching up with the rest of the world. But the way Úna thought about it, without folklore and traditions, surely Ireland didn't really exist? Surely it might as well just be England or France or anywhere else (give or take an endless soak of rain)? So just as there were those who preserved the country's mother tongue and those who saved up all the country's native stories, there were those like her father who devoted their lives to maintaining the country's old beliefs.

Úna closed her eyes and let the swell of pride rise up. Then she let the secret promise rise up too. Because she had made a vow that as soon as she finished school and became an adult, she was going to devote her life to those old beliefs too.

She hadn't told anyone—not even her mam—about her plan to become a Butcher. She knew she was still too young (even if she would be a teenager soon; even if she was sprouting new bits by the day). But most of all, she knew she should wait until she had proven herself and shown she could perform a slaughter in the proper way. Of course, to perform a slaughter you needed an animal—how else could you practise for real?—and still the mousetrap was empty every time she checked.

Eventually the afternoon bell thundered out. They had Civics next, which meant talking about the Troubles across the border. According to Mrs. Donoghue, the violence was nearly over. There was something called a "rally" next month for peace. Úna swallowed the last bite of her sandwich, wiped her mouth, and chucked the fist of tinfoil in the bin. As she passed it, she noticed a cardboard burger box poking out with a rim of brown grease. She checked around. No one was looking in her direction, too busy fussing towards the doors, except for the magpie who was perched black-blue and greedy on the fence. She swallowed again as she weighed up the thought. A single magpie. One for sorrow, wasn't it? Or were the Butchers allowed to believe in sayings like that?

Úna held her breath and reached her fingers inside the box until they encountered the oily remains of a chip. She shoved it into her pocket and ran for her next class. As she hurried past a giant poster in Irish—*Lá Fhéile Bríde*—she also wondered, since there were mother tongues, did that mean that there were father tongues too? And if so, which was easier for an almost-teenage daughter to learn?

When she arrived home that afternoon, Úna placed the chip in the trap and said a prayer to the Farmer's Widow. She raised her fingers to her nose, inhaled the salt and grease—just once—before she went to the bathroom and scrubbed them clean and sore.

She sat on her bed and made a start on her homework. In honour of St. Brigid's Day they had been asked to do a project on the patron saint. Apparently she had set up loads of communes around Ireland where religious women lived together without any men. Úna thought again of the Butchers' wives scattered all over the place and wondered if they should form a commune of their own? Although, were eight people even enough for a commune or did you technically need more?

At half past five she went downstairs to help wash and prepare the vegetables for the evening's stew. She asked her mam their usual dinnertime joke—"What's the special on the menu tonight?"—and waited for the usual reply:

You're the special, love!

But for whatever reason her mam must not have heard.

Úna watched her all through the meal and saw she barely ate a bite. True, the concoction wasn't very tasty—her mam had forgotten to add seasoning—but Úna knew that wasn't the reason. Her mam was never very hungry when she was in one of her sad moods. Úna already knew she would be served her mother's untouched portion, cold and slightly congealed, for dinner tomorrow night.

Úna went to bed worried. She lay there for hours unable to sleep. She tried counting sheep and then she tried magpies, but if one was for sorrow she couldn't remember what eight were supposed to be for.

In the morning, though, things had changed. Úna checked the cupboard on her way to breakfast and saw that a pink tail was waiting. She flicked open the trap and the mouse squeaked "hello" and instantly she felt very special indeed.

All day at school, she could think of nothing else. They submitted their projects and Car McGrath said Brigid was probably a *lesbian* and everyone sniggered. Úna stared at the clock on the wall, counting minutes instead of animals or birds.

Finally the day had crawled to an end and she was back in her bedroom with the door firmly locked. She surveyed her scene, seven Lego men arranged in a circle around the beast. It had taken her over an hour to get it right. To someone else it might have looked like she was playing a game of "zoo"—like a group of visitors had come to stare at some endangered animal. But this wasn't a zoo and it certainly wasn't a game. No, this was something other.

The animal's squeaks were high-pitched, nasal, almost as if Úna had put a strip of gaffer tape over its mouth as well as across its body. It was pinned tightly to the wooden floorboard. She only hoped the fur wouldn't dull the stick. The set-up was nearly there, though there was no denying the proportions were a little off. The Lego figures were the problem, their arms so short they had to be stood right up close to reach. Because they all had to be touching the animal when it died—seven yellow hands and Úna's the eighth, shaking eager by the head. That was the tradition. That was what her father had told her. That was everything.

She took out the knife—it was a paring blade she had filched from the kitchen drawer that afternoon. She held it up to the light and, as the ritual decreed, turned it three times towards her heart. The mouse began to struggle, which made Úna wonder if that meant animals knew about knives, their slashing and their cutting, and if so, what else about humans did they secretly understand? That her father was one of the Butchers? That it was February now, which meant he and the other men would be heading west? That it was crucial Úna got this right if she was ever going to prove she was special enough to join the group too?

Still the claws scrambled for traction on the floorboards. She smoothed down the tape and felt the nano-pump of the mouse's heart. Next she brought the blade to its neck, the tip parting the fluff to reveal a triangle of pink skin, no different from a human's, she supposed. Úna felt the pump of her own heart too, but she had to keep calm, to make her movements fluid, just one single slit to let the blood out. She closed her eyes and tried to picture her father doing it with the cows, but when she reached for him all she could feel was the goodbye kiss that was already starting to fade; the ache that wouldn't pass no matter how many times she traced his route on the map; the sense that—

"Úna?"

The tape ripped free and her eyes opened just in time to see the tail disappear beneath the bed. Úna lunged for it, falling heavily, crashing her nose flat to the floor. She missed.

"Úna? Special delivery!" her mam called through the door.

She lifted her face and checked behind where her fellow Butchers still stood, their expressions gleeful and unchanged.

The door opened. "Úna, love, is everything OK?"

When she rolled over, her mother was standing above her, concern in her voice and something hidden behind her back. Úna sat up, making sure the knife was covered. "I was just playing." Instantly she regretted how childish it sounded.

Her mam's smile didn't seem convinced. "Well, like I said—special delivery." She took a step back. "What I mean is, love, I bought you a present."

It was Úna's turn to look unconvinced—it was still nine months until her thirteenth birthday and she couldn't recall a present ever being plucked out of thin air. Úna knew it was to do with money—their house had come from her father's dead parents and their savings from her mother's dead parents, but after that there was barely any going spare. Úna always wondered how families managed when the parents' parents were still alive.

She wondered if there was such a thing as a grandmother tongue.

"Ta dah!"

But her wondering was swiped aside now for the big reveal. The uniform looked almost glamorous on its plastic hanger, a tag from the second-hand shop that said it was officially teenager-sized.

Her mam renewed her smile as best she could. "I noticed you had grown a bit big for your old one, so I went into town today. I'm sorry it's taken me so long, but I've just . . . Recently I've been feeling a bit . . ."

As the sentence stopped, the smile did too. Úna wished it would continue; wished her mother would explain what exactly she had been feeling.

"And I know we're not due for a couple of weeks, but I thought we could do haircuts tonight, if you liked? Complete your lovely new look?"

Úna felt the cold blade beneath her thigh. Behind her, the Lego faces seemed jeering now, mocking the awkward scene. "I think . . ." she stumbled over the lie. "I might try growing it out for a change." She knew her mam would see right through it—she had never refused a haircut session in her life. It was another ritual they had, sharp teeth combed across wet scalps; strands slowly snipped away until their heads—their whole beings—felt lighter again.

Her mam, though, only sighed. "Never mind, love." On her way out she hooked the uniform on the back of the door, which made it look a bit like a hanging body. Úna traced the pleats with her eyes, then felt guilty and glanced away, so it was only by accident that she noticed the blood. There wasn't much—only a tiny pool on the floor she could blot with her sock—but she supposed it was a start at least.

She gathered the Lego men back into their box and shoved it under her bed. She promised she would try again very soon. That way she could make a case to her father when he came back in June.

She promised she would find a way to fix her mother's gorgeous smile.

She promised she would become a Butcher yet.

CHAPTER TWO
Grá

County Cavan, March 1996

First she undid the button on her skirt and sashayed her hips to make it fall, then she took off her cotton underwear and threw it in the laundry bin. She dipped her hand to check the temperature. She wanted it even hotter and deeper than usual. A little indulgence, given it was a special occasion.

Grá held her breath.

Forty-one years old today.

The number still sounded like a mistake.

As she waited, she stole a glance at the mirror. She knew she had gotten thin. Her eyes always shone greener directly after she woke, even if she had barely slept the night before. And the more the reflection fogged, the more another face began to rise up from her memory—one she wasn't meant to think or talk about. Birthdays always had a habit of bringing it back. Grá supposed it was another, crueller kind of indulgence.

After the taps, the silence was so loud it took a moment to adjust. Grá held her breath and lowered herself in, watching her paleness coming out in blotches. She began with the soap, creaming suds along her clavicle, a waft of rose petals, old-world-smelling and sweet. Her hand went lower over ramps of ribs, down until the pine-needle trail of hairs began. She knew she was alone, so if she wanted to keep going she could. Úna was at school and her husband . . . her husband . . . But there wasn't so much as a tingle for it, her body far too tense. She worked up another lather and moved on to her calves.

As always, they had made love on Cúch's last night, but this year neither her heart nor her body had quite been in it. She knew she should have been cheered by his offer.

I could pop back.

Spend a bit of time with you both.

God knows she had been praying for something like it for years.

And yet, the more she replayed his words, the more a tiny part of her had felt pathetic—to be grateful for just a scrap of her husband's company? Was that really the kind of woman she had become? She had waited for Cúch to finish, then had rolled herself away.

So now she reached her fingers back beneath the surface and reminded herself that she didn't need him—not really—because after all, she was the one who knew her body best. She felt the water lapping her skin like a tongue, washing away the loneliness and the middle age and the rising sense of unease.

She jolted at the doorbell as if she had been caught outright. She released her fingers and pulled the plug. The water sucked away as if down a throat as she stood, her hair wet against her shoulders, Venus from a half-cracked shell.

"Happy birthday!" Mrs. P faltered as she took in the robe. "I'm sorry," she said. "I didn't realise you'd be—"

"Not a bother."

"I brought you a few bits."

"You shouldn't have."

They retreated to the kitchen where Mrs. P set down her load—a giant cake with an icing quiff, a silver envelope sealed with a tongue of spit, and a copy of today's *Anglo-Celt*.

Just as the older woman had predicted, the BSE had started to make all of the daily headlines. It seemed it really was true—the English cows were going mad again. But this time there was something more to it, because apparently there was a chance now the English people could catch it too. *Mad human disease.* Grá shuddered as she filled the kettle and picked out the mugs with the fewest chips.

"The scientists are still trying to prove the link." Mrs. P gestured towards the front page as she creaked down into her seat. "But if it's true, the rest of Europe might ban British beef altogether. It's a bit terrifying when you think about it, but I suppose it could be good news for the farmers over here. Picking up all the slack, you know?"

Grá spooned the leaves into the pot. Her head was still light from the heat of the bath, or maybe it was because she wasn't sure when she had last eaten. She wished, just for today, they could talk about anything other than men and cows.

"And did you hear about *Fair City*?" Mrs. P must have read her mind. "Apparently in Monday's episode two fellas are going to kiss! I know it's technically not illegal any more, but the complaints have been pouring in."

Grá opened the fridge and let the cool of it pour out.

Once the leaves had been dregged twice over, Mrs. P set off and Grá was alone again. They hadn't even touched the cake— it seemed far too pretty, somehow, to spoil. Grá noticed she had forgotten the card as well, so now she picked it up. *Happy Birthday Grá*, it read. *I will always cherish our strange sisterhood.*

Grá tried to steady her hand. She knew Mrs. P meant nothing but kindness by the words; knew she hadn't a clue of the nerve they would touch or the woman who had already been lurking on Grá's mind today. Eventually she made for the drawer to cut herself a slice of cake, but for some reason she couldn't see the knife she needed. It wasn't the first time recently she had found things out of place.

"Where are the candles?"

When Úna returned from school, Grá was still leafing her way through the *Anglo-Celt*. Most of the articles were about the peace talks in the North; about the six "Mitchell principles" for negotiating they had managed to agree upon. But the article she was reading now was about something different— Eoin Goldsmith or "The Bull" as he had come to be known. The photo was of him from Sunday's St Patrick's Day parade, a clump of shamrock adorning his lapel. Apparently Goldsmith basically ran the Irish meat industry—a small-town boy turned millionaire beef baron. Apparently he also had a mansion with a heated swimming pool. Grá imagined his beloved cows joining him for a splash.

"Mam?"

She looked up to find her daughter.

"The birthday candles. Where are they?"

It took a moment, then she remembered all over again.

Forty-one years old today.

She forced a smile. "There would be far too many of them to fit on one cake." She put down the paper. "Now tell me, love, how was school?"

"Well, we had History," Úna started, easily distracted. "We finally got our projects on St. Brigid back. Only, Car McGrath did his wrong, so instead of the patron saint he did some weird *pagan* woman who was also called Brigid and who supposedly lived around here too."

This time, Grá's smile came a bit more easily. She suspected they were probably the very same woman. She knew the way traditions and myths all evolved into one.

"And I made you this in Art." Her daughter produced a tattered card from her bag with three faces drawn across the front.

Grá saw that the greenest pencil had been used for her eyes. The shading was surprisingly good. "It's beautiful." She placed it on the table next to Mrs. P's. Side by side, the pair looked a little pitiful. She thought how you could tell a lot from birthday cards; could know how many or few people made up a single life.

When they first moved into the house, the local women had all popped by to pay her a visit, some even bearing home-made cakes of their own.

"I've heard about your kind, all right."

"I had a cousin who used to believe."

"And tell me, is it true one of you gave birth to a creature that was part child, part cow?"

Grá had laughed at that—the way myths of myths evolve as well.

But after a while, the women's visits had dried up—she was almost a disappointment once they realised her normality—far too strange to be welcome, far too dull to be news. Either way, she was to be left well alone.

Grá swallowed and reconsidered the phrase. *Un-well alone.*

"I've got homework." As ever, though, it was Úna who managed to bring her back from the edge. "And, Mam, can you age a steak for forty-one years? Or would it end up getting all wrinkly like you?"

"Go away out of that!" Grá laughed as her daughter scampered up the stairs.

In the fresh fall of silence, Grá felt a wave of gratitude towards her child. They were a perfect team—the two of them against the rest of the world. She knew the years of home schooling had been for both their benefits, really—it had given some purpose to Grá's days, just as it had given Úna a chance to grow into herself a bit before she was exposed to the other kids' inevitable cruelty. Of course, Grá knew it would have been best of all if they could have given Úna a sibling—a proper teammate of a similar age. Though Úna always insisted she preferred it this way.

Mam, I'm an only child just like you!

Surely that makes me more special?

Grá stood up now and glanced at the clock as if she would find the answers there. She reminded herself to check on the T-bones that were defrosting in the utility-room sink for tonight's birthday treat. And she reminded herself, of course, that having a sibling didn't guarantee anything.

I will always cherish our strange sisterhood.

Grá was only sixteen when her sister Lena had run away
to marry a non-believer; sixteen years and a single happy day.
So they had shared one last birthday cake between them, then
by morning Lena had vanished, nothing but an envelope with
Grá's name on the front underlined. Of course, she had told
Grá about the handsome man from Ulster who was down visiting his uncle's farm; had even invited Grá to leave with them
too, saying things about their parents being "stifling" and
"stuck in the past." But the shock was still total as Grá stared at
the unopened letter while her mam and dad called the police,
alleging discrimination when no assistance seemed to arrive.

That night, Grá set the letter alight with a match and regretted it just too late. Her sister had never sent another word.

From then on, Lena's name was not to be spoken in the house,
which meant most of the past was out of bounds too—a jagged
borderline drawn between "before" and "after." Lena's bedroom
was cleared, her twenty-one years as a family member erased in a
single night—her Hollywood film collection binned, her wardrobe and its moths all emptied out. Grá begged her parents to
let her keep the clothes—it was such a waste—she would grow
into them eventually. But there was some part of her parents that
seemed to believe that would mean her growing into the same
kind of woman. The black sacks were hauled to the dump where
the crows could peck out the buttons as if they were eyes.

Within three years, their mother passed away. Their father
blamed a betrayed and broken heart. He had grown frail himself, though he still managed to chastise Grá almost daily for
not finding a boyfriend of her own—one daughter a deserter

and the other left up on the shelf? It was hard to tell which was the bigger disgrace. But it wasn't like Grá could just go along to the local hop and hope the lad who asked her to dance was also a believer; could just take her chances while she hovered around the dented cups of lemonade. Plus, ever since Lena's departure, some of the other locals who still welcomed the Butchers had turned their back on them too—as if a fresh curse had been placed on the family name. That summer, her dad set her up with a lad who helped out with the mucking, Donal Heffernan, whose mother's people used to believe. They were on a walk to the village fair when he took her behind McGinley's fields and tried to shove his hand down her knickers.

"Don't be such a prude," he had snarled and tried again. "It's not like you're a fucking *Catholic*."

Grá had pushed him away and run, thinking of all the different names we give to each other and to ourselves:

Catholic.

Protestant.

Believer.

Prude.

When she made it home she announced she would definitely not be seeing Donal Heffernan again and her father punched the wall. The fist didn't seem frail in the slightest.

But that night, Grá had thought of Lena—probably off in some big city; probably watching some Hollywood flick with her Ulster man—and she didn't feel angry or ashamed any more. Instead, she lay awake until dawn feeling nothing but envy and admiration for the freedom her sister had managed to find.

It was another six months before the Butchers came to pay their annual visit. Usually they killed half a dozen beasts, then popped inside for a pot of tea. This time, while her father fawned over the men as if they were gods themselves, the youngest of the Butchers—only recently joined, apparently—caught her eye and gave her a smile. And Grá didn't know why she hadn't thought of it before—the way that she could make everything right—so that afternoon she made a choice and gave the new Butcher a smile back.

They wrote to one another for a whole year, her replies sent to the post office of whatever village was next on their route. She learned the words and jokes Cúch liked the best. She sometimes liked his jokes too. She made sure never to mention her older sister or the humiliation she had brought on the family. She tried not to think of the letter she had burned all those years ago.

For some reason when the Butchers returned for their next visit, Cúch seemed nervous to ask her father for her hand. But as soon as he did, the old man fell hushed like he had just received the ultimate benediction. He didn't say anything, but the tears softening the crust in his eyes were enough.

The day they married really was the best of her life, because finally she had done it—had paid for her sister's escape—the only person she had ever truly loved. As she walked down the aisle, the flowers in her hair stained the tips of her ears yellow with pollen. She had laughed when Cúch had licked his finger and rubbed it away.

But soon that laughter had disappeared. Cúch had inherited a house in the deserted borderlands of County Cavan. *An*

Cabhán. In Irish it meant, roughly, "the hollow." He returned to the road and Grá stared out at the hollowness with nothing to do except think of her beloved Lena and wonder what would have happened if she had let Donal Heffernan shove everything inside her that sunny afternoon.

•

"Just a small slice, *please?*"

The following morning it wasn't her birthday any more and somehow that made things easier again. She had forgotten to put the cake in the fridge so the icing had turned cracked and hard overnight.

"Come on—I *always* have sandwiches. I'm *desperate* for a change."

Grá looked at her daughter, laying on the theatricals in her brand-new uniform. "Go on then, just a small one." She opened the drawer. The knife was right where it always was.

Once Úna had departed, Grá switched on the radio to a channel where the voices weren't theatrical but sombre and low. They were discussing the latest developments to do with the BSE that was spreading all over England. One expert said if the human link was confirmed it could be a total disaster. Tens of thousands of deaths—a full-blown national plague.

Grá's stomach gave a growl, but she had got better recently at ignoring it. Next the expert moved on to all the precautionary measures Ireland was taking to keep the disease at bay. It was important to do things independently; to set themselves apart from England's mess. Grá listened until the report was finished, fetched her jumper and gloves, then slipped out into the chill air of the garden.

There had been rain overnight, but for now the sky was taking a few moments to catch its breath. The grass was a perfect slice of neatness, especially compared to the wildness that spooled away beyond the fence. But this cut of earth was Grá's and Grá's alone, so she kept it pristine, manicured, an entire lifetime of loyalty and care and boredom.

The snowdrops were still in bloom, their heads dripping white from thin and delicate necks. The bluebells were holding out a little longer. She checked the beds for daisies or dandelions. She tipped some nuts into the feeder, which was meant for the thrushes, not the fox, though Grá had more than a soft spot for them both. Next she was down on her hands and knees with a trowel, working the darker, denser earth. She had planted the vegetables in meticulous rows; had fertilised and turned the land around. It was pride as much as practicality— Cúch worked hard to provide their special Sunday meals, but every other day of the week, the dinner was down to her.

She had sown beans and courgettes; parsnips and potatoes. For a change she had decided to try the sweeter variety. From what her fingertips could make out, the roots had taken well enough.

Years ago, she had responded to a notice in the greengrocer's window looking for a couple of hours' help a week. When she went in to enquire about the role, the woman hissed at her that it had already been filled. Another time, Grá had put a sign on a lamppost advertising gardening skills at a competitive rate. The phone had sat silent for weeks until a newcomer to the village, Mrs. Casey, called. Grá had done a couple of shifts, mostly pruning back the roses planted by the previous owner, when Mrs. Casey came home one afternoon with her shopping and said in a low, cold voice: *You never told me you were married to a Butcher.* Grá had left in such a rush she had forgotten to take her clippers. She had never had the heart to go asking for them back.

When she was finished she stood up, straining backwards to ease the ache at the base of her spine. She wondered if she had turned into an old woman yesterday after all. She pulled off her gloves and boots, went inside and up to the bathroom where she stared down at the empty tub, but for whatever reason the prospect of it didn't hold the usual appeal. She rolled her eyes. She didn't know what was wrong with her at the moment. What if she just never had the heart again? But then she thought of Úna's dramatics this morning and she managed a smile.

I'm desperate *for a change.*

She grabbed a towel from the rail and took the stairs two at a time.

The land was a windsweep of grey and brown and for a second Grá was tempted to turn back. What the hell was she thinking? There could be no comfort here. But when she looked a little closer, she saw cowslip and cinquefoil; sheep's sorrel and even early dog violet, the petals a paler purple than the later, sweeter kind. Of course, they were technically weeds—in her own garden she would have ripped them merciless from the roots—but out here there was a different set of rules. Something about their colour, their wildness, resonated with her, even if she was aware her spontaneous outing was as much to do with being pushed as being pulled.

Eventually she found her way to the Mass path, the ancient rut barely visible through the grass, but it was the quickest route she knew to the nearest lake. They said there were 365 bodies of water all across the county—one for every damp day of the year. The number felt far too convenient to be the truth. She knew there was Lough Sheelin, or "the Lake of the Fairy Pool," down by the Westmeath border; there was Lough Gowna or "the Calf Lake," which was somewhere over Longford way. Local folklore said it had been named after the legend of a supernatural cow. Grá scoffed at the thought—bloody cattle everywhere she turned. And yet, these days you heard less and less about those ancient superstitions, all the old tales cast aside for future progress.

Modern Ireland.

That was the only narrative the locals were interested in now.

Who needs Cúchulann when you've got the Bull, hey?

Grá felt her stomach nagging again. The gorse in the next field smelled oddly sweet, like coconut. She sucked in the air. Maybe she should have had a bit of breakfast after all.

And maybe she should have known better, but she assumed that yesterday's rumination about her sister would have passed by this morning—the annual remembrance over and done with for another year. Whereas even out here in the open where the wind slapped her face and streaks of muck flicked up her calves, she could feel her sister's presence with her still.

Grá always assumed Lena had escaped to one of the big cities like Cork or even Dublin, where she lived in some modern apartment with concrete views and an endless stream of flashing lights. Grá had read about the bridge over the River Liffey where the government had just built the Millennium Clock, the digits projected on to the water, counting down to the twenty-first century. Oh, Modern Ireland was coming, all right, and it was going to be on time.

When Grá arrived at the clearing beside the lake, she stopped short at the view. Even her stomach went quiet. The water stretched out flat and still and vast—the opposite bank was a thin green line that seemed very far away. The only things projected on to the surface were the slant shapes of the clouds. Everything in between was space for her to breathe.

She might have expected a fisherman or a fellow stroller, but the place was truly deserted. Even the tourists didn't bother with places like this—they only wanted Ireland's lush and picture-perfect greens. In its own way, the emptiness made her feel a bit exposed. She thought of "Camera Mountain" on the Armagh border—the hill with all the watchtowers during the peak of the Troubles. She wondered if the privacy of the bathroom wasn't such a bad thing after all.

But thinking of the house only spurred her again. She crouched low into a clump of bog rush and stripped her layers away. She knew at this time of year, in only bra and knickers, there was no point trying to ease herself in. So instead she edged to the lip of the embankment and leapt—breath held—plunging beneath the water, where the cold was sharp as a million little knives; but she willed them to stab and stab, to cut to shreds whatever fug, whatever unease, had been blanketing her of late. She promised when she broke the surface again she would be renewed.

It was afterwards, while she was getting dressed, that she saw him on the rock. At first she thought the movement was just a bird—a heron or a grebe—though surely it was too early yet for them? Then there was the giant eye that confused her further, but when he lowered the camera the whole of him just about made sense. She fixed the button on her jeans and slipped her feet into her boots.

She hadn't been doing anything wrong and yet she felt, once again, as if she had been caught outright. She wondered how far his lens could zoom in; wondered if he could see her nipples poking out beneath her gardening gear. But then the wonder turned into a kind of rage, because what was he—some sort of pervert? Lurking here in the back of beyond, preying on whatever poor unfortunate creature he happened across?

"Excuse me?" The wind was up now and it was against her, making tendrils of her dripping hair. "Excuse me, you can't just go taking photos of people without their permission." She didn't quite recognise the sound of her voice, nor the formality of her words. "You know I could report you to the Gardaí?"

It was only when she was much closer that she felt her anger teetering. His hair was fair. His face was young. His sunglasses were perched on his head even though the sky above was still dark with clouds.

"I didn't mean to startle you."

When he spoke for the first time she frowned, resenting the implication that he had done anything to her at all.

"I promise I'm only interested in the landscape."

The second time she felt something closer to offence.

"Stunning, isn't it?"

It was his accent she noticed next—probably Dublin if she had to guess—but instead of asking, she followed his gaze towards the high bog where the conifers stood in formation, their roots living off the rot and bones of whatever had been swallowed there. "What are you, some kind of *naturist*?" She did her best to sound contrary. "Up from the big smoke to get your fix. Or are you—"

"A naturist?" He took a step forward from the rock, a hint of a smirk on his lips. "In this weather? You'd freeze! No, I'm a photographer," he said. "Ronan Monks. Doing a project on the borderlands."

She didn't acknowledge his joke, only focused on his name, which made her think of holy men in habits. She wondered— of all things—whether this stranger was a man of faith.

"Or at least, I'm trying to."

But when she focused back on his face, the smirk had already vanished.

"I've been out here all week," he said, "but my shots have been mostly rubbish. I don't suppose you have any suggestions?"

And for whatever reason, the question made Grá suddenly think, not of her long-lost sister or her precious daughter, but of her husband. A man of certainty, of absolutes. He had never asked her for a suggestion in his life. "Well, I'm afraid, Mr. Monks, I've no time to be playing *tour guide*." She hurried her arms over her chest. "I'll be swimming again tomorrow and I would *appreciate* some privacy." Her nipples were now throbbing with the cold.

It seemed the weather had at least decided to join in her fury, the clouds opening up as she turned for home, the rain stinging her face as she trampled the nettles and cottongrass. Upon returning, she slammed the front door and leaned her body against it, waiting for the breathlessness to pass. When it did she realised, very sharply, that her head was dizzy with hunger. She pulled a towel off the peg in the hallway and padded to the kitchen where she flicked on the radio and kettle, her two ever-loyal friends. As soon as she saw the cake, she reached for it with both hands. She didn't bother with knives or plates. She took it in fists and crammed it into her mouth; felt the icing smear around her lips, the crumbs digging deep under her nails.

She ate and ate until she began to feel sick, then she ate even more. Next she felt guilt, which always forced her to keep going; she had ruined everything so it was too late now to stop. It was only when half the cake was gone that she finally paused for breath and noticed the voices on the radio. It was the lunchtime news—apparently the scientists over in England had just confirmed it; apparently humans could definitely contract BSE. So British beef was now officially banned, though in some cases it was too late—the disease had already taken hold. Eight people were dead and counting.

And just like that, the rage fell out of Grá's body as she puddled to the kitchen floor. She rested her head against the cabinet door and closed her eyes. She tried to swallow, but already she could feel the sense of unease returning worse than ever, rising up in her throat with the icing like a grey and murky tide.

CHAPTER THREE
Fionn

County Monaghan, March 1996

He was already gobshite late, but he couldn't leave without sorting herself.

He had made boiled eggs and soldiers for his first breakfast and guzzled the whole lot down (to his mind, they had been British soldiers, of course—bite off their fecking heads). Then he had done a bowl of cornflakes, just to be sure—even if he wasn't buying or selling today, it was always important not to set off to the mart on an empty gut.

Fionn clicked the hob. The smell of the gas half reminded him of the drink. He shook his head and plonked the kettle over the flame.

After everything that had happened, he had sold off most of the acres and scaled things right down on the farm. "Smallholder" was the word for him now. "Semi-retired" he preferred. He still managed to pool together just enough milk to meet the quotas. The farming subsidies (if he jiggered them right) just about kept the place afloat.

Fionn noticed a spill of egg yolk hardening itself on the countertop. He flicked it off. The bitch would snuffle it up later for a salty treat.

He knew it would feel a bit strange showing up empty-handed, even though he also knew it was curiosity as much as anything that was sending him down to the livestock mart today. Because ever since the British beef ban earlier in the month there had been endless talk doing the rounds about all the opportunities this could now mean for Irish farmers. Apparently there were new jobs on the horizon; new contracts from Europe to be signed. "The Celtic Beef Boom," the papers were calling it. Fionn wondered who in shite had come up with that. But in fairness, if the rumours were true then it really could be a chance for the country to flourish; a chance to finally break away from England and prosper all on her own.

The kettle's rattle matched his enthusiasm. Fionn poured the water, then let it draw while he fetched the milk from the fridge.

But on top of his nosiness about the boom, there was another purpose to today's escapade: a face that needed to be found amongst the crowd and a question that needed to be asked. Fionn was well aware it was the reason he was a bit wired this morning, out milking the girls even earlier than usual. When he had finished, he hadn't washed his hands. It was an old superstition meant to bring good luck.

His boots went savage with the stairs, a shudder down to the foundations, a skip over the fourth step from the top, which always made the noisiest creak. But with every stage of the ascension Fionn felt himself relax, almost as if her aura were seeping underneath the door.

"Eileen?" He rapped lightly, then he pushed; breathed in the slightly stale air. He would leave a note telling Davey to change her sheets when he got home from school. "Morning, love." He tried a clumsy version of tiptoes, though still the duvet didn't budge as he set the cup next to the Bible he had left out on the stand.

Up close, he saw the eyes were shut, the new growth of hair matted flat into the pillow, but it was enough. He exhaled. He didn't feel wired any more. "Right, love, I'm off to the mart. According to the rumours, the mad cow stuff in England has been good news for the boyos over here—the prices are going through the roof!" He stopped. The optimism somehow felt a little cruel. He wondered if today would be one of her good days or one of her bad.

It was almost nine months since the last bit of treatment on the lump in Eileen's brain. The surgery had excavated the bulk (Fionn pictured a wee JCB digger), then the chemo had zapped the dregs. Her strength was returning, but now the doctors had her on more drugs in case of a seizure or epileptic fit. The pills left her knackered; caused dreadful headaches of their own. Some days she barely left the bed.

Fionn waited a moment longer, hoping to catch a glimpse of his wife's emerald greens. She always said the eye colour ran in her family, though as it happened he had never met any of the others. When her lids stayed shut, he sighed and set off. He told himself she would be better when he came home from the mart, especially if he was bearing some good news of his own.

Out on the road it was wild—Mother Nature at her most demented—no postcard bollocks as far as the eye could see; only whitebeam and blackthorn, bracken and broom, briars and brambles that would flay you to shreds. The hawthorn leaves had returned, thickening up the hedges, while elsewhere the fields were spliced by stone walls or barbed-wire fences—all the borderlines demarcating one man's slab of muck from the next.

Fionn revved the 4×4 a little harder, letting the familiar view work its wonders. He had been born and raised on the same farm and beaten about daily there as well. Though there had been a fistful of decent memories too—his father taking him off on junkets through these very roads, the shroud of blackness and petty criminality bringing them close.

Fionn did his first bit of cattle smuggling when he was just fourteen years of age. "Not that you'll be of any use," his daddy had slurred through the drink. "Just keep your gob shut and watch." Big Billy Tierney had been there that night, the Horgan duo nestled close in the lorry's cab, a violent stench of farts and prawn-cocktail crisps. They drove for an hour before they reached the unapproved road, crossed the border into the North, and met the pair of Proddy lads just after two. The cattle hides glowed fluorescent beneath the moon, but their cover was safe enough—their contact had charged a small fortune to ensure the guards wouldn't be on patrol tonight.

It had taken them ages to get the last of their livestock loaded up into the filthy container. When it was finally over, Fionn's daddy had pocketed the cash. And then he had offered his son a rare smile—a look that might have almost resembled love. It seemed that up in no man's land the usual rules just didn't apply.

Fionn had been dreaming of such escapades ever since he was a little lad. At school they had done the story of *Táin*

Bó Cúlainge, "The Cattle Raid of Cooley." It began with the Queen of Connacht storming Ulster to try to get her hands on Dáire mac Fiachna's bull. When she failed, the battles had begun—thousands of men led to the slaughter—all for the want of that fine specimen of a beast.

And Fionn had long imagined passing the famous story down to a son of his very own, picturing happy years and clandestine trips to come. Only, by the time he was married, the cattle smuggling had become a far more complicated thing. The Troubles were raging. Contact or no, the borderlands were no longer safe. Then in '74, the Dublin–Monaghan bombings had left thirty-three men, women, and children dead, which meant the patrols were even tighter than before. Eileen would sit glue-eyed to the violence on the tele, begging him to abandon his trips, while Fionn would try to explain: "It's nothing to do with politics, love—it's only cattle; only dodging the tariffs for a few extra quid." Until one night, Big Billy Tierney got himself murdered on a run, a bullet through the face while he was driving some Dexters to sell on the sly. Eileen had soothed the worst of Fionn's grief, then reminded him what he already knew: "In this country, love, cattle *are* politics."

Back on the road, Fionn spared a thought for his late friend, but also for what could have been—a rite of passage with his only child—the thing that might have finally brought them close. As it was, Davey had never shown any interest in the cattle or the farming, only in poetry and ancient books— Fionn wondered where in shite he had picked up all of that. Though he reminded himself, all things considered, it could have been a whole lot worse between them—compared to the bruises and bashes off his own daddy, it was grand. Fionn had sworn to himself he would never make the same mistakes; would never raise a fist to his family.

He had broken that promise only once, and God knows he would never go breaking it again.

From the moment he stepped out of the 4×4, the air was men and animals and it was mighty to him. Fionn inhaled, soaking it up, the throbbing buzz of baritones. There were tractors reversing and livestock groaning and *Northern Sound* blaring from car radios, traffic reports and weather forecasts and lists of all the recently deceased. Men supped from flasks of tea or stronger, trying to take all the edges off. Fionn paused. Christ above, he could have murdered a taste. But instead he tucked his T-shirt into his jocks, heaved another deep breath, and aimed his wellies in the direction of the hangar.

The closer he got, the more he realised just how busy things really were. Every pen was stuffed to the brink; every queue stretched for miles out the door. The air was like a carnival— like when the knackers brought the hurdy-gurdies to town—a look of anticipation lit across every unshaven face.

The Celtic Beef Boom.

Opportunities.

It turned out the rumours were absolutely true.

Eventually a few lads clocked his arrival. Fionn was a little wary how they would react. He knew he had never been the most popular—they considered him a bit of a tight bastard, a nasty drunk—same as his daddy before him. *And as for that odd-ball son?* Fionn cast his mind back to the house. He hoped Davey had checked on Eileen before he left for school. He hoped she had woken in time to take her tea while it was still warm.

"Thought you'd forgotten us down in your wee dairy retirement home." The first one to approach him was Derek O'Brien, or "DOB" as he was known—a nickname that made him sound almost as thick as he truly was. But Fionn was grateful to him all the same; a precedent set so now the rest would follow suit.

"Well, I heard ye were having the life of Reilly up here, so I figured I'd see about all the fuss."

"Never mind Reilly." DOB winked. "With the Brits firmly out of the picture, we're going to be able to buy and sell any Reilly for twice the fucking price."

Behind DOB now there was Mossy McGrath, Briain Ní Ghríofa, and the Sullivan twins. It seemed the atmosphere was so jubilant that any eejit was welcome—no matter your popularity or your daddy before you. So Fionn let his hand be pumped and let himself lap up the sense of occasion, matching the grins and nodding the head.

And yet.

His eyes remained peeled for Martin Fahey. A quiet wee word in his ear. A certain question meant for him and him alone.

"Right so." DOB slapped Fionn's back. "Come on, I've a heifer up next." Not waiting for an answer, only leading him inside where the atmosphere was tenser, so many men crammed under one roof it might collapse.

The farmers sat in tiers around the ring, leaning forward and licking lips like the creatures on show were for eating there and then, not for taking home to fatten up. The board told the weight and breed of the next lot, while the shiny new ads from Bank of Ireland wished them well from on high. Some lads fidgeted their hands in their pockets—almost dodgy-looking, like—but Fionn knew it was only for surreptitious strings of rosary beads, as if Our Blessed Lady might spare a moment from her divine routine to dabble in a bit of agricultural bargaining.

DOB's heifer was led in by the drover with cauliflower ears who whacked his stick a few times on the dirt. She had a fine broad muzzle and a straight enough back. Fionn thought of Glassy, his favourite girl, with her gorgeous nature and her wonky walk. He had purchased her in this very room, secretly heeding the superstition about lame cows giving the sweetest milk. It turned out the lore had served him very well indeed.

Now the bell rang out and the auctioneer began on the microphone, calling numbers and spotting twitches off men that meant a higher bid. The stream of words was almost unintelligible, racing a hundred miles an hour. It went so fast it took a minute for Fionn to get his ear back in, and even when the meaning arrived it still made little sense, because this was serious, the figures they were flinging—four, maybe five times what he used to get for a sale. He decided there must be an error on the board; must be a whole batch of heifers out back and this one just a sample specimen. DOB spotted the gorm on him and smirked. "Another contract arrived from France. Some English farmer had to let it go thanks to his woes so we hoovered it up. Cry me a river, Mr. Major, am I right?"

The cow had started to grow a bit angsty, her hooves twitching a dance in the dust. But even as the stakes went higher the men didn't blink, which let Fionn know that DOB was right—they could get their money back on the meat no bother—desperate times and desperate French and a round of pints in O'Connell's pub tonight singing a chorus of "God save the beef-banned Queen!"

But not for Fionn. He felt the fizz of him start to flatten—it was a world that suddenly felt very far away, while he was left behind with his semi-retirement and his oddball son and his beloved wife shrunken into herself.

Which reminded him.

Martin Fahey.

All done!

The auctioneer's hammer clanged a final price and Fionn slipped away while DOB whistled out a rebel song.

Martin Fahey's wife had been diagnosed a few years back with a rare and untreatable form of cancer. Some had suggested taking her to the old woman down in Carrickmacross who was said to have "The Cure"—the ancient Irish gift for healing. But instead, Fionn heard Martin had taken her to a clinic in Dublin where they ran "experimental" trials. He didn't know the details—he suspected it was far beyond what the semi-retirement could afford—but the least he could do was ask; the very very least.

Eventually Fionn spotted him amidst the crowd, a blue fleece zipped right up to the throat. "Martin, ya messer!" The ginger shag of hair had grown a bit long, though it seemed to be surviving the grey.

Martin took his time with his saunter. In the distance, the bell rang again as if the two men were squaring up for a box. Martin finally arrived: "Are we well, Mr. McCready?"

"Surviving, sure."

"Something else, this place, eh?"

"Nay bad, I have to say. Nay bad at all."

The men looked at one another. No doubt Martin would have heard about Eileen's health, so it was only polite that the enquiries would follow next. But Martin closed his lips and looked away as if he were already bored. Fionn rolled his shoulders. *Silly buggers, is it so?*

But whatever dignity he would have to forgo he was willing now to forgo. "Martin, I wanted to ask about that place in Dublin. The one you took your missis, like." Fionn felt clumsy, but he pushed on nonetheless. "I'm sure it cost a bob or two, it's just . . . Even though they got the tumour, the doctors warned Eileen it's very likely to come back, so I'm just—"

"Da, I've been looking for you everywhere!" When Fahey's youngest appeared by his side he looked every ginger inch his father's boy. He took no interest in Fionn or the pane he was after smashing up against. "Did you hear the rumour?" he panted. "Apparently the Bull's just brokered a deadly deal with Dubai. Apparently his mate the Taoiseach managed to pull him a load of strings." The boy got the news out, then started to cough. Fionn caught the strags of asthma on his lungs. He wondered what the woman in Carrickmacross would make of that. There were days Ireland felt Modern and days she felt anything but.

Martin didn't heed his son just yet, still piecing together the meaning of Fionn's half-formed plea. The name of the clinic would suffice; a ballpark figure to see if it was even feasible. And never mind Fionn's reputation or his bad phase with the drink—he hadn't touched the stuff in years—whereas a woman was sick, so really wasn't that all that mattered? Wasn't it clear he was trying to start a new phase altogether?

"Da, would you hurry?"

When Martin smiled, he revealed a gap in his gum where one of his incisors should have been. "Coming, Domhnall." He placed his hand on his son's shoulder, a look of hearty, shameless pride. He leaned into Fionn's ear and whispered the number once and only once, then added loud enough for anyone to hear: "Bet you're wishing you hadn't scaled things down after all, eh?"

Fionn crossed the car park with his hands balled tight. He could never afford the figure Martin Fahey had gloated in his ear; could barely resist the temptation to knock out another one of Martin Fahey's teeth. But even in his fury, Fionn knew it wouldn't be worth it—better not to give them the satisfaction. He would go from unpopular to an outcast altogether.

He spotted his 4×4 a mile off, the paint scratched and splattered with mud. Whereas the rest of the car-park rows sat clean and bright, new models with names he'd barely heard of, each with a number plate that had been registered this very year.

"Fionn?"

His own name made him freeze, though his pulse pumped faster. His first instinct was that someone had come to give him a hiding; to let him know he wasn't welcome here.

We've told you before, we don't sell to the McCready clan.
We thought you had retired, you scabby prick?

He supposed it was the one thing he could thank his daddy for—he had always had a decent nose for violence.

He forced himself to turn around. There were three of them in total, hands in their pockets to give the casual impression. Mossy McGrath and Briain Ní Ghríofa stood together. Fionn didn't recognise the third lad, only noticed a badger streak running through his hair.

"Fergus Hynes." The stranger stepped forward. "A first cousin of Mossy's. I wondered if I could have little word."

Fionn felt his sweat soaking his shirt down into his jocks, his muscles tightening in readiness. He wouldn't go down easily. He promised himself that at least.

"Tell me, Fionn." Fergus wore a belt around his jeans that had an awful shiny buckle. "I take it you have heard of a lad called Eoin Goldsmith?"

Fionn cocked his head. He had been caught off guard again, this time by the simplicity of the question. He tried to understand what was going on; tried to trace any sort of possible link.

Because there wasn't a man in the country who wasn't familiar with the Bull or the empire he had built. He was the brains of the meat industry—from processing plants to development plans; from offal and equipment to cattle feed. He had created employment and launched Ireland on to the international stage—his success story would be told for generations to come. Along the way, a couple of journalists had tried to make accusations; to spread certain reports about foul play. But mostly the stories had gone away—they were nothing but stupid rumours; nothing but begrudgers trying to take the mighty down.

"Well, you see," Fergus continued, "the Bull has put me in charge of a wee project you might be able to assist with. We're looking for someone with a *knowledge* such as your own."

It was only now Fionn started to realise that maybe it wasn't bruises the men were after. He felt the fear slink out of him like a ghost. Instead they needed something else—something to do with the border; a "business operation." Beef from the North that couldn't be sold on account of the recent British ban. Nothing dodgy, they assured, but it would just be useful to have someone with a certain *kind* of expertise if they were thinking to transport the stuff south.

"Ah, but them cattle smugglings were a fair time ago," Fionn reminded them, out of modesty and caution both. "I haven't been up that way in yonks."

But their flattery didn't stop, nor their nonchalance. It would just be a couple of runs—barely a commitment if he thought about it, really.

"Of course, Goldsmith would provide a decent fee for your trouble." It was Mossy who delivered the clincher. "Serious bob, like, assuming your discretion. He could even give you half in advance if you need?"

This time Fionn lingered on the sound of "need." They must have overheard him with Martin Fahey; must have caught just how extortionate the Dublin clinic really was.

But the lads said no more before they left—no further details; no indication about the where or the when of it all. And no mention either of Fionn's unpopularity—his stingy reputation or messy years with the booze. It seemed this was just men; this was just beef, simple as that.

This was just a line that needed to be crossed.

Back home, Fionn unwound the twine on the gate and pulled the 4×4 into the yard. He killed the engine, but he wasn't ready to move just yet. He glanced at Eileen's Fiesta. Her license had been revoked on account of the risk of seizures. Of all the side effects, he knew she despised that one the most.

When he had made his decision, Fionn opened the door and Blackfoot came barking out. He had named her in a moment of daftness. It was to do with some old superstition that said if your dog was called that, your herd would be safe from disease. Fionn scratched behind her ear in greeting. First he would give the girls their latest dose for the fluke, then he would head upstairs and change Eileen's sheets. He would promise her everything was going to be OK.

•

The call came a week later while he and Eileen were watching one of her old black-and-white films before bed. *Some Like It Hot.* It was one of her favourites—she knew all the lines by heart; could give the American accent a decent lash.

"Might be Faela for Davey," she drawled as the phone started ringing, but when Fionn went to the kitchen and picked up the receiver, it wasn't his son's girlfriend at the end of the line. Instead, the voice was male and unfamiliar. It told Fionn nothing except the time and place he was to be waiting. It said he would know the date in question because on that morning, the first half of his payment would arrive through the letterbox.

Fionn started to ask how they knew his address, but the call was already dead in his hand. He stared at the phone, then looked up and found his son standing in the doorway. "Jesus, lad, you put the heart crossways on me!"

Davey hovered a moment longer before turning. Fionn wondered how much he had overheard. He felt a flicker of panic, but then he had a different idea. He could invite Davey along on the job; could come to some kind of arrangement with Fergus Hynes. Because maybe this could be a chance to put things right between them—if it had worked for him and his own daddy, God knows it could work for them. Fionn jogged out to the hallway and glanced up the stairs where Davey was just heading back into his room. "Son, can I have a word?"

The door slammed instantly. Fionn waited, listening in case it was opened again. But of course, even after the apologies and the sobriety, he knew Davey had never forgiven him for the awful things he had done. Fionn sighed. He heard Marilyn Monroe and then he heard his wife's laugh. He returned to the living room.

"No matter how close I look," she said when he appeared, though her eyes didn't leave the screen, "I still can't tell she's pregnant. She lost it after six weeks, you know? Tried to kill herself again. Three times Arthur Miller had to save her life."

Fionn collapsed into the armchair. He knew the time and the place. Now all he had to do was sit and wait.

•

Three nights later and, even inside the van, the cold night air was knives against their necks. Fergus Hynes sat silent behind the frozen wheel, chewing his fingers to hangnail shreds. The pair of them scoured the view. Mossy and Briain were parked up in their own battered-looking van next to them, but other than that the world was nothing but shadow.

As far as Fionn could remember, this was one of the routes that had been blockaded during the worst of the Troubles, barriers and spikes in the middle of the road to stop anyone from trying to get across. Until last year, when the border-buster JCBs began to remove it all—the government had shut the checkpoints too—making way for cars; making way, it seemed, for peace.

Fionn checked his watch, the cheapo plastic kind with the squeezy light. It was meant for children, not for jaded smallholders breaking laws in the depths of no man's land. But it had always been a handy yoke for the smuggling operations back in the day—another thing about tonight that filled Fionn with old border memories. And yet, technically the scheme this time was the opposite way around—the olden days were about moving cattle north to sell at a higher price. Whereas here they were bringing beef south; taking down all the perfect wee steaks that had been crossed off for an embargo an ocean away.

As promised, he had found a brown envelope containing a wodge of cash on the doormat this morning. He had counted it twice. It was only the tip-and-a-bit of the iceberg, but he told himself it was a start.

"Right, you stay here."

Fergus's growl made Fionn jump, then squint out the window where he caught the skulk of black on black. To his left, the others gave him a hasty nod; a moon-glint of nerves. Fionn made the sign of the cross. Fergus Hynes approached the truck on foot and the driver hopped down in a leather jacket and a pair of loafers as if they were off to the pub, not out in the freezing cold shifting crates of contraband. They conferred until Fergus gave the signal and Fionn shimmied into the driver's seat. His hands were shaking as he turned the key, but the engine soon cricketed to life. The two vans reversed to the arse of the refrigerated truck, the doors laid open and awaiting. Fionn jumped out and saw the beef piled up. It would be a serious job to get it all across. But Briain was clearly here for his muscle, so he wasted no time in leaping up and jostling the first pallet to the edge. "Fionn, if you catch," he said, "Mossy can stamp and load. Let's make this quick." He proved his point with the first one tossed already out.

Fionn caught it just in time, taking a bit of a bruise, then paused for a moment to inspect the contents. Each cut of meat lay cellophaned in its carton with a simple sticker on the front inscribed with the date and weight.

Fionn stared at the beef; the Northern Irish beef. The British beef that had officially been banned. He passed it over, a little clumsy, just as Mossy produced a rubber stamp from his Umbro bag. Next Mossy dipped the stamp into a pad of ink and bashed it down on each label, quickly like he had done the whole thing before. Fionn watched as ink stains began to bloom on Mossy's fingertips, blue rims around the nails that would be a bugger to clean. And for the first time all night,

Fionn smiled, just as the next crate arrived in his arms ready to be turned into something else.

100%, the stamp said, no hint of doubt; no questions or anxieties when it made its way to the southern warehouses and overseas on to the supermarket shelves. No, just this:

100% Irish Beef.
Celtic Boom beef!

Fionn decided he was warming to the phrase after all.

On the drive back, he dozed a little. He had assumed they would be stashing their haul at one of the Bull's swanky facilities, but when he woke he saw they were turning down a narrow lane and pulling up by a dilapidated shed.

Inside the old cold store, the tiles were ruined with cracks. Half the hooks from the ceiling were blunt with rust. Fionn noticed the temperature. "Is it just me, or is it warmer in here than it is outside?"

And the last thing Fionn noticed was a portrait that had been mounted on the left-hand wall, Our Blessed Lady garbed in her traditional blue. This time he didn't need to say a thing.

"Don't look surprised." Fergus winked. "The Bull is a very religious man."

Shortly after they locked up, they drove past O'Connell's pub where Fergus said he and the lads would be celebrating later. "You should come," he said. "Toast to all our hard work. I'm sure the others wouldn't mind."

Fionn was touched by the invitation, even if he had to decline. He hadn't frequented the pub in almost three years. His logic was that, sober, he wouldn't make the same mistake again.

Once he was home, Fionn kicked off his wellies. Even Blackfoot was fast asleep. He made his way up the stairs, past Davey's room, then took a breath as he reached the next door and pushed. Eileen's body was so small a lump beneath the duvet he might have mistaken it for the feathers themselves. They used to keep hens—every morning she would cup the eggs warm in her hands and hold them out like a sacrament. As Fionn watched her now, he felt the exhaustion deep in his bones—from the heavy lifting of the night, but also from the memory of everything else that he had done. Even three painful years on, he still couldn't quite get over the horror of his crime. Not that he could actually remember a thing of the incident—oh no, the quantity of drink had made very sure of that. But he could remember the morning after—the mess of her lip and the swell of her jaw; the blood in her startled eyes where the love used to be but could surely never be again. To this day, Fionn didn't understand how he had let it go so far; couldn't pinpoint the moment he had turned into the father he'd so despised.

Carefully now, he sat down on the edge of the bed. His face contorted as he removed his socks. Outside, the first shreds of morning fell across the giant beech where a coil of rope hung down from a branch. Fionn traced the length of it with his eyes all the way to the end where it should have held a tyre or maybe a swing, but when he thought back to his childhood, he couldn't remember it ever holding a thing.

For all his exhaustion, though, for all his shame, Fionn knew this morning was about looking forward, not back. Because what if this was a chance, finally, to make amends? To eliminate that wretched tumour for good? Very slowly, he lifted the duvet and slid his way beneath. He moved an inch closer to his sleeping wife. He breathed in her scent, the heat off her back, wanting to touch, but not quite trusting himself to.

When he opened his eyes, he rolled on to his left only to discover his shoulders were in knots and that Eileen was gone. He swallowed. The back of his throat was pure scratch. He would need a rake of honey to stave off the worst of last night's chill. He wondered what hour it was, then heard the footsteps and saw Eileen appear, fully dressed.

"Well, there's a sight for sore eyes!" She hugged a pile of fresh laundry to the bones of her chest. "The dead arose and appeared to many."

"Eileen, you shouldn't—" Fionn coughed before he went again. "Leave that, would you? Davey can—"

"Davey has enough to be getting on with at the moment." Eileen opened the drawer and slammed it a little too hard. "I'm fine."

He swallowed again and tried a different tack. "How did you sleep?"

She yanked the curtains. "Not bad." But then she stopped where she stood as if something in the view had caught her attention. "Although I had that strange dream again—you remember me telling you? The one about the Butchers?"

Fionn closed his eyes. Jesus, his shoulders really were fucked.

Eileen was right—it wasn't the first time in the last few weeks she had told him about her strange dream. For Fionn, its recurrence—its presence at all—was one of the strongest signs that her brain still wasn't quite right. He had considered telling the doctors about it, but ultimately he had decided against. It would have required far too much in the way of explanation.

Because before she got ill, those words hadn't been uttered between them for almost twenty-five years. *The Butchers.* Not since the day they were married and she left her old life behind; not since the day she announced she didn't want to be called Lena any more.

Fionn stared at her now, her frail body angled away to soak up the morning light. Even through her cardigan, her shoulder blades jutted out. He thought of a milk-dry heifer being led off to the slaughterhouse.

"Mam—breakfast!"

When she was gone, Fionn buried his head into the goodness of the pillow. He would sleep another hour, get up and milk the girls. Then he would call that Dublin clinic and get the appointment booked in. For his sins, he would pay the very highest price.

CHAPTER FOUR

Davey

County Monaghan, April 1996

Davey held his face an inch from the book as if he were drying the ink with his breath. Or as if by peering close enough he would be able to catch a glimpse of the beast the words described. The Minotaur. "Part man, part bull," Ovid said, though the poet was never explicit as to exactly how much of each part there was.

Davey thought of the animals down in the byre. He thought of the bullish man doing their milk.

It was King Minos who had hired Daedalus to construct a labyrinth for the Minotaur, a maze of such complex twists and turns the creature would never manage to escape. In the margin, Davey saw he had once doodled a sketch—a higgledy swirl encased by a circle. In the middle there was a dot with a tiny pair of horns.

But despite its captivity, still the savage Minotaur was sustained on Athenian blood. Every seven years, lots were drawn to select seven men and seven women to be sent into the maze to feed the beast. Davey could remember the numbers, though he saw now that one of the sevens was underlined. Mr. Fitz had said in some accounts it was every *nine* years instead.

Davey paused, committing the fact to memory. It was the kind of thing that might come up on the exam.

Until one year, the mighty Theseus declared that he would be the one to enter the maze, whereupon he would kill the Minotaur. They all thought him crazy—nobody who had gone in there had ever survived—but Minos's daughter, Ariadne, gave him a spool of thread to unravel as he sought out the beast. Then, after he had slaughtered the thing with suitable classical quantities of blood and guts and gore, he had traced the thread back into the light; back to freedom.

Theseus, against the odds, had managed to escape.

Davey felt the usual surge of triumph as he reached the climax of the tale. He sat up straight, away from the book, a nagging protest in his lower back. Out the window, the late-afternoon sky had started to turn pink. He listened. There was no sound of life from his mother's room.

All around him on the desk, the books were piled high in perfect columns, even if only one of them had been opened all day. It was eight weeks until his Leaving Cert—the six exams that would decide his future plans. He could have sat Classical Studies in the morning, full marks. Mr. Fitz had nurtured Davey's unlikely love of the ancients, loaning him books and awarding him As. He had even offered to read some of Davey's own poetry (that was, if Davey ever wanted to share). The other teachers, though, didn't really approve.

Why in God's name are you reading all that?

Sure, we've plenty of legends of our own.

Never mind your man Oedipus—what about Táin Bó Cúlainge?

Meanwhile, his classmates only took it as yet another reason to rip the piss. They already thought Davey was a weirdo with his notebook and his highfalutin notions.

A poet you want to be, is it?

Here, I've a poem for you—what rhymes with "massive hunt"?

But for all their teasing, Davey couldn't help his infatuation. Maybe it was the imagery, maybe it was just the pure strangeness, but something about the foreign tales stirred him far more than anything in this place ever had.

He glanced again out the window. Already the pink was a deeper hue, leaving bloodshot rims around the black trees on the hill.

After Theseus defeated the Minotaur, the story of his bravery had spread far and wide. The people of Calydon came calling—a wild boar had been slaying their children and animals so they needed a hero to come and save the day. Some legends said the boar embodied the spirit of Diana, goddess of the moon, while others said—

"Ah, the poet's lair. I thought I would find you here, all right."

Davey's spirit dropped down on to the page. The slam of the bedroom door shuddered through the rafters. If his mother had been asleep, she certainly wasn't any more.

He took a moment, then straightened up just in time for Faela to slump upon him. She kissed his neck and squeezed his shoulders, the knots of his muscles ever-tied.

"I was getting a bit worried." His girlfriend hoisted herself on to the desk in her miniskirt and battered Nike runners. "You weren't even at Mass yesterday?"

Davey wondered if the wood would hold. "I wasn't."

"Heathen!" she cried. "And on Good Friday and everything? Father Devlin will be raging. You'd better have at least fasted and abstained?" Here she paused, eyes glinting. "I assumed that's why you were avoiding me. Abstinence, hey? *Do not lead me into—*"

"I was studying."

"Oh, bollocks to that." Faela swatted his words like a fly. "Haven't you heard the news—no need for college any more. Thanks to the Bull and the eejit Brits, we're going to be *rolling in it soon.*" Her laugh was as bright as her ginger hair while she produced today's newspaper and slapped it down on the desk. Her nails had "J-E-S-U-S" Tippexed across, the only expression of vanity the nuns were willing to overlook. "Do you want to go to the pictures tonight?" The newspaper was folded in four, but half the cover photograph was still visible. "Apparently that *Trainspotting* one's supposed to be deadly. I reckon the Scots are just a more knackery version of us."

Even from this angle, Davey could recognise the Bull pinned in his three-piece suit. Next to him was the Minister for Agriculture, the pair of them grinning like it had been a very good Friday indeed.

Faela followed his gaze. "Oh, *him?* They say he's got all sorts of sneaky wee moneymaking schemes on the go. Speaking of which, have you noticed your old man acting *unusual* at all?"

Davey ignored her. He didn't want to talk about his father—he never did. Instead, he unfolded the newspaper, leaned in close, and scanned the headlines.

McDonald's Rejects British Beef!

Irish Farmers Kill Fatted Calves!

The Bull's face had the look of pure mischief. The brown hair had the unmistakable look of a comb. And this time it wasn't an ancient tale on Davey's tongue, but an ancient word. *Hubris.* The arrogance of the invincible; the confidence that nothing could possibly go wrong. He thought of Daedalus again, fashioning a pair of wings so his son Icarus might fly away from prison, only for the lad to get greedy and soar too close to the sun.

Davey closed his eyes. The failed escape. It had always been his least favourite of the myths.

"So this is where the magic happens, eh?"

When he opened them again, he saw that Faela had found his black leather notebook. It had an elastic band wound tight around as if to hold the poems in. "Give me that." He reached for her, but she was nimbler than she looked, slinking off the desk and knocking a piece of paper with her—a white feather slowly floating to the floor.

Faela tossed the notebook on to the bed and picked up the fallen page instead. "What's this?" She held it as close to her face as he did his books—it was one of the few traits they had in common. It was one of the few things Davey knew that he would miss.

"Your CAO." She answered her own question as she began to read. His Central Applications Office form; his college choices listed in order of preference and ready to submit. "You've put Dublin first and second."

Instead of answering, Davey returned to the window. The beech tree stood with its coil of rope hanging down. Davey could never see it and not consider a noose. Behind it, the pink had begun to recede like a shoreline when the tide is out. Davey itched for his notebook on the bed—it would be a decent enough start for a poem. "I have."

Faela snatched at his words. "But I thought we discussed—"

"We did."

"So what, you just *lied* to me? Davey, we had a whole plan. You and me over at the Tech. Together."

Eventually he had no choice at all but to look at her. Her anger burned even brighter than her hair. Yet Davey soon saw it fade; saw her eyebrows wilt and her face soften in understanding. "Davey, I know you want to get away, but I've told you—you won't need to be near him any more. We can stay in halls. I've heard they even do double rooms, so we—"

"It's not just him."

At this, the softening stopped. She was still holding the CAO form. As always, the Tippex on her right nails was much more smudged than on her left.

"It's everything." He tried his best to keep it simple—he hadn't expected this conversation so soon, but he had known it was coming all the same. So now he searched for a way to explain what had been mounting for months or maybe even years; to translate it into words they might both understand. "I don't belong here."

Faela's brows stiffened, reversing any mercy. "And what about me? Do you *belong* with me?"

Davey tried—he could have sworn he did—to hold her stare. But soon he was looking at the books instead; the window; the rope; the newspaper folded over. He had never really noticed the chisel of the Bull's jaw.

When the bedroom door slammed for a second time, the front page lifted up in the draught, then settled into itself. Faela's footsteps stomped down the stairs and across the yard until they had disappeared. Both the regret and the relief settled over him at once. Behind her, there was no thread spooled out for Davey to find his way back.

For the next half an hour he tried to read on, but his concentration was broken. He closed the book and stuck it on top of one of the piles. His needed some air. He had to yank the door extra hard to free it from its frame after Faela's dramatic departure. He made for the stairs, then paused outside his mum's room. She had been up for the morning, but had gone back to bed at lunch, her face an ashy grey. Very softly, he opened the door.

Her form was barely a blip beneath the piles of tartan blankets. It seemed they were all worried about her getting cold— the things we can control; the very very least. Davey noticed the various mugs and empty pill bottles scattered across her bedside table. He would tidy them up when she woke; would peel off a layer or two to let her breathe.

It was hard to believe it was only a couple of years since she had been rushing about on the farm. Davey used to love watching her feed the newborn calves from the giant tubs with the plastic tits. He knew that, without her, his father had had to do away with the calving altogether this year. He knew that, without her, his father was struggling to cope.

The good news was the treatment was finally finished— the hospital visits which left her vomiting into plastic bowls for days. Davey had offered to take her along since she wasn't allowed to drive herself any more. But she had always refused, insisting there was no way he could be missing school at a time like this. He supposed it really was the least his father could do.

"I take it that's things finished with Faela Quin, so?" Her words appeared over the crest of the blanket pile, even though her body didn't move. Davey was as surprised by their arrival as by what they seemed to intuit. He walked around the bed so that he could see her face. Sure enough, her eyes were pure green and clear.

"It is," he said.

"I'd say you won't be long over that."

Davey smiled. "I'd say you might be right."

He felt the knots in him loosen a bit, guilty always of assuming the worst. Just because her body was ill, didn't mean her mind hadn't as much of a handle on the place as ever. But Davey suddenly tightened again, because did that mean she could also glean about the CAO? About his escape plan of counting off four more months and then away? "How much did you . . . ? I thought you were asleep."

With only a trace of a wince, she sat herself up. Her chest was a xylophone of bones. "Ach, I was," she said, then she paused. A frown passed across her face like a cloud. "But I keep having this mad dream which wakes me. Have I mentioned it before—the one about the Butchers?"

Davey felt the cloud pass across him too.

His mother had first told him about the Butchers when he was only a little lad, explaining about the mythical curse;

about the eight men with their eight touches who used to visit her parents' home. But she had also told him her parents were dead now and she had become a Catholic like his daddy, so it was important not to mention any of that again.

Since then, the only time Davey heard mention of the Butchers was when the lads at school were spreading nasty rumours, usually around June when the group came to visit the handful of believers who were said to live nearby.

I heard they ride the cow before they kill it.

I heard they suck it off.

My da told me they slaughter a human every five years too.

But even despite these sordid versions, there was something about the whole thing that had always appealed a bit to Davey—more akin to Ovid or Sophocles than anything else this country had to offer. He thought of the Minotaur, "part man, part bull." He thought of Zeus turning Io into a cow. Maybe when he got to Dublin he would write a book of poetry that linked it all up.

"And it's not just the dream." His mother's voice pulled him back now. "The Butchers have been on my mind quite a lot recently. I think—you'll call me daft—but I have the strangest urge to see them one last time—"

"Were your family always believers?" Davey cut her off sharply. He knew the answer, of course, but he couldn't listen to the phrase "one last time." Anything but that.

"Both my parents were raised in strict households, so ours was the very same. Not that, between you and me, I was ever totally convinced. My father claimed he could trace his ancestors back to the widow who made the original curse." Here she smiled; half rolled her eyes. "Trust me, if you had met my father, that would come as no surprise."

She had explained these things to Davey many times over the years, but it was still nice to hear them again—how her parents would count down to the annual visit; how she and her sister would be made to get all dressed up.

"But then you just left?" Davey looked at his mother. The newly grown wisps of hair were held in place by a thin film of sweat. He would draw a bath for her this evening. She used to be a great woman for the baths.

But when she sighed, it didn't sound great at all. "I thought leaving my family would set me free. Give me the chance to really *find* myself, you know?" She paused. "Now look at me." She glanced down as if taking her own advice.

Davey turned away. He would fill the tub with bubbles and all.

Through the darkness, the outline of the trees loomed up either side of the road. Most of them wore a suck of ivy right up to their necks, covering their modesty. Davey paused. He felt the corners of his notebook digging sharp into his pocket. Truth be told, he hadn't written in the thing for weeks.

He set off again, thinking of Faela and her absolute fury this afternoon. Despite everything, he knew he would miss her more than a bit. There had been something so calming about the constant noise of her while he could just sit there and safely go unnoticed. He had joined her and her friends a couple of weekends drinking in the furthest of Hogan's fields, but mostly the girls just got scuttered on cider and squealed things like, *He's so fecking polite!* He imagined Faela up there with them now, spitting venom between sugary gulps. *And to think, I was even going to give him the ride. Not that he ever asked for it, mind you . . .*

Davey went rambling along the roads most nights, strolling the land for want of writing it. It was the only time he could allow his mind to unfurl the full extent of itself. Out here, there was no risk of bumping into anyone from school; no risk of people reading bits of paper they weren't supposed to read.

He would walk for hours sometimes, nothing but the elegant stare of horses for company. Or the full-beams of a distant souped-up car going ninety an hour, the little boy racers blaring "Born Slippy" on brand-new subs. But apart from the neighs and the techno blips, the only sound was the echo of the ancient myths in his head. Sometimes it was Euripides and other times it was Aeschylus. Like the one where Prince Thyestes slept with his brother's wife, so in return his brother cooked him an almighty feast. It was only after Thyestes guzzled it down that he discovered the flesh he had eaten was that of his sons. In the end, it was the cannibalism more than the grief that turned him mad.

Davey thought of his father back on the farm, guzzling his dinner.

He had heard the old man's footsteps in the wee hours the other night. Between that and the strange phone call last week, he knew Fionn was up to something dodgy. How had Faela put it? *All sorts of sneaky wee moneymaking schemes.* Davey rolled his eyes. It was bloody typical. Because never mind that the farmers had had this stroke of luck that was about to line their pockets three sheets thick—"the Celtic Beef Boom," the papers were calling it, nice and twee as only Ireland could ever be—but some of them still had to go one better; still had to take the absolute piss; rules broken and things passed under the counter because it was their time to shine so they may as well make the very most of it.

Regardless of what Fionn was up to, Davey had to stay focused, because he also had a wee scheme under way—a plan to nail his exams, then get his results, then book his train ticket out—a one-way escape! After that he would stroll the Dublin streets every day as opposed to these dilapidated country roads; would join a few societies, gather up a few pals, see the Dublin girls. The Dublin lads. He would perfect his Latin and his Ancient Greek and finally find a language that matched his thoughts and turned his ideas into beautiful poetry.

But even as he conjured it, the dream didn't take. Because who on earth was he codding? He was only an eejit with an empty notebook and a thousand notions and never a clue how to make them come true. From some dark branch above, an owl called him out. Davey thought of ancient augurs who could read signs in the organs of beasts, like the shape of a liver or a kidney that might mean love or the coming of a death.

And as well as an eejit, Davey knew he was a traitor—his poor mother still recovering while her own son plotted to abandon her—the same son who had failed her before while her drunken husband did his worst. Davey hunched his thin shoulders; shame always made him smaller. From his right, he heard a noise in the undergrowth. It might have been a fox or a badger; the land hid all sorts in her skirts.

He heard his mother's voice from earlier.

The Butchers have been on my mind quite a lot recently.

I have the strangest urge to see them one last time.

Only when he reached the top of the hill did Davey pay attention to the new idea that was beginning to form. He placed his hands on his hips to catch his breath and squinted in the direction he thought was north. Somewhere in the distance, the Republic ended and the United Kingdom began—an invisible line they all believed was worth fighting for.

And what—or who—was worth it for him?

Even as the idea grew legs, Davey tried to tackle it down— the logistics alone would be a nightmare. The rumours said the group passed this way in June, but when exactly? And how would he possibly contact them? But Davey reminded himself about focus; about his vow to start making his notions actually come true. It would be nice to do something special for his mother before he disappeared. It was the least he could do.

He sucked the night air into his chest and held it there. He felt the sentence reform itself.

It would be nice to do something special for his mother before she *disappeared.*

He glanced towards the borderlands one last time and began his descent.

INTERLUDE

New York, January 2018

Five days after the launch, he has no choice but to return to the museum. He has never known the meaning of "separation anxiety" before. He thinks of long-distance lovers, pining. He thinks of widows left behind after their husbands' deaths.

All day long the snow has been relentless, muffling Manhattan an eerie white, but finally it seems to have coughed and spluttered to an end. He knots his scarf a little higher up his neck and skids down the side of Central Park, past the solid, shining mass of the lake.

The exhibition posters are visible from the end of the block. The marketing department decided to go with the pouting shot of the IRA boys. And then the title below in bold:

RONAN MONKS: BORDERLINE IRISH

He knows there is every sort of pun intended.

But he also knows that he cannot complain since, thanks to the Brexit talks and the anniversary of the Good Friday Agreement, the Irish border is suddenly back "in vogue." Which means his early work is suddenly in demand, giving him just enough leverage to insist on the inclusion of an unknown photograph—not quite border-related, though it wasn't taken a million miles away either.

Behind the ticket desk, the two turtle-necks don't even bother to glance up from the snow-glow of their Apple screens. Ronan tries to remember seeing them at the launch. There was a half-decent crowd, he supposes. As usual, he spent most of the evening drowning his nerves in drink while other people discussed his images—the diesel smugglers from South Armagh; the Murray house that straddles both sides of the border.

I heard they have one postman from the North and one from the South.

I find it quite the poignant metaphor.

But amidst all the pretentious posturing, he didn't catch a single peep about *The Butcher*. Of course, part of him was relieved—too many questions could have led somewhere he didn't want to go. Another part, though, couldn't deny its disappointment—even just a word or two of praise:

The light in those eyes barely makes him look dead at all.

Mr. Monks, you have a way with the morbid that's incredibly striking, you know?

What he *does* know is that he can't stop thinking about him—twenty-two years they have lived together—so this afternoon he has braved the great, bollock-shrivelling outdoors to drop by for a brief reunion.

When he finds the girl, she is sitting cross-legged on the museum floor, gazing up at the photograph. Instantly, Ronan's heart begins to hurtle. He isn't sure if it is anxiety or delight or both. He tries to scrutinise her from behind. She is much younger than him, with hair that would probably be described as mousy, though even sitting down it is clear she is tall and broad like a very different animal.

He takes a step closer. She pays no notice. He traces a line from her eyes to the abandoned cold store and back, trying to see what it is she sees. Until eventually he dares: "Staggering, isn't it?"

She doesn't turn. "I can't get over it."

"Personally, I think," he dares himself a little further, "it might be Monks's finest work."

When she does turn, the first thing he notices is that her irises are a shocking shade of green. They are also, he sees, a little shocked. "Ronan? Is that you?"

This time his heart races so fast it hurts. His cover has been blown—she will think him such a wanker! It has been the same all his life, giving off the impression of arrogance when, secretly, he is as insecure as they come.

The stranger, though, doesn't seem to mind. She bundles herself upright. "I didn't realise you would be here." Next he notices her accent and wonders if she is visiting or if she is an expat—an exile? an immigrant?—just like him. "It's my last night in New York and I heard about the show, so I . . ." She stands and smooths her trousers. "Ronan Monks. I can't actually believe it." She comes closer until he can see her freckles, great scatters of them across her cheeks, which seem strange for this time of year. He was right, she is tall—almost the same height as him. Her hair is in need of a brush. But the more of her he takes in, the more he begins to feel it, the tug of recognition. Or at least, the sense that he has definitely seen this face somewhere before. Other galleries? Other admirers of his work? There have been almost twenty hazy years of them. Maybe back in Dublin or over in London? Or even Berlin, Paris, Tel Aviv?

"Coffee?" she says.

He is a little taken aback—they don't usually move as swiftly as this.

"I'd love to ask you a few questions." She turns to the photograph. "About this, I mean. I can't believe . . . this changes everything."

And there is something about the way she says it that makes him, just for a moment, hesitate; something telling him that, just maybe, this isn't quite as good as it seems.

His ego tells him otherwise: *What's your problem? She likes the photograph.*

While another part insists: *You definitely know that face.*

"I know a decent diner down on Sixth?"

She tucks a strand of hair behind her ear. The lobe is pierced, but it is empty. It could even just be another freckle.

"Let's go."

CHAPTER FIVE
Úna

County Cavan, April 1996

Finally it was spring, which meant a new smell in the air—
the sour tang of silage and the sweetness of bracken. It meant
splays of early foxgloves along the roadsides and beads of sweat
along hairlines after they had done their usual walk to Mrs.
P's. And once they arrived, it seemed spring also meant better-
than-biscuits, because Mrs. P welcomed them with bowls of
homemade pudding, the syrup scalding fat blisters on their
tongues. Úna sometimes wondered what Mrs. P's loneliness
did to her arrangements of flour and eggs—a secret ingredient
that turned the texture extra close.

As Úna ate, she half listened to the women launching
into their usual catch-up. Most of their chat was still to do
with the BSE drama that was unfolding over in England.
Just as the experts had predicted, more human lives had
started to be claimed by the disease. Only yesterday it was
announced that a fifteen-year-old girl from Manchester had
passed away.

"The doctors say it was from eating hamburgers," Mrs. P
reported, bowing her head. "Isn't it a shocking thing? Thanks
be to goodness we're safe and sound over here."

Úna's mam bowed her head in agreement, though in truth she didn't look particularly shocked—her eyes were too bright, her whole face tinged with the glow Úna kept noticing recently. It might have been the weather that was responsible—the bit of sunshine finally melting whatever glacier of sadness had hardened inside her—but Úna could have sworn there was something else behind her mam's newly brightened mood.

As it happened, Úna had a "something else" of her own that had been making her glow recently, because as of Tuesday night her task was finally, bloodily complete. It had been tomato with mustard that did the trick, which meant that when Úna eventually came across the mouse its fur was smeared so yellow it looked more like a freshly hatched chick.

She had taken it out to the back garden with the knife and the seven Lego men; had found a paving slab behind the shed where she could tape them firmly down. She had checked the moon in the evening sky, turned the blade three times towards her heart, and then—at last—she had begun.

Once she had the rodent bled and skinned (for this she used a razor blade from her dad's shelf in the bathroom cabinet), she hung it by its feet from a rusty nail. She cleaned the mess with kitchen roll; took the men apart to wipe between their plastic cracks. When she was finished, Úna closed her eyes and thought of the Farmer's Widow and her awful grief. She thought of her father and how proud he would be when she told him what she had achieved. And then for some reason, Úna thought of the English and their dying animals; of the plague of death that was slowly spreading across their fields.

She had gone inside and scrubbed the mouse guts from beneath her nails.

Despite the temptation, though—despite the buzz of triumph that charged the following days—still Úna hadn't said anything to her mam. One kill was well and good, but it was hardly sufficient evidence to prove she was fully qualified Butcher material just yet. She would have to bide her time and try for another slaughter—maybe something bigger (she thought again of the garden fox)—then when her father came back in June she could announce her intention to join the group.

Úna took another bite of her pudding. The syrup had cooled thick and sticky as glue. She wondered if she could take some home to use as bait.

•

"So who can tell me who this here is?"

The following Monday, they were sat in Civics class playing the usual game of "name the eejit in the photograph." Mrs. Donoghue held up a picture of Gerry Adams, the beardy leader of the IRA. Most of the arms in the room went dashing up, including Úna's, though hers wasn't selected. She told herself that maybe next time it would be. She tried to make herself believe the lie.

"And what about this?" For the second photograph, the crop of arms thinned right out. Apparently the president (*Really? But she's a woman?*) was far less common amongst the classroom's repertoire.

"And finally, this lad here?" The third portrait, though, had the entire place reaching for the sky, stretching stretching like the bigger they made themselves the more intelligent they might appear.

The teacher took her time, savouring her power. "Siobhán?"

The arms collapsed, slapping down with the injustice.

"That's the Bull, Miss." Siobhán Maguire's voice struck its usual sing-song tone. "My da—"

"Ah yes, the Bull, very good. But Siobhán, can you tell us his *real* name, please?"

Úna spotted the hesitation, the blush, while the arms spotted a final chance; a sliver of hope that all might not yet be lost.

Me me me!

Car McGrath was the selection—"Eoin Goldsmith, Miss"—the teacher unable to resist the novelty of the class messer having a clue about anything for once. "And tell me, Car, what does Mr. Goldsmith do?"

"He's the country's leading beef baron, Miss. Especially at the moment, like—thanks to him, my da says we're going to break away from the Brits and be *minted*!"

The entire place was nodding now, lips muttering various versions of the same boom-time tale. Their fathers were feeling flush—Máire Casey had already shown off the new Skechers shoes she had been bought for Easter; Siobhán Maguire said she had been promised a pony. So now Mrs. Donoghue saw her chance: "Well, you know, the Bull wasn't always a wealthy man. In fact, he grew up on a small farm like many of ye. But he worked very hard and made a few bob and after that his empire grew and grew. So remember, boys and girls, if there is something you want, you just have to put in the graft. If there's something you believe in, don't let anybody—"

The bell rang out, as it always did, at the worst possible moment. The chair legs screeched away, a herd of savages back into the wild. Still, as she packed her things, Úna clung to the weight of the words. It was as if they had been uttered for her and her alone.

She wondered if her father had ever met the Bull on his travels.

She wondered if a pony could contract BSE as well.

"Thanks, Miss."

And she was wondering still when she stepped into the corridor and found herself grabbed and shoved against the wall. Next, something was forced into her face; something round and wet, squelching into her skin. Úna struggled to break free, but the strong hands held her firm, and only then could she smell it. Her panic overflowed. It was the worst possible thing.

It was meat.

"Yeehaw!"

The unseen hand pushed the burger a bit harder as salty liquid dripped off Úna's chin, her breath building up and up and up with no escape. She thought she might pass out; she thought of that poor girl in Manchester who had passed away.

Isn't it a shocking thing?

Thanks be to goodness we're safe and sound over here.

She heard the scream before she realised it was coming from her. Instantly she stopped, mortified. But at least it had been enough to finally get them off. She wiped the juices from her eyes and saw the group arranged in a semicircle, cracking up like she had just said the funniest thing in the world. Car McGrath was in the centre, the Big Mac mangled in his palm, but still he held it out in her direction.

Úna's stomach cartwheeled afresh. She looked at Car, his fair hair, his wide sneer. She knew he had been held back a year in school so he was bigger and older than the rest. She knew what he was going to say even before he did.

"Eat it."

She tried to back away, but she was cornered.

"Take a bite, cowgirl." Car thrust the burger towards her again and her gorge rose. "It's lovely and fresh."

Úna gagged.

"I said eat it, freak!" This time Car's temper burst ferocious, a spray of spit for added punctuation. "You know you're tempted." Then his voice turned wheedling. "You know you're curious. You know you're sick of being the only one in the entire school who can't—"

Úna's vomit poured up and out of her in a perfect yellow arc. Car jolted back, but not before the splatter found him, sopping the tips of his Kappa runners. The laughter turned to cries of disgust.

"I bet it's poisonous!"

"Car, you're cursed!"

"You'll never be clean again!"

Úna wiped her mouth on her sleeve, staring at the mess on the floor—her insides out for all to see. She was so hot she couldn't move; couldn't even bring herself to look up. Which meant she didn't meet Car's eyes as he uttered his final pronouncement and made the sign of the cross. "I told you she's fucking *diseased.*"

Úna felt her own eyes wet with something that wasn't grease.

On the walk home that afternoon, she dissected her shame, picking it apart like a crow going at a piece of roadkill. All around her the fields were empty—no farmers, no animals, only the occasional row of hay bales wrapped in black plastic so they looked like giant marshmallows, charred. Next week, though, it would be Bealtaine—the first day of May—which meant the cows would finally be put out to pasture again. Úna wondered if the animals realised; if they were counting down the days. She wondered if they went a bit mad just from being cooped up.

She knew her shame was mostly to do with having so many people see her in distress, but she was also ashamed that she even cared at all. Because didn't she *want* to be singled out? Wasn't that all *part* of being "special"? So then why did it bother her so much? It wasn't like she needed her classmates to be her friends; all she needed was her faith and her family and her dedication to the cause.

She suddenly caught the smell of vomit on her jumper. She realised, with a small smile, what she really needed was a bath.

By the time she had made it home, she felt calmer again. Car McGrath—of all the eejits. And him just cocky after getting the only question right in his life.

Thanks to him, my da says we're going to break away from the Brits and be minted!

So remember, boys and girls, if there is something you want, you just have to put in the graft. If there's something you believe in, don't let anybody—

The voices were so fresh in her head, the voices in the kitchen took a bit longer to register. When she entered, they stood up. Her mam wore a purple T-shirt and a fresh dose of her newfound glow. But it wasn't her that Úna noticed most, it was the man-shape waiting next to her, his skinny hand held eager out.

"This is Ronan," her mam began. "He's a friend I made a few weeks ago so I decided to invite him round for some tea."

Úna glanced at the mugs, not knowing what they proved.

All she needed was her faith and her family and her dedication to the cause.

"Pleased to meet you." When the stranger spoke, his voice was strange indeed; his vowels flat and low. "I've heard all about you. Your mother—"

"He's from Dublin," her mam cut in, reading her mind. "He's a photographer. Isn't that fun? I've been making a few suggestions to try and help him with his project."

It was only then that Úna saw the device sitting bulky on the table, the black leather strap hanging careless off the edge. The stranger wore jeans and a chequered shirt. He was very tall, like the men in the pictures from Civics class.

"I was just explaining," he spoke next, "that I was up photographing some IRA boys yesterday and they were telling me how they used to organise cock fights along the border. It's funny—they said they would start in the South until the Gardaí came along, then they would move north until the RUC showed up. And if there were both, the men had a raft in the middle of the river and they moved the cockerels on to that so they couldn't—"

"I've got homework." Usually Úna had a snack when she got in from school, but for now her biggest craving was for silence; for a bath full of water and a bar of rose soap that would slough off the stains of the day. She wished the man from Dublin good luck with his pictures and the raft for his cockerels. She wondered if the men kept the birds in cages just to turn them crazy and make for a better, nastier fight.

A while later she heard the front door close, then a *knock knock* on the bathroom door. She lowered her head under the water and heard the *thump thump* of her pulse. She placed all eight of her fingers against her skin, but she didn't feel any better. Truthfully, she didn't really feel a thing.

·

She didn't see Ronan the photographer again for a while, though her mother did mention him a couple of times. Apparently he was building a portfolio. Apparently, on her mam's suggestion, he had photographed the famous Murray house that straddled the border. It was said they had two different addresses and two different postmen to deliver their letters. Úna thought how confusing that would be, not that she had ever received a letter in her life. Still her mam's mood was a brighter shade, and Úna reminded herself that that was nothing but a good thing. Even if, for some reason, she couldn't help wondering whether Mrs. P knew about Ronan or not.

For some reason Úna already knew not to say anything in front of her.

At school, she did her best to avoid Car McGrath and his gang. She ate her lunch down behind the prefabs or perched high on the toilet like a king on his throne. But she needn't have worried, because soon her classmates were all distracted by other things, the arrival of Bealtaine bringing a brand-new kind of buzz.

The first of May always meant celebrations—streamers and cakes and plenty of music; fireworks smuggled south illegally for the parties that would officially herald in the summer. Apparently the biggest festivities were over in Westmeath, on a place they called the Hill of Uisneach, where they set up torches and ribbons and all sorts of pagan stuff. They would dress the cows in hawthorn blossoms and walk them around the bonfires for good luck, then people would leap across the flames to banish demons and get positive omens for the year ahead. Of course, Úna had never attended the festivities herself—the Butchers didn't keep those traditions. Although, now that she thought of it, weren't the Catholics supposed to have stopped believing in all that too?

She sighed. She wondered if it was legal for the Murray family to set off screamers and Catherine wheels from one side of their house, but illegal for them to do it from the other.

On the day itself, the boys stayed home to help their fathers lead the cattle out to the fields, so the classroom was all girls, all of them gathered in the front two rows. They were messing about with an ancient game that supposedly predicted their future husbands. Siobhán Maguire foretold she would marry one of the Gallaghers from Oasis; Máire Casey foretold Car

McGrath, and the rest of the group fell about the place until she warned them with narrowed eyes. The riddle was another Bealtaine tradition—the girls insisted they knew it was total rubbish, but they played along with it all morning just the same. Mrs. Donoghue sat at her desk attacking a tower of copybooks with the red point of her pen. Úna sat in the back row and wondered if the teacher had a husband of her own.

Mostly, though, Úna thought of her father. The Butchers would be looping back through Longford this week, loosening the triple knots of their boots to accommodate the warmer weather.

She wondered if it was wrong to kill a cow that had blossom in its hair.

She wondered, for the thousandth time, who got to decide one tradition was right and another was wrong.

For a treat, the school day ended at lunch. When Úna got home, Ronan and his camera were sitting in the kitchen. In the middle of the table a jam jar had been stuffed with tiny flowers. Úna didn't recognise them from the garden.

"Happy May Day, love," her mam called. "Are you hungry?"

Úna dropped her empty schoolbag to the floor.

"I thought you might be." Her mam kissed the top of her head even though Úna hadn't said a word. "I'm just heating the soup—it'll be ready in no time. And actually, it's tomato, so it really will be *reddy*!"

Úna blushed, embarrassed for a stranger to overhear their private jokes.

Her mam left her for the hob. Still Úna hadn't sat. She looked at Ronan slouched so comfortably in his wooden chair.

But then he leaned forward. "Úna, tell me—I want to learn about the Butchers. And your mother says their history is your speciality."

Instantly Úna assumed it was some kind of trap, even though she couldn't help but like the word. *Speciality.* She glanced at her mam and found only the back of her, humming beneath her breath. "What . . . what do you want to know?"

She had barely whispered the question, but it was still enough to make Ronan smile. "Everything," he said. "I had never heard of the group before this trip. It started with a curse, am I right?"

Úna gripped the shoulder of the kitchen chair and nodded. Then, "Yes," she said, just to be clear.

"An ancient widow," he coaxed. "Who had lost her children, so—"

"She lost her husband, too—no wonder she was angry!" The outburst was more than she had intended. She noticed her mam stiffen, but she didn't turn. Feeling self-conscious as much as anything, Úna sat.

The soup took a long time to boil. She went slowly with Ronan's questions, cagey still that this wasn't all some elaborate trick. She explained how a farmer's wife had lost her entire family way back in some ancient war, so in her devastation, she had placed a curse which dictated certain rules around killing cattle.

Henceforth, no man could slaughter alone;
Instead, seven others had to be by his side . . .

And ever since then, Úna warned, these rules had had to be adhered to or else the widow's grief would be forgotten and the whole of Ireland would become diseased. Here she paused to catch Ronan's laughter, but his face remained pure smooth. Her mam had taken bread from the oven. The smell was yeasty, crusty fresh.

So Úna continued, explaining how the Butchers paid a visit to a believer's farm once a year where some cows had been set aside for the occasion; how, depending on the position of the moon, they burned certain herbs and decided who amongst them would stand at the head and do the kill. And then how the rest of them—very gently—touched the beast as it was brought to death, thinking of grief and all the loved ones they had ever lost.

Úna heard a crack in her voice. She coughed to cover it up and glanced behind. Her mother was beginning to ladle out.

"They hang each animal by its feet, bleed and skin it, check the organs. Then they clean and process—that means butchering it all into cuts. Then on the last day of their travels, they do a special ritual for the final cow. They split the meat between all eight of them to take home to us, their families." The bowls arrived before them steaming. Úna picked up her tarnished spoon. "And it's tastier than any of that rubbish you would find at McDonald's!"

The soup was sweet and it was scalding, little green herbs flecked across the top. Úna realised she hadn't seen her mother eat so greedily in weeks. But in a funny twist, Úna was the one who wasn't interested in food any more, only in answering question after question as they came.

"How many used to believe?"

"And how many are left?"

"What about the knives? Three times in which direction?"

Ronan seemed genuinely fascinated by everything she had to say.

Úna replied as best she could—none of it was ever written down, only passed orally from one generation to the next—but she had been careful to store up as much as she could from her father over the years. And the more she spoke, the more she found she didn't care about Car McGrath or Bealtaine celebrations or her mother's changing moods—all that mattered was the pride she felt as she spelled out this glorious history. Not to mention this glorious future: "Then when I grow up, I've decided I'm going to be a Butcher too."

She made her confession before she had fully realised what she was doing. But it didn't matter—why should she hide her intentions any longer? She knew it was years away, but why shouldn't she tell her mother and her friend about her plan?

And why—why was her mother laughing?

Úna turned to her mam, her gorgeous face scrunched with some joke Úna couldn't for the life of her make out. "What's so funny?" She tried to keep the question calm, but already she could hear the crack in her voice coming back.

"Oh, darling, you can't be a Butcher."

Úna had been fingering her slice of bread, but now her hand went slack. "Why?"

"You're a girl."

Instantly, Úna looked at Ronan. "So?"

"So there has never been a girl Butcher. No—you'll be the one left behind twiddling your thumbs and making soup for eleven months of the year." Then, as if to sweeten the bitterness that had started to creep in to her voice, her mother reached across and squeezed her hand.

In the silence, Úna noticed her eyes turning wet. Maybe it was the steam from the soup. Maybe it was another spring symptom—the hay fever starting to do its rounds. But whatever it was, she couldn't stop it; most of all, she couldn't stand the weight of Ronan's stare.

When she pushed back from the table, some of the soup spilled over the rim of her bowl. She saw it seep red into the wood.

Úna kept her rage down as she crossed the garden until she was safely inside the shed, then she kicked out in fury, slamming her anger against the freezer door, which burst open, almost as if it were erupting too. Through her tears, she saw the cuts of meat inside, more purple than they were red, the white marbling of fat pressed up against the plastic. They had been stacked in such a way to fit the maximum amount. A year of cow—properly killed. A weekly treat for the ones who were left behind.

Úna steadied her breath and went to close the door, but she found her hands reaching in instead. First she pulled out a shank, cartoon-fat and wrapped in cellophane. They would save it for a special occasion—a birthday or an anniversary or even an extra visit home to them in June.

As it thudded against the wall, the whole shed shook. The tools tinkled from their shelves like bells. Úna reached again. This time it was a pair of sirloins. She lashed them straight for the pots of nails and screws on the shelf, the spill like a shower of bullet casings; like the Troubles they kept saying were nearly over. She went again with fillets and rumps, a T-bone that cracked the window, though the sunlight that poured in was nothing against the billows of dirt and dust. Úna threw one frozen lump and then another, until the bottom drawer was almost done—the offal that meant they were down to the very last of it. She wondered which one was the heart so she could throw it extra hard, break it in two or maybe even three, because in the end, that was all a family was—just three different bits that would never understand each other no matter how many questions you asked; no matter how many secret rituals you had; no matter how hard you ignored the bullies and the loneliness and the strangers slouching around your kitchen table.

"What's going on?"

Through the dust, Úna saw her mam out on the grass, her green eyes flitting over the carnage. Úna thought, of all things, of the fox. She hadn't seen or heard her in a while.

"Úna, what the hell—"

"I hate you." She couldn't deny the flicker of satisfaction she felt as she watched her mam wince. But she also knew the statement wasn't quite right. So instead of taking it back, she tried again. "I hate the Butchers."

Sure enough, this seemed to hurt her mother even more. "You don't mean that, love," she said. "I'm sorry I laughed. I'm sorry—"

"I hope that something bad happens to them out there."

But for all the things that were said that afternoon—that beautiful Bealtaine afternoon—they both knew this one was the worst. They stared at each other, a mother and a daughter surrounded by a mess of muscle and flesh; a mother and a daughter who sometimes felt so lonely they shared one bed. A chill ran through Úna's bones, a shiver that lingered long after her mam had pulled her close, murmuring into her hair while Úna sobbed into her chest, and the freezer fuse had blown itself to bits.

CHAPTER SIX
Grá

County Cavan, May 1996

She could still hear the bath draining itself, the sound a wet and mangled choke. She unwound her towel and stared at her reflection. For better or worse, a little weight had come back on.

She opened her drawer for knickers and a bra and tried not to notice herself selecting. The radio on the side was yapping about the Eurovision Song Contest that was happening in Norway next week. Ireland was going for its seventh win—such an accolade!—with a song called "The Voice." Grá turned it off, then immediately regretted the silence.

Earlier, she had cooked Úna's favourite meal and waited for her to utter those all-important words: *What's the special on the menu tonight?* Since last week, her daughter hadn't asked the question once. After dinner, they had packed Úna's bag and walked against a sunset over to Mrs. P's. The older woman was delighted to welcome her guest, if just a little too curious about the reasons for her overnight stay. "A book club, you said?"

"I saw it advertised in the *Anglo-Celt.*"

"You never mentioned."

"I thought it might be nice to do something for myself for once."

"Finishes late, does it?"

The air between them had stiffened, Mrs. P squinting like she could suddenly read it all. But then she had softened. "My Sol takes a couple of books with him on the road. I always ask if he could take me in his bag instead and he promises that, one year, he will."

In her bedroom now, Grá looked at the blue dress hanging lifeless from the silver hanger. The sleeves were long, but the neckline low. She thought about earrings, but didn't want to overdo it. Her hair was static from the bath's condensation— she would brush and spray it if she had the time. Cúch always preferred it up; but she, what did she prefer?

"And how has she *been*?" Mrs. P had shifted tack next, lowering her voice and flicking her eyes towards the kitchen door where her guest had already sprinted to discover what array of delicious treats had been prepared.

Grá had barely explained the half of what she had found in the garden last week, only that Úna had had a little *episode*. She hadn't mentioned the meat across the grass or the things that had been said—the real and the ridiculous and the devastating.

She hadn't mentioned, for various reasons, Ronan.

He had quit the house straight away so that Grá could tend to her hyperventilating daughter. She had pressed eight fingertips against Úna's sweat-soaked skin until she found her breath again. Together they had managed to change the freezer fuse and save most of the meat, but they both knew the words, no, the words could not be saved.

I hope that something bad happens to them out there.

Grá could tell Úna was trying to figure out what exactly made a curse a curse.

But it wasn't superstition that had kept Grá awake that night as she spooned her darling daughter; wasn't even sadness or fear for what it all might mean. Instead, it was rage—pure rage aimed out across the blackness, over the sleeping fields to where a group of eight men had set up camp at the side of the road. Because the price of her husband's absence she could just about pay (even if, recently, she had been struggling with it more and more), but at some point she had obviously lost sight of just how much it was hurting their child. Grá had tossed in bed all night, the anger soaking her own skin in sweat.

By morning it had dried, but in its wake a new instinct had been born. Because what if she were to hurt him back?

The taxi's horn sounded just as she was applying the bottle to her neck and the underside of her wrists. She ran to the kitchen and slipped the hardback into her handbag. It weighed a tonne. She had decided if she took the alibi along with her she would be safe from getting caught out—another strange instinct she somehow knew to trust.

"Evening, love." The driver's eyes were fat and greedy with her in the rear-view mirror.

She gave the gist of the address.

"Hot date on the town?"

She ignored him and looked out the window. She realised she had forgotten to rinse the tidemark from the tub.

Night lay down everywhere, draping the land in a dense, funereal black. Though really, Grá knew this was the season of birth, the fields twitching giddy with brand-new infant tribes.

She sometimes caught the gleam of the purple afterbirths strewn slick across the grass before they disappeared beneath a starving swoop of birds.

It had taken them years to get her pregnant. They had tried everything—had spent Cúch's entire month home in bed; had even discussed her meeting him halfway round the route to have another go. It wasn't until she reached twenty-seven that something had clicked and her stomach had finally begun to swell. Every day she had walked to the village, half ignoring, half relishing the remarks the local women hissed her way.

"I heard she was barren."

"Must be carrying a calf in there."

"I heard they sometimes eat their own young—it's another one of their *traditions*, don't you know?"

But after the birth, she didn't care what anyone said; she finally understood the meaning of true love. She had thought of her sister; had wanted to give Úna her name (though that would have meant revealing everything to Cúch). As for him, she had assumed from that point onwards he wouldn't be off travelling as much. There were two of them now and only one of him—it was basic maths; basic family. But it soon became clear nothing was going to change. If anything, being a father only seemed to make him more fixed in his ways. Because that was tradition; that was the comfort of ancient certainties; that was the reason she loved him.

Wasn't it?

The hazard lights flashed before her eyes.

"Here you are."

Her heart skipped as she handed over the note. She tried to remember the last time she had spent so much money on a single journey.

"I'll come back and get you for the price of a kiss?"

She opened the door and felt the weight of the book in her bag. She imagined the brutal hurt it could cause if she smashed it hard enough into his face.

The restaurant was a glammed-up thing fashioned awkwardly out of the ribs of a pub. There was a decent crowd for a Wednesday night, George Michael on the stereo singing them all along, extolling the virtues of having *faith, faith, faith*.

She saw the back of him first, the lean sweep of his neck and the shiny flop of his golden hair. She had worn earrings after all, though she still worried it was too much. "I know," she said. "I'm late."

The words came out colder than she intended. "It's fine," he said. "I only just—"

"I said I know," she repeated as she sat. There was a glass of water on the table, which she downed in one. The bath always left her dehydrated.

When she finally focused, she saw he was wearing a white shirt and a pale blue tie. She wondered if he'd already packed the formal wear in his suitcase, or if he'd had to buy it especially for tonight. Either way, he looked different—she was used to him in scuffed jeans and walking boots; a pair of black sunglasses for eyes; a camera slung around his neck and a finger on the button always ready, very gently, to press.

After that first encounter by the lake, she had spotted him the following afternoon when she went down for her swim. She felt his eyes tracing her every stroke; felt a thrill that was more startling than she understood. When she was dry he approached, repeating his request for suggestions. She realised she must have been preparing her answer overnight. She turned north, the opposite direction from the house. "Follow me." When he did, it thrilled her all over again.

For the next few weeks they had spent most afternoons venturing higher and higher into the borderlands. Grá knew that, up here, it was a lawless kind of place; that, up here, different rules applied. He did most of the talking, mostly to do with his work, his various plans and ambitions and dreams—how they would exhibit his work in the museums of London and New York; how his pictures would take him very far from home. As she listened, Grá felt as if she were being transported too. She found herself thinking more and more of her sister. She found that, the day after their walks, her limbs were stiff and sore in ways they hadn't been in years.

"You look incredible."

Tonight, though, their limbs weren't side by side, they were facing one another across a candlelit table. Grá felt herself blushing, so to cover it she reached for the bottle of red that sat open, breathing and ready.

"I mean it, I'd barely recognise you."

She picked up her glass and he did the same. She very rarely took a drink. She wondered if he knew it was the best thing he could have possibly said.

They turned to the menus and this time Grá felt herself blushing at the prices, even though he had insisted it was his treat. That was the whole point of the dinner when he first suggested it—a "thank you" for her assistance with the project. He was heading back to Dublin shortly so it was the least that he could do.

It was, Grá knew, the last borderland venture they might have.

She hadn't accepted right away, but then last week after the incident with Úna, her anger had spurred her to tell him that yes, she would come. At the time, Ronan had been crouched behind a mound of sedge photographing a heron that had, just then, taken flight. Grá thought now of that bird; thought again of her sister. She wondered if Lena would recognise her after so many years apart. She wondered if, in the last few weeks, they had actually grown more alike.

"Right so, are yous ready?"

Grá looked up. She could take the waitress's question as loaded or she could just let herself smile and order the fish. With the menus removed, it somehow felt the first hurdle was out of the way. Soon they fell into their usual rhythm—him prattling about his project, all the latest ideas and developments.

A bread basket appeared, which gave her something to do with her mouth.

"I took your suggestion about your man Eoin Goldsmith." As he spoke, Ronan tore the crusts away from the edges like a child. "Strolled up Monaghan way, made a few enquiries. And you were spot on—the Bull does seem to be at the heart of this boom. Although, did you hear about the suspected case in Cork they reported this afternoon? If the BSE has arrived over here, the boom might be fucked after all."

Grá nodded along even if, being honest, she had fallen out of interest in the poor mad cows. She had had more than enough on her mind (and her body) to keep her occupied. She tried to remember the last time she had even been to a restaurant—probably Mrs. P's sixtieth birthday lunch a few years ago, the older woman getting wobbly on two glasses of sparkling wine, then bemoaning Sol's absence for the whole bus journey home.

"Anyway, I've decided the Bull might be the last photo I need. I'm still lacking a killer shot to pull it all together. And if I can't—"

"You mean to say you went walking without me?" She was teasing him, but she got a small buzz out of seeing him flinch. She decided the shirt and tie made him look younger, but what she couldn't decide was whether that was bad or good.

"Grá." His voice came out wounded. "You told me you couldn't . . . You said you needed the day to get ready." And then: "It was worth it—you look incredible."

"You already said that."

For another moment his eyes sparkled, the pair of them wide and terrified. But when she smiled, he exhaled and looked up at her, a bashful wee grin. "Well, it's true." Until his confidence returned, his gaze travelling down her throat to the low-cut border of skin and dress. She reached out for the bottle, the gesture stretching the neckline so there was a glimpse into the shadows beneath. As she poured, she tried so hard to keep her hand from shaking.

She took one look at the salmon and knew there would be invisible bones she would have to search out with her tongue.

The first bottle had somehow vanished so they ordered another. He had asked for his ribeye well done.

"Worried it might make you mad?" She sent her hand across the space between them to help herself to one of his chips.

"Ah sure, I reckon I'm already a bit cracked."

She knew he was joking, though he had mentioned his moods more than once before. It was something to do with depression; with a cocktail of pills he took to keep him up or keep him down. By all accounts he'd had a tricky childhood— a father who'd abandoned him young and moved back across to England. Grá had listened, though she didn't much care for the details, except to wonder if every family had their runaway.

She wondered if there was ever room for more than one.

"And did you hear about the Gardaí?"

She watched him now, still going, still obsessed, furiously working his elbow to saw through the black lump of meat. "They've just launched a new operation to barricade the border shut. It's costing the government thousands of pounds." He raised his fork to his lips. She tried not to pay too much attention to the smell. "Apparently some illegal smugglers have started sneaking in contaminated cattle from the North, so the guards want to catch the bastards and lock them up." He took the bite and began to chew; swallowed so quickly it must have hurt. "And the whole initiative has been given *quite* the name." With this, though, he took a moment, savouring the punchline before he spat it out. He smiled. He really was handsome. "*Operation Matador.*"

She took a moment too; felt the mischief building in her. "Matador?"

"That's right."

She leaned in over the table. "Now there," she said, "is your killer shot." As she pictured it, her smile began to spread. "The Gardaí lined up in a row along the border. All dressed in their bright red capes." Their laughter rang out as one and it felt glorious.

By the time they had settled again, she looked down and saw her plate was empty. She couldn't remember the last time she had finished a meal.

"You enjoyed that."

She looked at him. "I did."

"Dessert?"

She shook her head. "I couldn't."

"I think you probably could." His lips had gone blue from the wine, which meant hers probably had too, so now the transformation was complete. She was a different creature, beyond recognition entirely.

In the back of the taxi, the camera case sat between them—it turned out he'd had it stashed under the table all along. She had teased him—"all work and no play"—and he had said not to worry, he was feeling very playful indeed. As if to prove a point, they had drained the second bottle, then rolled on to some Irish coffees, the smack of whiskey spinning their words and their heads out the door and into this sticky leather-look back seat.

She suddenly wondered if what she longed for, more than anything, was for him to just take her photograph; to be committed to film, as if she mattered.

For now, the device sat between them untouched, like a border, a barricade, a new operation—*Matador!*—could you believe it? And beyond the device was his body, also untouched, though she could feel its heat from here, a bright red flag to a fired-up bull. She tried to distract herself by singing songs in her head—*faith, faith, faith*—but she kept slipping over the words. They had told the driver the first stop would be her address. If anything more had been decided, it hadn't been said aloud.

She wanted to roll down the window. She needed air; needed water. Or maybe she needed something else entirely. She saw where the clouds had started coming into themselves, squaring up like broad-shouldered men—there would be rain within the hour. She reminded herself it would be good for the garden, though truth be told she hadn't tended to the thing recently. In just a few short weeks it had started to grow, she knew, wild.

"Right—here you are."

She looked up. Yes, suddenly, here they were—two strangers in the back of a taxi, nothing between them except a black camera case and three weeks of desire. The hazard lights tried so hard to warn them. She looked at his face and knew this was the last time she would ever see it. She could taste the dark fruit of the second bottle, which made her think of the locals who still believed rowan berries kept you safe from being captured by the fairies. Oh yes, some beliefs never died. *Faith, faith, faith.*

"He can walk from here," she told the driver as she lurched herself out of the car, leaving Ronan to pay the price. She wondered, not for the first time, how he was supporting himself while he worked on his project. She wondered, not for the first time, whether there were other women he went walking with too.

Outside, the night air was as damp as it looked. There was the crunch of her footsteps on the gravel. And there was a stranger sound. She stopped to listen—the fox's bark. It was getting very close. Next she heard his footsteps and the tyres roll away so she staggered as far as the front door before she turned. He came to join her, their bodies only inches apart, though still they hadn't laid a finger. Suddenly she remembered. "I have something for you." She reached into her bag while he stood there, confused, his eyes stretched wide and terrified again. It was as if he were worried she might eat him alive. It was everything in the world she wanted to do. She felt the first spits of rain on her skin, little pricks of delight, as she handed over the book. *The Butcher Boy*. His laughter was more like a gasp of relief and hers was more like a howl, an animal sound.

When their laughter stopped the only noise was the droplets of water, faster now, and the silence of all the days ahead when there would be no more walks, no more dreams, only her husband's absence and her daughter's despair; only her friend's dependence and her long-lost sister's bravery. There would only be hours drowning in the bath trying to touch herself, trying to claw for something—anything—more.

She grabbed the back of his head. Her tongue searched out the dark fruit of his.

The heavens finally opened themselves wide up.

•

When she woke, she was alone in her bed, a steady beat thrumming against the four walls of her skull. She staggered up to her elbows. It was barely dawn, so there wasn't much yet in the way of light. She thought of the darkroom Ronan had once described to her. The process there sounded like a kind of magic. She had left her earrings in, so the flesh of her lobes thrummed a steady beat too.

"Before I go, can I ask you something?"

It was only when he came into focus, his shirt buttoned, that she fully noticed her nakedness. Her limbs were cold, a little stiff, though it would be hours—or maybe days, maybe weeks—before last night would fully sink in.

"You don't have to answer if you don't want, but I was wondering . . . Do you by any chance know what county the Butchers are headed for next?" Ronan paused to lick his dry lips. "Do you think they would sit for me? Never mind the Bull, I've realised *that's* the killer shot I need."

While she listened, the bedsheet fell below her breasts, but Grá didn't move to pick it up. Her anger started low, her voice very careful not to trigger the looming pain in her head. "So that's what this was about?" she growled. "Your great artistic strategy—using the women to get at the men? The ones with the lives that are actually *worth* capturing?" But just as soon as it got going, her tirade stopped. Around them, the room was already lighter. Much to both their surprise, her moans had been loud enough to fill all four walls to the brim. "Monaghan," she said as

113

she sighed and rolled over. "They'll be arriving there in the next couple of days." Because she knew women sometimes used men too; knew, in the end, that was all bodies were really for.

By noon, Grá could no longer delay the walk to Mrs. P's to collect her only child. She had drawn a bath, though she already knew she would draw another, even hotter one, that night. From the sideboard, the radio struck a sombre note. The suspected case Ronan had mentioned down in Cork had just been confirmed. Which meant it was official—the BSE had somehow managed to make its way to Ireland.

I hope that something bad happens to them out there.

Grá thought of her daughter's words and then she thought of the taxi driver who had dropped them off together. She thought how she had almost ordered steak at the restaurant, but then hadn't—it seemed, despite everything, some loyalties were harder to break. And when she grabbed her coat and opened the front door, she thought the fox's tongue was just lolling out because it was thirsty—because it needed Grá to go back inside and fetch her a bowl of water—but the contortion of limbs across the front step said otherwise.

The night's torrential rain had finally run itself dry. The breeze blew soft furrows through the tail. Up close, the animal wasn't orange and it wasn't brown and it wasn't breathing either. *Madra rua* it was called in Irish. "Red dog."

It really will be reddy!

Grá scanned beyond the road towards the sodden fields, searching for any lurking predator. There was only dirt and then there was nothing; only the endless, lifelong nothing. Maybe the taxi had hit the poor creature with its bumper. Or maybe it had eaten a dose of rat poison a farmer left out. Or maybe it had been infected by a widow's curse or an English disease, which, despite their best efforts, had found its way across the Irish Sea. But Grá realised the explanation didn't matter one bit when she heard the sound of the cubs mewling somewhere close, calling for their mother to please, please, come home.

CHAPTER SEVEN
Fionn

County Monaghan, June 1996

Ever since the borderland operation, Fionn had been riding a bit of a high. He could still feel the adrenalin of the smuggle rushing merry through his blood; could still taste the anxiety of the wait followed by the exultation of the refrigerated truck's eventual arrival. And more than anything, he could savour the reassurance of the cash tucked safely away in the kitty. He would have Eileen up to that Dublin clinic before she knew it.

So when Fergus Hynes phoned about another expedition, Fionn didn't even have to consider his reply. He only had to help Eileen to bed after the second half of *Casablanca*, then slip out into the sideways rain. He drove to O'Connell's where Fergus had told him to be waiting, parked up and stepped out into the mizzle, humming the tune from the closing credits beneath his garlic dinner breath.

From inside the pub, Fionn could hear the men cracking up; could imagine the creamy taste of their pints. He shoved his hands in his pockets and hummed a little louder.

As it happened, last Sunday after Mass he had bumped into DOB, who said he'd heard Fionn was involved in one of the Bull's "secret operations." Fionn had panicked until DOB reassured: "Sure, aren't we all? Making the most of this boom while it lasts!" But then DOB had gone a bit serious. "Just be careful—they say those Matador cunts are keeping a beady eye. God knows the Bull would hang you from a hook if you got caught."

"Right, you gobshite!"

Fionn looked up now to where Fergus Hynes and his badger streak had appeared across the O'Connell's car park.

"Let's get this show on the road. Jesus, I'll tell you what— that new *Ballykissangel* programme is a total waste of space."

Fionn shook out his head and forced a smile; tried to remember the jaunty thread of his tune.

"Bloody BBC makes rural Ireland look awful dull."

An hour later and they had arrived in the borderlands, Mossy and Briain parked up with a trailer alongside. Fionn wondered whose turn it would be with the rubber stamp; who would be marked with the bright-blue ink around their nails. Then, when the smugglers appeared—their vehicle so large it was clear tonight's haul was at least twice the size of the last— Fionn wondered if he would be getting paid twice as much.

He wondered if DOB might need an extra pair of hands for his own "secret operation."

He wondered, out of nowhere, if the Bull even knew his name.

What he didn't know until he was out in the sodden air and the vehicle doors had been wrenched apart was that tonight's haul was a different variety altogether. Fionn gasped, then tried to swallow it back and got a lungful of drizzle for his troubles.

"Anything the matter?" Fergus Hynes asked, pure neutral, as if he had mentioned the change in plan all along.

Fionn knew better than to give an answer; knew enough to just stay quiet and shake his head. Fergus Hynes just added four more words—"it was Goldsmith's idea"—as much a statement as a sort of warning. It was the first time Fionn had felt anything but kindness towards the beef baron and his secret operations.

Because this wasn't beef at all—no, these were beasts and they were very much alive, their breaths steaming like kettles, their feet kicking up like Riverdance, their lows sounding a deep and panicked chorus. Fionn turned to Mossy, expecting an ally in confusion or consternation at least, but Mossy was already busy setting up—not with a stamp and a pad of ink, but with a batch of tags and a plastic hook.

Fionn stumbled to piece the bits together. From what he could tell, the new plan of attack was to remove the tag from each cow's ear, then clip in a shiny new one before it was loaded up and taken south. That way it would be marked as an Irish cow—as *uninfected*—and nothing ever else, a fresh counterfeit passport hanging down from its cartilage.

Fionn had seen many things in his time—litres of whiskey smuggled inside a cattle carcass; huge sides of beef wrapped in bales of hay and driven right under a border guard's nose—but even in the olden days, he had never seen the likes of this. He had thought false tags were a notorious bugger to get away with. He sighed and didn't even bother to swallow it back.

Briain led the first cow out and shoved her neck through the contraption they were using as a makeshift head gate, then hooked the remover and yanked too quickly so that he ripped the flesh of the ear. The beast kicked out in discomfort while Fionn flinched too. There was no need to be so rough. The pliers clipped the new ID in through the open wound.

But Fionn had to set his discomfort aside because there was a job that had to be done, even if it wasn't technically the job he had been hired to do. He tried to soothe the animals as best he could as he led them up the ramp into the empty livestock trailer. He tried to keep one eye on the horizon in case anyone was watching.

By the time he made it home the rain had finally stopped, though when he locked up his 4×4 and made his way into the byre he could hear a steady trickle of water. There were holes in the roof and decay in the joists. There was an entire bloodline held together by tape and twine. Fionn still felt agitated, so he decided he would stay up and get started on the morning milk. He knew it would help calm down the worst of his jitters.

The fields were silent as he jimmied open the bolt. Even after such a torrential few days, Fionn knew the girls were delighted to be back out in the paddock. He had moved the fences yesterday to give them a brand-new strip to graze.

He led them into the parlour six at a time, then positioned himself in the middle pit. He cleaned down the tits and attached the clusters. He always wondered if it tickled. He caressed the damp velvet of their flanks while they filled the containers with the flow of their warm white milk, every drop sucked away to the giant refrigerated tank next door. They chewed the meal which he bought off one of the Bull's side companies at a very reasonable price. It made Fionn glad that, even after scaling things down on the farm, he could still afford to keep his girls well fed.

He worked through them slowly, one batch at a time, going even more gently than usual, then made sure to finish up with Glassy, his wee pet. She was an Irish Moiled with brown map-of-the-world shapes strewn across her back and face. Her walk may have been a bit wonky, but the rest of her was a dream. He had named her after Glas Ghaibhleann, the great Irish cow whose milk was so plentiful it managed to satisfy the multitudes. According to the myth, she had travelled all four provinces filling vessel after vessel, her bounty knowing no end. So now the place names across the country bore testament to her generosity:

Knockglas.
Glasnevin.
Finglas.

Fionn listed them out as he worked, an incantation to ward off any worry, any residue of fear.

After he led the girls back to the field, he hosed the parlour down, scraping the muck and rinsing the dung, the water running wretched then crystal clear into the drains. The Lakeland lorry would come tomorrow to test the batch for butter content. Fionn gulped the glass he had kept for himself, unpasteurised and wicked-fat upon his lips.

He had been right—already his jitters had calmed. Sure, what did it matter that Fergus hadn't mentioned the change in cargo? Hadn't they managed just fine? And wouldn't the Bull be only delighted with their work? Fionn hadn't counted the envelope yet, but he was pretty sure the heft in his pocket felt bigger than last time around. If anything, it was the best result he could have hoped for.

He watched the sun crawl up through the mist, a reddish hue that revealed rowan trees and bracken clumps; hawthorn flowers with their dirty white petals and their sickly sweet scent. The view might not have been beautiful to some, but for him the familiarity was pure comfort, the copper light collecting in the furrows that streaked through the muck a bit like veins. And he was almost ready for his bed—almost ready to exhale— if it weren't for the linger of some silly, throwaway words.

Just be careful.

Fionn flicked his gaze and found the coil of rope hanging down from the tree.

They say those Matador cunts are keeping a beady eye.

He shook his head and licked the cream from his lips.

God knows the Bull would hang you from a hook if you got caught.

He didn't go to bed till long after the mist had burned off.

•

The following week, thanks be to God, Fionn's paranoia had died a quick and painless death. He had counted the notes in the envelope—sure enough, there was an extra bit thrown in. And now he had another operation to be focusing on, not up in the borderlands or down the back of a midnight trailer, but right here waiting on his own front doorstep just as the Angelus bells tolled six o'clock.

Fionn stared out at the men, all eight arranged in a perfect semicircle. He thought they looked a bit like a group of carol singers come to sing "Once in Royal David's City." Then he remembered—*feck's sake!*—they probably didn't celebrate Christmas or the Angelus or any of that. Fionn's paranoia was gone, but that didn't mean he wasn't nervous.

Of course, the whole thing had been Davey's idea—an elaborate plan he had managed to concoct in between the study notes and revision guides that were piled up on his desk. And all in response to that "strange dream" Eileen had been having recently.

You remember me telling you?

The one about the Butchers?

Fionn knew, at least for now, the main chunk of the tumour had been excavated from her brain. There were times he wondered if something else had taken root there instead.

Eileen's family had been believers since way back, whereas Fionn's family had always been Catholic to the core, so when their whirlwind romance began he insisted he ate what he liked and worshipped Christ and that, if she loved him, she would do the very same. Surprisingly, she had agreed—if anything, it seemed to make her even keener on the whole affair—any excuse to gobsmack her backward clan. Although she did say there was a little sister she would miss something terrible; said she would try to convince her to run away with them too (truthfully Fionn hadn't been so keen on that part of the plan).

For the duration of their marriage, though, the Butchers had never been mentioned again. It was only recently that Eileen, out of the blue, had started to utter their name. And then Davey had uttered it too when he approached his dad in the yard one evening and explained his idea; his logic, despite Fionn's better instinct, actually made a bit of sense.

It will make her happy.

We owe her that at least.

Sure, what have we got to lose?

But the answer to that, Fionn knew, was plenty—especially at this particular moment in time. Because what if Fergus and the lads found out? Fionn was only beginning to gain their respect—the last thing he needed was to draw the wrong kind of attention. He swallowed. He wondered if the Bull and the Butchers had ever crossed paths somewhere on the road. He wondered, daftly, if the Butchers had a cure for BSE.

As it happened, on the last borderland expedition, there had been a bit of chatter about the ancient group; about their imminent arrival to the county to visit the few locals who were still rumoured to believe.

"I once knew a lad," said Briain Ní Ghríofa, "who reckoned they could cure a cow of blindness—could touch its eyes with mud and make it see."

"Sure, some say they come from the Holy Land."

"Well, I heard the old bitch who made the curse was descended from St. Patrick himself!"

Fergus Hynes, though, hadn't shared their curiosity. "Glorified knackers. Still stuck in the past." His spite had reminded Fionn of his daddy—God knows he had always detested the Butchers too.

But Fionn had to remember that this wasn't about the other men and it certainly wasn't about his father. This was about Eileen—she had been through so much—the tumour, the seizures, the drugs, the beating delivered from his own two hands. The waiting list for the clinic was probably as long as the Shannon, but in the short term it seemed this would make her smile.

And really, wasn't that everything to him?

So eventually he had said "yes" to Davey, and Eileen had said "thank you" when he told her the date.

"You're very welcome." He had placed his hand on top of hers.

She had looked at it, taking a moment to find her focus and make a choice. She hadn't taken her hand away.

"You're very welcome." This time the words were meant for eight sets of hands, not just one. "Fionn McCready. Pleasure to make your acquaintance." His attempt at formality betrayed the full extent of his nerves. He had thought of combing his hair earlier, then felt a total thick. But luckily two of the men stepped forward now to meet the introduction smiling— an old lad called Sol and a slightly younger one called Cúch. Fionn checked over their shoulders, terrified for who might be driving by. Thanks be to God, the road was silent as a prayer.

Eileen had advised that the best thing to do was to let the Butchers get on with their killing, then to invite them inside afterwards for a pot of tea. So Fionn led them through the yard, watching the way all eight of them walked; the way all eight of them were dressed. They wore overalls and sturdy boots that were tied in double—or maybe they were triple?—knots.

There was a calmness about them that was almost serene; something that wasn't easy to describe.

Apart from the sag in the middle of the roof, the byre was looking halfway decent. Fionn had spent the afternoon cleaning and laying fresh bedding, while Eileen had busied herself with the tidying of the house. For all Fionn's reservations, it seemed Davey's theory had been spot on—already the visit had done her good. She was a bundle of energy; had even applied a swipe of lipstick.

Fionn tried to remember the last time his wife had put on make-up for him.

Out in the byre, it was all business, the men asquint as they adjusted to the semi-darkness. In the corner was the pen where Fionn usually kept the newborns. Sol and Cúch stepped forward to inspect the animals.

"So here are the girls," Fionn began. "I didn't know if you needed anything *specific* so I've given you a couple of options. This is Aoife and Bó, both about eleven hundred pounds and still milking like the clappers." Here he paused, a bit self-conscious. He breathed in the earthy closeness of the animals' hides. "Then we have their mother, Glassy. As you can see she is a slightly bigger animal. Although there's not a whole lot of milk left in her, I'm afraid, even despite the name!" Here Fionn tried to laugh, but suddenly his self-consciousness had turned into a kind of guilt. He stared at his pet. Half her eyelashes were brown and the other half were white. She was fidgeting—lately her hind legs had been giving her more trouble than usual—but even if she wasn't long for this world, what the hell was he thinking? Why had he chosen to bring her here and offer her up?

"Have you been busy?" In his panic, Fionn offered small talk to try to slow the proceedings down.

Sol kept studying the livestock. "Oh absolutely, it has been a very good year so far."

"People seem to be feeling flush," Cúch elaborated. "More inclined to welcome us in; put on a bit of a spread. Let's hope this Celtic Beef Boom is here to stay!" As he spoke, his eyes did a scour of the place, taking in the sag of the roof and the peel of the rust.

Fionn felt himself blush. "As you can see, I might have jumped off the bandwagon a little early."

But now Sol looked away from the animals. "Well, if you ask me, you're wise—I suspect things are probably about to turn. Another case of BSE has been confirmed. People are being very reckless—I suspect the disease will be everywhere before we—"

"That's a load of bollocks!" No sooner was it out, Fionn regretted the snap. He tried for another laugh to cover it up. "I mean, touch wood or fingers crossed or whatever you're into yourself." But it was too late—the conversation had already slunk off into the opposite corner of the byre. The Butchers returned to their business, mumbling quietly between themselves.

Fionn held his breath. Glassy looked straight at him with slow, knowing blinks. Thanks to some miracle, they opted for Bó and Fionn exhaled audibly. He wondered if the Butchers had a sixth sense for these sorts of things.

"We'll let you know when we are finished."

Fionn heard Sol's words, but still it took him a moment to realise they wanted him to bugger off. He bristled, just for a second, then stepped outside where the air had grown cooler. As he waited on the other side of the corrugation, Fionn tried to resist the urge to press his eye up against it for a sneaky peek. He had heard there was a special prayer the men recited. Others said they all kissed the cow on the head. Others suggested far ruder things, but Fionn assumed that was only dirty talk—God knows there would be none of that queer stuff under his roof, that was for sure.

Fionn folded his arms and thought back to the house, wondering if Eileen had started pouring the hot water into the mugs to get them warmed up, while Davey hovered by her side for company. Or maybe he had disappeared upstairs, his face glued deep into his books, his mind a million miles and worlds away.

Fionn heard a lowing from next door. It was very steady, very calm—nothing like the panicked, painful squeals from the factory floor.

As always, thinking about his son flooded Fionn with a deep sense of regret. He had agreed to this whole idea for Eileen's sake—to bring a bit of joy to her housebound days. But he had also agreed because it was Davey's suggestion—a secret father-son operation at last. Fionn knew it might be the closest they would ever get.

Next he heard a thump, which meant Bó was gone. Fionn assumed they would string her up now by the feet—probably with ropes or chains from the byre joists—then slowly start the bleeding out.

That being said, even after Fionn had made the arrangements—had managed to get word to the Butchers on the sly—still Davey had been acting distant as ever. Maybe he was just nervous about those exams. Maybe he was still moping from his break-up with Faela Quin. Maybe there was something else Davey was keeping from him—a barrier locked with ropes and chains to keep Fionn firmly out.

This time it wasn't a sound he caught but a smell. It was a bit like burning; a bit like something herbal. Fionn closed his eyes and sucked it deep into his lungs.

And thinking about his son always got Fionn thinking back to his own daddy, for better or for worse. No doubt if the old man were here now he would suggest a couple of ways Fionn could snap Davey out of his spell. But there were traditions that should live and others that should be left to curl up and die alone.

"She passed peacefully."

When Fionn opened his eyes, the youngest Butcher was standing before him. Fionn could remember being introduced to the lad as Con, not much older than Davey by the looks of him, but a good deal broader in the back.

"We'll start preparing her now—it shouldn't take long. If you could just let us know where we'd find your freezer and your—"

"But you'll come in?"

"What?"

"Afterwards. For a pot of tea."

"Well, I'd have to—"

"No you must," Fionn said. "It's for the missis, you see." He wondered if he should explain about Eileen's poor health or, again, if the men had a special sense for these sorts of things.

"We'd be delighted!" It was the older lad called Cúch who appeared next and who seemed to have the full meaning of the scene. "I've a serious thirst on me," he said. "And trust me, I know very well what wives can be like."

Fionn laughed with relief and set off, realising it was true that all men were the very same no matter their prayers or their traditions or their terrible mistakes.

By the time the Butchers had cleaned up and presented themselves at the house, Fionn saw that Eileen's lipstick had been reapplied. He tried to catch Davey's eye, but didn't succeed. "Allow me to introduce the Butchers." He took control as best as he could, holding out the kitchen chairs as if they were thrones and indicating that the men should take a seat.

Soon the room was full to capacity—elbows and teacups, local gossip and national politics—until the air almost had a touch of celebration to it. They discussed the Stormont Talks and the latest ceasefire; they discussed the Euro '96 soccer tournament that had started on Saturday. Fionn glanced one more time for Davey, but in amongst the bodies he could no longer find his son's.

"And how long have you been a member?" he heard Eileen asking next. She was sitting opposite Sol, his wrinkled face lit up by her attention. "Not that you look, of course, a day over twenty-one." The old man threw back his head, the pleats of his neck stretched tight, young again. "And you must call to the same families every year, but what about when they move house? Or when the children leave home? Or—"

"Eileen, leave off with the inquisition and pour our guest a drop of hot!" Fionn barked the order to try to save her— he could tell the barrage of questions was a cover for her exhaustion setting in. But in fairness, by now they were all a little weary—nicely, like, from the success of the afternoon. The men had started to disperse, some nipping outside to stretch their legs or have a bit of tobacco. Blackfoot weaved between their legs, ferreting out any fallen crumbs.

Eventually, Cúch announced that they would do one last sweep of the place to ensure they hadn't forgotten anything, then they would get out of Fionn's hair.

"Ah, you're not in my—"

"Fionn, why don't you go out and give Cúch a hand?"

Fionn looked at his wife. Her eyes were as green and sweet as freshly cut grass. "You don't mind, do you?" she said. "Only Sol here is in the middle of telling me a wonderful story."

The two men walked outside and while Cúch checked the carts, Fionn told him he would check the byre to make sure nothing had been left behind. He wondered, just for a second, how he would look in a pair of overalls. He wondered if he might start doing his laces in triple knots.

The dusk was a mild and purple thing spread soft like a blanket over the yard. Fionn had moved Eileen's Fiesta further out of the way. It was good to run the engine every so often to stop the battery from dying altogether. The fields beyond lay motionless, the trees poised with their arms raised to the sky. Fionn sighed into the view. He felt more relaxed in himself than he had in a long long while.

He was approaching the byre when he first heard the noise. It sounded as if somebody was crying. "Davey, is that you?" He could have sworn he saw a movement by the back door; a sound a bit like footsteps sprinting out. But when he flicked on the light everything was still again—the rakes, the hoes, the meal sacks lined up along the side—and in the middle, the black water marks tinged with pink.

Fionn looked up and tried to picture it. The joist was far above him—he hadn't a notion how they would have got the animal up there. He thought he could see a white chafe in the wood where the chains must have looped around. And suddenly Fionn thought of that coil of rope hanging from the tree in the yard and remembered what his father used to tie there. Dead crows—black eyes, black feathers, black beaks—dangling upside down. It was an old trick to scare the other crows away; to warn them what would happen otherwise. Fionn turned off the light. He wondered how much all traditions had to do, really, with fear.

Before they set off, Fionn made a point of shaking each of the Butchers' hands in turn. He somehow knew he wouldn't wash his own hand tonight; somehow knew it would bring him luck. Eileen joined him on the front step, waving goodbye until the carts had receded from view; then she did something Fionn couldn't remember her doing in months or maybe, he conceded, years.

After the kiss, he opened his eyes. The wind had blown a wetness into hers. "You are a good man, Fionn McCready," she said. "A good good man."

He opened his mouth to say something back, like *I'm so sorry* or *I will make you better* or *You are my wonderful story*, but the only sound was the horses' hooves, the clop as steady and sure as a human heart.

•

Within a couple of nights, the good luck had already started kicking in. Fergus Hynes was on the phone about a last-minute job; a generous envelope. Fionn did the dishes after dinner and made Eileen a hot chocolate to take with her to bed. He smiled. He was feeling more than a little indulgent.

But when he arrived at the O'Connell's car park and transferred into Fergus's passenger seat, he had a different sort of feeling. "How's she cutting?" His greeting earned him no reply—not so much as a nod of the head. The engine revved throatily before he had even done his safety belt.

They drove in silence. The moon was so full and low it looked as if it might fall out of the sky. "Are we talking livestock or steaks this evening?" They weren't, of course, talking at all. But Fionn decided he could at least ease the strange atmosphere by focusing on the night's proceedings. "Did Mossy and Briain go on ahead or are they following after? Who's in charge of the stamps, or—"

"Would you ever shut your fucking face?"

And suddenly Fionn went cold, very cold, because he realised that, clearly, Fergus Hynes knew everything. About the Butchers. About their visit and the overwhelming joy Fionn had derived from the whole affair. He had counted the cuts they managed to fit in the overflow freezer—Jesus, there was more than they would possibly get through—but for some reason Fionn wanted to wait for a special occasion to try the first, like a wedding anniversary or a clinic appointment finally booked in. And he had convinced himself he'd been fierce discreet with the whole arrangement, but God knows nothing around here ever stayed a secret. Fionn thought of Davey. Had the boy let something slip? And if so, had it been an accident or out of that same old spite Fionn couldn't seem to shift? Either way, Fergus Hynes had found out, and now he was taking Fionn to no man's land to teach him a lesson; to remind him about loyalty and priorities and the proper order of things. *Glorified knackers.* Wasn't that what he had called the Butchers? *Still stuck in the past.* Whereas the Bull and his cronies were all about "Modern Ireland" and progress and the Celtic Beef Boom—they couldn't be seen fraternising with the likes of *them.*

Fionn tried his best to breathe as they drove higher and higher, up where nobody would ever find him. The borderlands had always been a place to take items you wanted to dispose of—burned-out cars and old bits of fly-tipped junk. He had seen broken fridges, the spiral coils of their backs exposed; battered toys and teddy bears, their stuffing ripped out and blown into some nearby twigs to be mistaken for a sheep snag of wool. And then, during the peak of the Troubles, they said far more sinister things had been dumped up here—men murdered and fed into the borderland bogs, their bodies swallowed by the viscous muck. "The Disappeared."

The proper order of things.

"Ach, Fionn, I'm sorry." When Fergus spoke, Fionn swallowed his thoughts. "Things are starting . . . It's all getting a bit out of control." Fergus wrenched the clutch and changed to a higher gear. "Tonight might be a bit of a dodgy one."

Fionn knew he should probably feel some kind of anxiety at this, but he felt only a rush of relief. His secret was safe. The Butchers' luck remained untouched.

"You should probably open that."

Next Fergus raised his eyebrows high and cocked his head towards the glove compartment. Fionn also knew, somehow, what he would find inside; knew that, even in the darkness, the gun would be small and black like a child's battered toy. Very slowly, he clicked the latch.

As he held it in his hands, Fionn thought of his daddy's friend Big Billy Tierney; of a bullet through his face on a cattle run long ago.

When they arrived, the other side were already waiting. Fergus parked up close and they all leapt out in unison. With the metal tucked into his waist, Fionn's trousers stretched tight across his gut. He realised he was desperate for a piss. Even outside, the air was mostly silence, which of course should have let him know the situation straight away, but when he reached the open doors of the trailer he was still surprised by what he found inside.

The bodies had been flung, one on top of the other, in an awkward black-and-white heap. A splay of broken limbs. A whole pile of unwanted junk, fly-tipped and never to be seen again. Fionn tried to trace the outlines, the flanks and the haunches, until he could just about trace one of the heads. There was a hole in the middle where the animal's brains had splurted out.

"We need to hurry." The main lad had an accent that was thick Armagh. "Them Matador pricks are on patrol tonight."

He bounded up and started hooshing the first body forwards. "If you lads grab the front legs, I'll take the rear."

Fionn saw the animals were only young. He saw where one of the hooves had tangled with another. It looked like a pair of lovers linking arms. "How much do they even *weigh*?" Of all the questions, Fionn didn't know why he chose to ask this one, when what he really wanted to know was where the calves had come from and why the calves had been shot and if the calves had tested positive for BSE?

Fergus answered them all at once. "We didn't have time to make proper arrangements."

"Ah, Fergus, you can't be serious."

But Fergus Hynes was very serious as he nestled his shoulder under the dead calf's flank like a pallbearer at a funeral. "Didn't you hear the lad? We need to hurry."

Would you ever shut your fucking face?

So Fionn shut his face and crouched his back, bracing himself for the force of the impact. He staggered, trying to guide the young animal into place. He could have sworn the hide was still warm. And he could have sworn the glare was just the fat moon again, lending a bit of extra light to their terrible task, but then he saw the flashes of red and blue which sent Fergus bolting and the calf tumbling and its leg clocking Fionn in the back of the skull. He tried to get up, but found that he couldn't, so instead he just lay down in the muck with his head spinning, his eyes watering, his lips whispering to Eileen that everything would be OK—he had done the maths and it was only one more job to go until the kitty was full and ready. Maybe they could book a hotel in Dublin—make a proper weekend of it, like?—and never mind the Garda cars approaching with their sirens screeching like banshees or that full moon in the sky above like a white mark on a black scan of a brain that says it's come back it's come back it's come back.

CHAPTER EIGHT
Davey

County Monaghan, June 1996
"One hour to go, lads. One hour to go."

Davey glanced up at the invigilator, Mr. Twomey, but already the old man had turned the other way, indifferent entirely to the significance of his words.

One hour to go.

Of this exam.

Of all the exams.

One hour to go of this whole portion of your life.

Davey jiggered in his seat, flicked his pen, bounced his knee, every bit of him an awkward metronome sounding a different beat. From the desk in front, Mickey Flavin turned and glared at him to stop his fidgeting. From above the stage, Jesus watched down, splayed upon the cross.

But Davey couldn't help it, because apart from the fact of this being the very last paper, there was another reason his nerves were firmly on the glitch. Ever since last week he had been consumed with shame (or at least, something he was pretty sure was shame). Ever since, that is, they paid their visit.

He swallowed. Ever since the Butchers.

Davey reached for his top button and relieved his throat. The hall was hot, beastly so, summer having managed as ever to coordinate her finest weather with the examination period. Though by now, most of the other lads were free to enjoy the sunshine, having raced through their core subjects and generic "Business Organisation" options. It was only Davey and three reluctant Classicists left scribbling the final paper, the rest of the desks stacked high and empty all around.

One hour to go.

To Dublin.

One hour to go away from here.

Davey looked at his script. It appeared he was answering a question on *Prometheus Bound*, his favourite of the ancient plays. It was the one where your man Prometheus got chained to a rock so that an eagle could visit him daily and gnaw out his liver. Mr. Fitz's preferred translation hadn't gone lightly on the gore: the spew and coil of entrails; the guttural roar of a man racked out of his mind with pain. Especially since, every night, the wound would heal again, the organ somehow replenishing itself, so that the next day the savaging could be inflicted from the top. And all because Prometheus had refused to conform to the Tyrants' rule. A deviator. A voice that needed to be suppressed.

Davey swallowed again and wiped the moisture from his forehead with the back of his sleeve. The sweat was enough to set his agitation off anew.

Because there had been sweat the other night, too—sweat and bodies and things he still couldn't quite translate into words. Just a name on his lips, a single syllable he let fill his mouth.

Con.

He wanted to make it the first line of a poem.

But no—he had to keep going. Keep writing. Keep listing all the "crimes" Prometheus had committed. The most famous, of course, was that he had introduced the humans to fire. But he had also taught them how to yoke and harness their animals; how to trap and tame them for good use. So now it was the irony of ironies that Prometheus had been tethered to a rock, reduced to nothing more than a beast himself.

Davey pictured him there with his arms stretched out, splayed.

But the image of the rock was a bit like the low stone wall where Davey had been sitting the other night, the one where he could still hear the chatter from inside the house—the Butchers and his mother and her endless pots of tea. He had been holding his notebook open to the sky as if some of it might just fall in, fully formed, when the question had arrived. "How long ago was her chemo?" Davey jolted at the voice, but also by what it seemed to intuit.

He had already noticed the face in the kitchen, similar to his in age and framed with a mop of golden curls. Even out in the shadows, Davey could tell the Butcher's overalls were a bit tight around the shoulders. "My old lad had it. Pancreatic to begin, then it spread until he was riddled." The stranger began to approach. "Not that, between you and me, it was any great loss." When he sat, he chose a spot on the wall a little closer to Davey than it might have been—his position almost as bold, almost as candid, as his words.

Davey had glanced down at his notebook; had noticed the stranger doing the same. He had shoved it into his pocket and looked up.

"Con." The eyes were there waiting.

"Davey." His vowels were croaked.

A hand took his, holding too tight and too long. "Pleasure."

The way the buzz had raced through him, it was as if his body already knew; as if it could already sense what was about to occur; as if—

Mr. Twomey gave a roar. Davey reared his head in terror as if he had finally been caught outright. He was just in time to see the sneeze follow through. The teacher fumbled a handkerchief to his nose, the germs floating up and away, joining the dust clouds captured by the windows' light.

Above, Jesus looked more agonised than ever.

"Are you still in school?" Con had asked next.

"Final year."

"What subjects?"

Davey had rattled the list from bottom to top.

"Classical Studies, eh? Who knew they taught it round here?"

Davey thought of Mr. Fitz and the other teachers. "Most of them don't approve."

"Ah sure, they never approve."

For some reason, this caused a little pause.

"And what's next? With all that Latin you could become a priest."

Davey half smiled. "College. Dublin, hopefully."

"You don't sound very convinced."

Davey had paused again and looked at Con, though it was hard to make out much in the darkness. And maybe that was why he had suddenly felt inclined to explain; to lay it bare for this half-hidden stranger. "I'm not," he sighed. "Convinced, I mean. I'm winging it entirely."

"Sure, Davey, aren't we all?"

"Twenty minutes, lads," Mr. Twomey heckled. "Last-chance saloon stuff, here."

Davey squinted down at the page. He was on to the final question—not literature this time but architecture. *List the differences between Doric and Corinthian columns.* The trick, always, was to start from the base and work your way up to the scrolls at the top.

Con, though, had had other opinions. "Well, I think you're fierce brave."

"What?"

"It takes a lot, like, to follow your dreams. Especially when everyone expects you to be one thing and not the other."

"You mean like you?" Davey didn't like to presume, but for some reason he felt he had a measure of the stranger.

It was the first time Con had been the one to falter. Davey wished he could see his blush. "Yeah, a bit like me. Of course, I'm cuter, though you're not too bad yourself."

If the line itself hadn't thrown him, the touch on Davey's leg would have been more than enough. Because even in the blackness, the rise in his trousers was instant. And now he felt it again here in the hall—the ache that kept cropping up these last few days. He flushed with embarrassment, forced one hand over his crotch, still trying to write with the other.

The architrave.
The triglyph.
The metope.
"Right, lads—pens down."

Davey dropped his Bic to the desk. Mr. Twomey snatched his paper and added it to the pile. Davey looked up at the cross and breathed his last.

It was done.

Out in the playground, his classmates were already drenched head to toe from the pelt of celebratory water bombs, the playground littered with the neon skins of burst balloons. Davey kept his own head down and beelined for the gate. His eyes flicked up to check, purely on instinct, but of course he knew nobody would be waiting there to celebrate with him.

He had always walked the two miles home from school, except on the very last day of the academic year when his mother would come and collect him in her beloved blue Fiesta. She would wear sunglasses and a scarf tied over her head—Davey knew she must have seen the image in a film somewhere before; knew she was trying to make their life, just for a moment, as beautiful as that. It was a tradition as gorgeous as it was, he supposed, suffused with a kind of longing. He passed through the empty gates now and hurried down the road.

At the end, he turned left and left again. He cocked his leg and mounted the wonky stile. He hadn't taken the cut-through in a while, but today felt just the occasion for it. He jumped another fence, then ducked another, ignoring the barbed-wire knots and the furious signs. *KEEP OUT! TRESPASSERS*

BEWARE! In the next field along, some cattle were drinking water from a rusty bathtub. The sun was at its highest point. Davey licked his dry lips. He thought of Jesus supping vinegar on a stick.

He had read just yesterday that another case of BSE had been confirmed down in Tipperary. According to the scientists, the disease affected the protein plaques in the cattle's brains. Apparently the first symptom was a dodgy walk, the animals stumbling around like drunkards from a pub, before they grew aggressive and turned violent on their owners.

Davey considered the owners themselves now, all of them dodgy, all of them plotting different moneymaking scams. He thought of karma and what a bugger it could be—as far as he was concerned they deserved everything they got. He stopped for a moment to take in the view, using one hand to save his eyes from the gorgeous cruelty of the sun. From here he could see for miles, right to where the drumlins began their ascent, working their way up in rugged increments to the sky. Below, the grass lay skewed to the side like a lad's hair that had been slept on awkwardly overnight. Davey thought of insomnia; of tossing and turning until dawn thinking thoughts he knew he wasn't supposed to think.

Thinking what it meant to be a deviator; what it meant to be suppressed.

But then Davey blinked a little harder and realised exactly where he was standing—O'Connell's pub wasn't very far away. So there was a much better idea to be getting on with (or at least, the only idea he could manage for now). He resumed his walk down through the woods, the tree trunks as close and warm as bodies, past the dilapidated cold store that hadn't been used in years. Although, when Davey glanced at the gap underneath the door, he could have sworn the lights inside had been left on.

He supposed he had assumed the pub would be a bit subdued, given the climate of uncertainty that had started to creep in; the doubts around the farmers and their "untouchable" boom. But in reality, O'Connell's was lepping—no sign of anxiety; no trace of disease or violent cows—unless, of course, the buzz was just a cover-up to take their poor minds off.

And sure, wasn't that why Davey had come—to take his mind off, too?

He had frequented O'Connell's only a handful of times before, but from the doorway he could remember the features precisely: the tricolour hung on high, the crumbling dart-board, the plinth with the ancient hurl painted in the county colours which they kissed on match days to bring the local team good luck. Davey noticed the paint flaking away in parts. He thought of lips against the grain.

He thought of Con, but Jesus, he couldn't risk his trousers spiking now.

He made his way to the bar, wading through the air that was fugged with smoke and sweat, taking care not to meet a single bloodshot eye. He pictured his classmates gearing up for their own celebrations—he knew the plan was to see off a few cans tonight, watch the Germany–Italy match, then on Saturday head out to the boglands for an epic end-of-exam rave.

They had managed to acquire a decent boombox and a haul of ecstasy. They would stumble around with haywire brains just like the cows, only for the lads it would be pure bliss.

"Well, here's a surprise."

When Faela Quin popped up from beneath the counter, Davey started. Her hair was a little longer than when he saw her last; her face, all things considered, a little less filled with rage.

"No need to look quite so petrified," she assured. "Didn't I tell you about my summer job? Jesus, Davey, why are you still wearing *that*?"

He looked down at his uniform. "We have to. For the exams."

"They're still going?"

"Last one today."

"And what, a pint on your Toblerone to celebrate? Ring a fucking ding!" Even as her laughter began, Faela must have sensed the nerve she had touched. Davey ripped off his jumper while she compensated. "You're a rare breed, Davey McCready, do you know that?" She smiled. "A rare bloody breed."

He tried to take it as a compliment; tried to mumble something between a thank-you and an apology when she stood him a pint—God knows, after everything, he didn't deserve her kindness. But she waved his words away and moved on to the next customer. He noticed her fingernails weren't Tippexed any more.

He settled into a stool by the bar and started on his stout, big gulps to satisfy his thirst. His head began to lighten, the booze pushing away months of figures and facts and finickity acronyms learned by rote. He watched as more men began to arrive fresh from the fields. Davey checked for his father—he said he hadn't stepped foot in a pub for years, but Davey didn't trust him as far as he could throw him. He wondered if he ever really had.

Davey felt his head grow even lighter. He passed an hour with a bag of barbecue crisps. He thought of Prometheus; of Theseus and the Minotaur and a maze that had been built to keep a wretched beast at bay.

He thought of an eagle eating a contaminated liver and contracting BSE.

He thought of calling it *mad part man part bull disease.*

He watched Faela flit through the room with towers of empties. He watched a stranger enter the pub with curious eyes. When the lad didn't find what he was looking for, he took a low stool in the corner. It was only then that Davey noticed the camera round his neck.

The more the place filled up, the more Davey found himself catching threads of the punters' conversations, all of them discussing the recent arrival of the BSE. Last time the disease had flared up in England, the scientists had discovered it was caused by MBM—meat and bone meal—a kind of cheap animal feed that was made from the nasty, boiled-down scraps of cattle carcasses. Davey rolled his eyes at the idea. Had they really needed fancy scientists to tell them that turning a cow into a cannibal sent it fucking nuts? He thought of Prince Thyestes eating a stew made from his children's boiled-down flesh. Had he really not been able to tell the difference?

But since that discovery, the MBM had been completely banned in Ireland, so now they needed the scientists back to tell them how the BSE had suddenly reappeared over here. Could there be another source? Could the disease have evolved like one of those super-viruses? Could they be certain the Irish food chain was safe? Whatever the answer, government inspectors had started doing spot checks on herds across the country. Meanwhile, an arrest had been made on the border a few days ago. A group of eejits had been caught smuggling infected cattle from the North. If they weren't careful, they would end up on their arses no different from the Brits after all!

Plenty of the punters, though, remained perfectly calm. Never mind a couple of freak cases, Irish beef was clean—hadn't they seen the ads in the paper saying as much? And no matter what happened, the Bull would be sure to protect the industry. Oh yes, if there was one man who could look after them now, it was him. Davey rolled his eyes even more vigorously at this—*talk about a Messiah fucking complex!* He gave a little laugh, his humour lubricated by the cream of his second pint. Even if he had already decided he probably wouldn't be having a third. His body was craving a shower. His belly was craving a bit of dinner. His mother would be craving an update of how he had got on with the last exam. As it happened, she had been acting sort of funny this week, asking a load of strange questions.

Do you know, love, if there's a direct bus you can take from here to County Cavan?

Did you ever hear of anyone hitchhiking around these parts?

As soon as he stood up, though, Davey heard a voice next to his that was the strangest thing of all.

"Two bottles of whiskey, please, to take away."

Davey stiffened, still facing the bar. He held his breath; counted the rows of brown-glass bottles that hadn't been touched in years. His body was suddenly craving something else.

"Well well well," the voice went on. "How are we—"

"What are you doing here?"

"I could ask you the very same thing. Hot date, is it? You obviously dressed up for the occasion."

But that was all it took for Davey's stiffness to vanish. He turned so that they were face to face. Davey stared at the grin on Con's lips and noticed the stubble on his chin that hadn't been there before.

The Butcher explained that there had been a change of plan. One of the believers on their route was after failing a BSE inspection, which meant he'd had to sign his whole herd over for the cull. In his despair, he had hung himself from a beam in his barn. The following morning, his wife had found him. The following morning, the Butchers had found her and turned back the way they'd come.

And Davey was listening—of course he was—he couldn't take his eyes or ears anywhere else, but when he made to reply, Con was looking away. "Oh, for fuck's sake, what is *he* doing here?"

For some reason, Davey assumed he was talking about his father—that Fionn had finally shown up, just as Davey knew he would. He thought of the byre the other night when the old man had called his name and they had had to stop what they were doing and run. But when he followed Con's glare, he saw he meant the man with the camera. "You know him?" The flicker of jealousy was almost swallowed, but not quite.

"Our *stalker*? Wait till you hear—he says he wants to capture us *as we truly are*. As if we need another bloody version of us doing the rounds."

Davey tried another laugh, though he had suddenly noticed quite how close Con's body was.

"We told him to feck off, but he got a bit pushy. Typical Dub, thinking he can tell the culchies what to do."

When a fresh group of men swarmed up to the bar, they were pushed even nearer, Con's leg grazing against his.

"Thinking we're something exotic. Something primitive. What an arse! Although I will admit he's a bit of a ride, don't you—"

"Sorry, I couldn't find it anywh—" Faela's arrival cut through Con's words and then she cut through her own as well. She placed the bottles, very carefully, on the counter. Both were wrapped in a brown paper bag for the purpose of discretion. She looked at Davey with a bit of a squint. He felt his heart lurch up from his chest all the way to his throat.

To capture us as we truly are.

But soon Faela's face resolved into that same kindness Davey didn't quite deserve or understand. "Enjoy your evening," she said, and nothing more. Davey watched her go, wondering what she had seen—what there even was to see.

While Con had other questions. "Shall we get out of here?" He wedged the parcels into his pockets. "Your man's just clocked me, and . . . I've been to your home, so I suppose it's my turn to show you ours." He placed a couple of coins on the bar for a tip.

Davey felt his heart retreat back down his neck, though it was still beating something furious. He picked up his school jumper, then changed his mind. He left it draped across the wooden stool.

"About bloody time!"

The camp was only around a ten-minute walk—their feet moved in sync; they didn't say a word—though something about it felt a bit like stepping into another world. Davey smelled the bonfire long before he saw it, the same smoky tang as his tongue from the barbecue crisps. Con hesitated, just for a moment, then showed him in.

Dusk was falling, but still Davey could make out the carts hitched side by side at the edge of the clearing; the makeshift tents that seemed nothing more than off-white sheets draped like a children's game of a fort; the horses tethered to the trunks of trees, chewing gobfuls of hay from a low and golden pile, their coats so glossy they looked as if they were soaking wet.

"I thought we'd *die* of thirst." On a stump to the right, one of the Butchers sat with a knife and a stone in either hand.

Con ignored him. "This is Davey." He took the whiskey from his pockets, but he didn't hand it over just yet.

"Ah, so you're the one to blame for him taking so bloody long?"

Davey looked the man in the face, trying to remember him from the house last week; trying not to glance down at the sharpened blade. "If you were so desperate, you should have just come to the pub yourself."

The chorus of laughs and whoops arrived from all directions as the outlines of the other men emerged. Davey hadn't meant to be rude. The Butcher clearly disagreed. "As if we'd be welcome. Everyone's all smiles when things are going well, but as soon as they start to turn—"

"Don't mind Mik—he's a grumpy git." For some reason Davey could remember that the man talking now was called Cúch. "Anyway, the grub is much better here." He smiled. "Take a seat, lads, and I'll bring you both a plate."

Cúch was right—the grub was much better, a stew earthy with sticks of herbs Davey snapped like little bones with his teeth. Even though he was famished, he tried to go slowly; to use the eating as an excuse to just watch and listen and take it all in. The camp was relaxed, but busy too—each of the men focused on completing their respective tasks—scraping out pots or buffing up boots; rinsing off dishes or pegging shirts on a line. There was something almost domestic to the whole arrangement; something, Davey thought, almost feminine.

"You're Lena's boy?" After a while, the older man—was it Sol?—approached with a grin, his hand held out to relieve them of their clean plates.

Davey hesitated. "My mother's called Eileen, but—"

"Of course, my mistake. Lovely woman. I remember when she was only a girl."

"Wait, you knew her back—"

"Are you OK to take it neat?" Con cut in, offering the bottle and placing his hand on Davey's thigh to ask the question. Davey looked at it; felt a rush of heat to that single point—the flames of the bonfire and so much more. When he looked up, though, Sol was already ambling away. None of the other men were paying attention. The horses had lost interest in their

153

hay. Davey took the bottle and placed it between his lips and felt his insides burning too.

Soon the daylight had been diluted. A couple more men drifted over to sit and pass the whiskey round. Davey noticed that when they received it, they didn't bother to wipe the rim. There was a low swell of chatter, banter bobbing back and forth across the camp. Mik seemed more relaxed now that he had taken a drink. Davey thought of his father, then he didn't again.

And Davey also thought how the whole thing just wasn't really what he had been expecting; that somewhere along the way he must have envisaged them all sitting around swapping folk tales and ancient songs. Instead, one lad lay on his back with a copy of yesterday's *Anglo-Celt*, filling in the crossword. "Three down. A haphazard rhyme. Six and seven letters."

Meanwhile two other men—like all the men who ever lived—were engaged in a deep debate over directions and routes; the best way one might get from Ballintober to Ballina.

"What about the new modern stretch by Castlebar?"

"Ah yes, another lovely European-funded road."

Davey thought of his mother and her recent questions.

. . . a direct bus you can take from here to County Cavan?

. . . anyone hitchhiking around these parts?

He wondered if it was something to do with her haphazard dreams.

Helter-skelter.

He wondered if the lad had managed to figure out the crossword clue.

"Right, before we turn in . . ." It was the oldest amongst them, though, who did finally inject a bit of ceremony into the evening. As Sol spoke, the debate petered out, though a consensus still hadn't been agreed upon. "I'd like to propose a toast. To Paddy Dwyer."

Davey felt confused, then he felt something else. Con's breath was hot on his neck. "The guy we were supposed to visit today," he whispered. "The one who hung himself in his barn."

Since they hadn't been using cups, most of the men just raised their fists in acknowledgement.

"The loss of a believer," one agreed, "is always a tragedy."

But Sol was quick to correct. "It's a tragedy for *any* man. And for his wife to find him like that? God knows my missis would be beyond cure." His face dug deep with empathy, all the higgledy lines like an ancient map full of well-trodden routes. "Here's to the Farmer's Widow, that we may honour her grief. Right, lads, we've an early start. And Davey?" Here the pain gave way to a gentle nod. "It's been a pleasure. You're very welcome here any time you like."

Again, they walked in silence. Davey could feel the whiskey in his forehead. He didn't want to go home. He wanted to know what a word like "home" meant to men who slept under makeshift tents.

Of all the things, he spoke of the old man. "Sol said he remembers my mum."

"Wouldn't be surprised," Con replied. "He's been at this almost fifty years—he remembers everyone. Apparently his wife made him promise to stop when they had kids, but it turned out they weren't able. Then he offered to retire when he was sixty—his health hasn't been great—but by then she could see how much he loved it; how much he wanted to keep going. So in the end she agreed—said a promise was a promise was a promise—and now he calls her 'Mrs. P' for short." Con stopped. "Which reminds me—I'll have to think of a cute nickname for you."

Davey felt a fresh rush of heat to his face. He racked his brains for a coy suggestion. Then he realised they had made it back to the main road, and he wasn't coy at all. "When will I see you again?"

Con cast his eyes across the fields. A flock of shorn sheep were trying out their new skin. His own hair fell over his ears in pale yellow curls. "The change in route has cocked things up," he said. "And if some farms really are contaminated, we're going to have to reassess." When he looked back, though, he must have seen Davey's expression. "I suppose I could . . . Will you be in O'Connell's on Saturday night?"

Davey tried very hard not to pounce on the offer. Instead he just nodded. "You should all come along. I promise no one will mind." He thought again of Faela's kindness this afternoon; of what she may or may not have seen. And he tried very hard not to flinch when Con leaned forward to place his mouth on his—not with tongues and teeth; not with clambered hands and stifled shock like in the byre—but with a tenderness that left Davey even more confused; even more aroused.

He walked home slowly, a whiskey weave, making up crossword clues in his head. He didn't know how he was supposed to fit them all together. He only knew that Saturday night would be the beginning—or maybe the end—of everything.

I promise no one will mind.

He knew now that a promise was a promise was a promise.

CHAPTER NINE
Fionn

County Monaghan, June 1996

"Fergus, it's Fionn. Fionn McCready. It's just gone half past seven on Saturday evening. Or I suppose at this stage, Saturday night, depending on your particular persuasion. I was just calling to see how you were getting on. It's been over a week now and I was wondering . . . I appreciate the last border run was a messy business, but you will let me know when the next one is happening, won't you? Or frankly, if there are any other jobs the Bull might be needing a hand with. It's just . . . anyway, look. Speak soon, OK?"

Fionn nestled the phone into its cradle and waited as if it might suddenly jolt back to life, Lazarus from the dead. The cord loop-the-looped down to his knees and back again. He was trying to limit himself to three phone calls a day—he was familiar with the concept of "overkill." He was also familiar with the concept of "laying low." He knew last week's operation was, all things considered, a spectacular fuck-up; knew just how tickled pink the Gardaí were when they threw him and Fergus into the piss-dingy confines of that station cell. And he knew how fuming they were when they appeared the following morning to say there had been a "change in circumstance." Never mind how much the Bull had slipped into the back pocket of their bosses' uniforms, it clearly pained the honest lads to see them walking free.

So of course, those wankers from Operation Matador couldn't be given an opportunity to catch them out again. But even apart from the border antics, Fionn knew the Bull had other moneymaking tricks up his bespoke tailored sleeve. So he just needed to get through to Fergus Hynes and make it clear that he was willing to do whatever it took; just needed to get that kitty topped up all the way before everything else was spectacularly fucked up too.

"I thought I heard you talking to someone?"

Fionn jolted back to life. "Jesus."

"No, just me." Eileen's laugh was a gentle thing. "Guilty conscience?"

Fionn was aware she was only teasing, and yet.

She wore a matted dressing gown and a towel wrapped around her head like some queen from a faraway land. The arrangement at least hid how little hair there was underneath. Fionn caught a heady waft of lavender. "Nice bath?"

"Fionn, we wouldn't happen to have any maps?" If she heard his question, she was ignoring it. She hadn't commented on his absence the other day. She had probably assumed he was just so busy mucking the fields he had decided not to come in for lunch. Inside the cell, his biggest fear had been that—Murphy's Law—that would be the day Eileen's brain would finally decide to glitch and throw a seizure. He had pictured her lying there, twitching like a moth around a bulb. God knows her wings were as delicate.

"Maps?" But even if his nightmare hadn't been realised, here was more proof that her brain was still awry. He glanced at the telephone. If only he had an address for Fergus Hynes. "You mean like an atlas, love?"

"Just Ordnance Survey. Local roads, neighbouring counties—that sort of thing."

Fionn frowned; he wondered if this was something to do with her latest batch of dreams. "How about—"

His answer, though, was cut short by the pounding of footsteps down the stairs. Davey hurtled breathless into the kitchen. He wore a shirt that had courted an iron and an excessive slick of gel in his hair. He looked from one parent to the other. It was so rare to have all three of them in the same room together. "I'm going out," he said quickly. "Look after yourself, Mum."

"You too, pet."

Fionn saw them share a look of untarnished love. He saw they didn't share it with him.

Just as quickly as he had arrived, Davey vanished again. Fionn thought he caught another waft—a sort of musk. When he was gone, he asked: "Should we be worried about him? He's acting even odder than usual."

Eileen laughed the same gentle laugh as before. "No, pet, I don't think we need to worry. He's just finding his way." And as she vanished too, Fionn felt an unexpected pang, wondering if his wife would live to see the day their oddball son walked some oddball girl down the aisle.

To cheer himself up, Fionn thought back—as he so often did—to the moment he clapped eyes on Eileen for the very first time. He had been sent down for a few weeks to his dying uncle's farm to lend a hand for the calving season. Fionn would stay awake into the wee hours, the jack and the iodine and the ropes ready by his side. He had learned it was nearly time when the girls started walking in circles, standing up, sitting down, sniffing the dirt to see if anything had yet come out.

There had been ten calves so far, or eleven if you counted the one that hadn't managed to make it all the way. The hide had been such a shocking shade of blue it was clear the infant had been gone from this world for a while. The mother had licked it anyway, determined that love and instinct were more than enough to make a miracle. Fionn's uncle lived on the farm by himself. He had never had any children of his own.

And even by then, Fionn had wondered if he might end up the very same—it wasn't uncommon, lads too devoted to their land to bother with the seeking out or shacking up. Some waited until the eleventh hour, then moseyed over to the Ballroom of Romance—the infamous Leitrim dancehall filled with waltzes and hormones and desperate last-ditch attempts. Then of course, Lisdoonvarna hosted the annual Matchmaking Festival where surveys were filled out and pairings formally arranged. Rumour had it the weekend was fair old craic—they got in some decent country bands to play. They said the conversion rate was reasonably high.

But after the twelfth calf just about made it, Fionn had taken a celebratory saunter through his uncle's village. He picked up a battered sausage and chips for his tea, a double portion as a treat. Outside the video shop he had found her staring at the poster in the window, Elizabeth Taylor with her sultry eyes and her pouting lips. When he enquired, she said her name was Lena and that she had been born just up the road; said she loved going to the pictures, but that otherwise she was bored out of her skull. She didn't say anything about her sister or her family's beliefs (though they would have to deal with all of that soon enough). She didn't ask before dipping one of his chips into his ketchup pool.

Within just four weeks his uncle passed away, the twelve calves were sold, and Eileen agreed to be his leading lady. Two decades later, Fionn drank himself into such a stupor that his fists broke her nose and her jaw and her heart. Another year and she was diagnosed with a lump in her brain and he knew, without a doubt, it was all his fault.

He thought he had finally discovered how to make amends. It suddenly seemed his plan might not make it all the way.

He paused just outside the door to O'Connell's, trying to decide whether he was about to make yet another catastrophic mistake. Behind him, the car park was rammed—come midnight, they would all navigate the country roads home in a stupor with astonishing swerves. Above him, the clouds were soaked in a violent crimson.

Red sky at night, shepherd's delight.

Fionn spared a thought for the Butchers. God knows he believed in superstitions more than ever these days.

It had been three years since he last stepped inside O'Connell's—or any other pub, for that matter. He licked his lips and practised his order in his head. *A pint of red lemonade, no ice.* It was like learning a foreign language. He had decided he would give it an hour and if there was no sign of Fergus Hynes he would cut his losses, but when Fionn held his breath and stepped inside, the first thing he noticed was the badger streak across the room. The second thing he noticed was the wall of stale beer and stale heat that greeted him, so thick and solid it could almost be chewed. He squeezed through the swell of the crowd; heard someone humming a few notes, tuning up to let an old ballad rip.

"I don't believe it!" Fergus's exclamation was so aggressive it caused the rest of the booth to sit up straight. "The dairy dickhead himself." A ripple of phlegmatic laughs. "And it just so happens, the next one's your round."

Fionn opened his mouth, then closed it; simply nodded and made his way towards the bar, circumnavigating the mob gathered below the tele. He presumed it was for the soccer—he knew two of the Euro '96 quarterfinals were being played today. But Fionn saw it was actually the president of the Irish Farmers' Association on the screen, making yet another speech—demanding that more be done to protect Irish beef. Still consumer confidence was dwindling; still no source for the BSE coming to Ireland had been officially confirmed. At this rate, everything could fall apart at the hastily stitched seams.

Fionn felt his own seams hanging on by the thinnest of threads.

"Mr. McCready, what can I get you?"

Faela Quin was a surprise, not because Fionn hadn't heard that she was working here now, but because he had assumed she was the reason behind Davey's agitation and fancy get-up tonight—a reunion date. He must have had it arseways, though—there must have been another girl on the scene—another thing about his son Fionn didn't know or understand.

"Ages since you've been here." The next time Faela spoke, Fionn could have sworn there was a hint of implication in her words, but of course he knew the situation wasn't how it looked. He knew the sooner the pints were poured, the sooner he could have a quiet word in Fergus's ear, then get the hell out of this godforsaken place.

"What do you reckon, Milky Moo?"

Faela had at least provided a tray so he was able to lower the whole batch on to the table in one go. The hands shot out quickly to lay their grubby claim. There wasn't so much as a grunt of gratitude.

"Reckon about what?"

"Oh, Mossy is just raging because another importer from Europe cancelled on him yesterday. He's worried if he goes broke, his missis will do a runner."

"And she could," Mossy wailed. "Properly like. Thanks to this new bloody *law*."

Fionn sat. He knew Mossy was referring to the Divorce Bill that was after going through on Monday. It was official—a marriage no longer had to be for ever.

"Can you believe it?" Fergus slurred next to him. "What's the country coming to? First the gays and now this."

Fergus, meanwhile, was referring to the other new law that had been brought in three years ago—the one that meant being a homosexual was no longer a crime. Oh Modern Ireland was on its way, all right, but no one had warned them it came at a very modern price. "A nation of faggots and divorcees."

Properly or otherwise, Fionn had been terrified Eileen would leave him after what he had done, but instead she had stood by her vow—*for better and for worse*—and now he was standing by his—*in sickness and in health*. He thought of twenty-five years of marriage. He wanted there to be so many more. "Fergus," he muttered, "I was wondering if I could have a wee word?"

"That's what the priest said in Mass this evening." It was Briain Ní Ghríofa talking next. "That the country's soul is going up in flames."

"Maybe *that's* what brought the BSE over here—punishment from an angry God."

"Bit Old fucking Testament, wouldn't you say?"

Fionn gobbed his lemonade and wondered if Eileen might join him at Mass tomorrow; wondered if he should just go the whole hog and take her off for a pilgrimage to Lourdes—sure, wasn't that where the devout brought all their sick to be healed? A quick splash-about with the Virgin Mary and any tumours or seizures would do a runner for good?

"Fergus, it's about the work," he tried again. "I'm keen to keep going, you see?"

"Well, have *yous* any better ideas where it came from?"

"What about that pesticide they're saying has some dodgy chemical in it? Same as the Nazis used to use?"

"Fergus," Fionn whispered louder, "*please.*"

"Or what about the badgers—weren't they to blame for spreading the TB?"

"Let's shoot the bastards before it's too late."

"Shoot those Matadors, more like."

"She'll leave me," Mossy wailed. "I just know!"

Until finally, Fergus put his glass down and lumbered his torso round. He pawed his hand through his hair, the dirty black mass with the tarnished silver lining. "The Bull," he slurred, "has no more jobs." He thrust his face forward so his jowls were only inches from Fionn's. His breath was a cesspit of stout. "In fact, do you want to know a secret, Milky Moo?" And Fionn simply nodded again to indicate that yes, he did. "It's over," Fergus said with a smirk. "The whole thing is fucking kaput."

Fionn stood up in such a panic that he clobbered the table, a searing pain in his left kneecap for his troubles. As he dragged his dead leg away he thought of Glassy and her wonky walk, a spastic jive every time she entered the yard.

By now the pub was full to bursting, standing room only, so he had to use his elbows to shove his way through. The heat of the mob was thick to inhale. A couple of the drunker bodies shoved back. *Watch where you're going, lad!* The glass pane on the front door was dripping wet, and next to it sat a boy on a stool. He was surrounded by an air of such inordinate neatness that he stood out a mile from this foul place. "Davey?" Fionn's brain struggled, yet again, to make sense of what was happening. "What are you doing here?" But soon enough it caught up—his son was obviously just waiting for Faela; was obviously taking her out once she finished her shift. Somewhere beneath his panic, Fionn felt joy or maybe even relief that the two youngsters were an item again.

Davey stood up to meet him. "Don't you think that's a bit rich coming from *you*?" He suddenly looked bigger than usual, almost a full head taller than Fionn.

"I only just arrived." Fionn tried his best to stay calm. "And now I'm going home, all right?" But of course, everything wasn't all right—even if Fergus hadn't told him as much, Fionn could feel it now, rising up on the stale air. The heat and the drink; the mob tuning up and shoving back. "Davey," he said, "I don't think you should be in here."

"Pardon?"

"Things are getting sloppy," Fionn continued, still as calm as he could. "With everything that's been going on, and the president's speech this afternoon . . . I mean it, I'm sure Faela won't mind—would you not come home with me?"

His son's eyes stared straight into the question, searching for something Fionn prayed that they would find. Fionn's eyes stared straight back, searching for some clue to all the things about his son he didn't know or understand.

Do you want to know a secret, Milky Moo?

But when the pub door swung open, their eyes were yanked away to watch the men enter, very slowly, in single file. After the eighth, the door clicked shut—a sound that rang out because the whole place, just like that, had fallen hush.

Nobody moved, the heaving room now frozen stiff, waiting for somebody—anybody—to decide what happened next. Fionn glanced at the tele, which had turned to the weather: more rain. He glanced at Davey, whose cheeks had turned a violent crimson.

The silence stretched and stretched, then it stretched just a moment too far, before Martin Fahey finally stood up and did the honours. "You're very welcome." Fionn hadn't even realised he was in here. "Get your boys a drink now and we'll carry on as we were." The command was subtle, but it was clear—a set of instructions to both sides; an unspoken kind of warning or truce. The punters exhaled and resumed their drunken complaints and disease-spreading theories. God knows they had bigger things to be worrying about than some gypsy eejits in overalls.

"Careful!" From behind, a lad in a check shirt tried to jostle his way through, holding a camera above his head to save it from the crush of the crowd.

Fionn watched him go—probably some Yank tourist on some twee ancestry tour—then turned back to Davey. "We should get going," he repeated. Then more firmly: "I'm serious, son. I don't like the feel of the place at all. Your Ma will be—"

The smash of glass stopped him short. That huge silence came again—that collective breath held. This time it stretched much too far to be safe. This time, even Martin Fahey kept shtum.

Fionn whipped around to see where the violence had come from; who had broken, so quickly, the peace. Across the room, Fergus Hynes had managed to stagger himself upright. The broken shards glistened on the table beneath him. "What about those cunts?"

The accusation was so vague, so indistinct, and yet instantly the whole place knew exactly what he meant, which showed that despite the pretence, they had already been harbouring their own deep-seated suspicions along the same lines.

"Let's call a spade a spade," Fergus pushed on, a bit louder, a bit less slurred. "*They're* the source of the disease spreading over here. Them with their Satanic shite and their sinister curses. We all know they're pikey scum, stuck in the past."

Fionn flinched, but not as much as he saw Sol and Cúch flinching too. He didn't know if they had yet picked him out of the crowd. In another circumstance, another life, he would have invited them all to get a table in the corner; to just sit down and have a chat.

"Oh, would you ever piss off." In this circumstance, though, it was one of the other Butchers who stepped forward to take Fergus Hynes on. "You lot have brought this upon yourselves." He was a young lad, bright-eyed and a sort of Curly Sue situation on his head. "All your scams and your deals and—"

"Con, don't. Please, he's not worth it."

The final person to step forward, though, made Fionn flinch the most. Davey knew the Butcher's name. Davey was laying a hand on the Butcher's hand and their fingers, just for a second, were intertwined.

So now Fionn's brain was reeling back through the week, through the station cell and the arrest, back to the Butchers' visit and the strange noise he heard out in the byre, something like a man's voice sobbing—or were there two men? he asked now—something like footsteps running away.

Next, he heard Fergus's words from earlier:

A nation of faggots and divorcees.

And then:

First the gays and now this.

He heard the tourist with the camera above his head:
Careful!

He had heard more than enough.

"Don't." And suddenly the room was his, whether he wanted it or not. Fionn looked at his son with his Vaseline hair. He looked at the men all around them waiting to pounce—waiting for an easy target to take out their frothing rage. "Get away from him." In truth, he barely touched Con—only gave a wee push and swiped Davey's hand away. Like he was a child again, reaching for something he wasn't allowed to touch; something that was forbidden or would cause him pain. But that was all it took to shatter the moment into a thousand razor-sharp smithereens. DOB launched the first punch, landing it right on the bridge of Cúch's nose. The blood came exploding black as stout. And then the next blow rang out, another shatter of glass, months of hate and frustration erupting in eight different directions. Fionn thought of a gun in a glove compartment, loaded and waiting, the trigger finally pulled.

INTERLUDE

New York, January 2018

Three blocks down from the museum, the diner is heaving hot and wet, the whole of Manhattan seeking comfort food from the slush-drift of the streets. In the snug of their booth they order two cups of coffee and one slice of blueberry pie. Ronan flicks a sachet of Sweet'N Low, even though he has no intention in the world of opening it.

Across from him, the girl still wears her coat despite the swelter of the place. She still wears a face he is certain he has seen somewhere before.

"Here we go, folks." When the waitress leans low to fill their cups, Ronan makes a point of averting his eyes. In the booth behind, an elderly couple sits draped in matching red woollen scarves. They are feeding each other from a glistening pancake stack, despite the fact that it is almost dark outside. Ronan is tempted to reach for his camera. The world in snapshots when you expect it the very least.

"So I wanted to ask you a few questions about *The Butcher.*"

The sweetener sachet bursts at the seam. He sweeps up the granules with the side of his hand, then cuts the pile into neat white lines, a ghost of his previous life smirking near but oh so far. Already her eyes seem an even more vibrant green, as if they have thawed out from the cold.

"OK." He sips his coffee. "What do you want to know?"

"The man in the photograph," she begins. "He belonged to a group of travelling slaughterers, am I right?"

He nods.

"Which existed for hundreds of years until they split in '96?"

Ronan wonders what age she would have been back then.

"And am I right in saying that was the same year as all the drama with the BSE? Talk about a shitty time to be in cattle, hey?"

Unlike the others, this question makes him laugh. He remembers her saying this was her last night in New York. He wonders what hotel she is staying in.

Despite the insecurities and the pills, he has managed a couple of relationships down the years, though usually they end in the same argument. Something to do with him being aloof, putting his career ahead of everything—and everyone— else. But he points out that he isn't aloof at all—that, clearly, he is very easy to read—because they are right, his photography has always been the priority.

He has been clean for five years now, though he has grown no less devoted to his work. In fact, even to this day it remains the only part of himself that he feels vaguely secure about.

Why, then, are her questions unnerving him?

"Blueberry with whipped?" The waitress has returned with a steaming slice of pie and a snowball of stiff cream on the side.

"You sure you don't want some?" The girl wastes no time with her attack, seizing her fork and undoing the pastry lattice bite for bite.

Even as she eats, her movements spark something so familiar in him. He racks his brains—he is getting close. Though as she scrapes the juices up, he has a sense that she is getting close to something too.

"And wasn't it June that same year there was the carnage in O'Connell's?" She has demolished the main chunk of the crust. She makes light work of the rest. "When the locals saw red one night and lost their minds and beat the Butchers to a pulp?" She places her weapon down on the table. She knows far more than she first let on.

Over her shoulder, Ronan sees the couple wrapping up. They wind their matching scarves tightly around their necks. In his mind's eye he sees a floor covered in shards of broken glass. He sees one man squeezing another man's throat until it makes a "pop."

The bell above the door rings as the couple leaves, bringing Ronan back to the diner. He watches the couple through the window, hurrying across the intersection and into the night. He would shoot their image in black and white so only they would ever know that their scarves were the same colour. He has learned that some secrets are never meant to be shared.

"Then a few days later, one of the Butchers was found dead, hanging from a hook, and someone called the Gardaí and—"

"Folks, are we all done here?"

When he jumps, Ronan could swear the girl lets off a grin. The waitress doesn't notice, only whisks the plate away. "Can I get you anything else?"

He shakes his head. When they are alone again, it is finally his turn for questions. "Who are you?" he asks.

This time the girl's grin is more than obvious. The steam from her coffee rises up to meet her cheeks. "You really don't remember, do you?"

He suddenly feels faint. He should have ordered a slice of something after all. He closes his eyes and waits for the terrible blizzard in his head to pass. But it turns out it was just a bit of darkness he needed all along, because at last he has it. He has her. And now his head is out of the diner, hurtling east over the Hudson, travelling block after block until he reaches his Williamsburg studio where another unknown photograph sits—the only one in his portfolio he didn't take himself. He found it weeks after their night together when he was developing the film. She must have stolen the camera while he was sleeping; must have stared straight into the lens and pressed the button.

She must have wanted, he realised far too late, just to be seen.

So this evening must be more of the same. He opens his eyes and says her name. He notices the features—so obvious now. The savage green eyes. The freckle constellations. The teeth not quite straight, but close enough. "Grá," he says again, this time a little less convincingly. He knows that it is short for "Gráinne," which is Irish for "grace," but that also on its own it is the Irish, simply, for "love."

He also knows it has been over twenty years, so maybe he is hallucinating? Even without the pills, his system still isn't right—he sometimes has terrors in his sleep. He looks down at the black sludge of his cup and he realises. There are no hallucinations; there is only a final question that needs to be asked: "Tell me, Úna, what is it that you want from me?"

And Úna grins her best grin yet, commending him—finally—for joining all the dots; for lining up the granules in a row. "I told you, Ronan, I just want to ask some questions about what happened." The berries have stained her lips a dark and dripping purple. "I just need you to tell me the truth."

CHAPTER TEN
Grá

County Cavan, July 1996

They walked the barren field in silence, their heads bowed as if in prayer. They must have looked like a procession of mourners—for a dead person or perhaps a dead fox—but that wasn't it. Or at least, not just yet.

Instead Mrs. P bowed her head to watch her step—she was a little older now, a little less stable on her feet—while Úna bowed to scour the grass for treasures, the magpie-hunger of a child not quite gone from her yet. And Grá's head was bowed by the weight of her thoughts and her guilt. She didn't need to watch her step—she knew the lake route off by heart. She had visited daily for a time, first alone, then not alone, then utterly alone.

She paused, creaking her neck to the left and the right. She had lost weight again, her body back to bones.

Being honest, she might have preferred to make today a solo trip, but it was summer holidays now, which meant Úna was around all the time. Back in the home-schooling days, Úna had relished such freedom—had spent days on end in her own little world—while Grá had delighted in being asked, very occasionally, to join. But since that afternoon with the throwing of the meat, Úna hadn't been quite the same. Grá

179

had entered the kitchen this morning and found her staring listlessly into her lap. She had thought of the fox cubs. "Would you come for a swim with me, love?" She had thought Úna would reply straight away. Instead, she had taken a moment before she looked up, all smiles. "A girls' day out?"

The weather could have been a bit kinder—the breeze was brisk, almost autumnal—though Grá was trying not to think about seasons. Because thinking about seasons meant thinking about dates. Which, of course, meant remembering that June was over.

Which meant Cúch hadn't come home like he'd promised. "This way?"

Grá glanced up. Mrs. P was on ahead, frowning next to a stile.

"Afraid so." Grá tried to make her voice sound summer bright. She lowered her eyes again to give the older woman some privacy. No doubt it would be a graceless climb.

But Grá could pretend she was ignoring the date all she liked, when really she knew it was another reason behind the entire outing. Because the last few days of just sitting there, counting down the month and staring at the front door, hadn't worked.

A watched pot never boils.

A longed-for husband never arrives.

For goodness' sake, of course he hadn't come.

Whereas by vacating the house, then surely his promise (give or take a day late) would finally come to pass; surely fate would conspire to have him arrive ten minutes after they left, so that when they returned from their swim he would be standing there, smiling.

What time do you call this?

The irony of him awaiting them would not be nothing.

Grá hadn't told the other two about Cúch's promise to come home halfway round this year. She couldn't decide if it was greed or something else. She could only imagine what Mrs. P would give for Sol to pay a visit.

I could pop back.

Spend a bit of time with you both.

As it happened, Mrs. P had come by this morning while they were getting ready to depart. She had brought biscuits—chocolate chip, still warm. Grá had taken one look, then yanked her by the arm out the door. Her last thought had been at least Cúch would have something to nibble on while he waited.

The land began to descend, the smell growing stronger of muck and marsh. The air around the lake always tasted different. There was another one across the border they said was cursed by an ancient hag. Lough Doghra or "the Lake of Sorrow." In her sorrier moments, Grá had decided that Cúch's no-show was intentional—that he had discovered what she'd done and was deliberately punishing her. Other days, it was karma—that because of her transgression, some ill had befallen him. Other days it was this:

I hope that something bad happens to them out there.

Grá hesitated at the memory. She thought again of the cursed lake. Goodness knows she had never underestimated her daughter before.

But now Úna was calling—"I can see it!"—running the last of the way to the water, and Grá had to admit the view was not without its effects. The surface was brighter than the sky, glass-smooth and untouched, save for a distant corner where a group of grey-white birds had gathered.

They began to strip, their feet wincing against the spikes of the rush. Not a single toe amongst them was painted. Grá had known from practice to wear her swimming togs under her clothes so she was ready in a swipe. While she waited, she stole little glances at her daughter. The skin was pale as ever, but there was a newish stretch to it too. The beginning of hips. An underarm shadow. Something, maybe, about the chest.

And Grá had another memory then—weeks ago in the kitchen, when Úna had revealed the full extent of her dreams:

I've decided I'm going to be a Butcher too.

Grá's reply had been pure laughter:

Oh, darling, you can't be a Butcher.

And then:

You're a girl.

Grá had hated the words—had hated herself for saying them—though that didn't mean they were any less true. Because these would always be their bodies; those would always be the rules. She knew now that breaking them only made the pain worse.

"Mam, I'm *ready* and you're greeny!" As ever, Úna brought Grá back to herself. They ran to the edge of the bank. On the count of three they held each other's hands and leapt in unison.

Úna could do handstands; could dive to the bottom; could swim under their legs. "Now do me! Now do me!" Even Mrs. P was laughing, not because she was thinking of some memory of her and Sol once swimming together—it was just laughing. Just here. Just because.

Grá took in the view on every side, the distant mazes of gorse, the swathes of rapeseed so beautiful even despite the violence of the name. Local lore said the entire county had been founded by the O'Reilly clan, which was where the saying had first been born.

The life of Reilly.

Grá treaded the water and wondered about O'Reilly's wife; about the kind of life she might have led.

Closer to the bank, she saw the scatter of rocks and stones amidst the grass; the limestone slabs that lay flung about. Some were altars where the druids had performed their sacred rituals, some were dolmens which were portals to another world. But one chunk of rock held a different association altogether—a man in sunglasses lurking for the very first time. Quickly Grá tried to turn her back on the land, though of course she knew by now such a thing could never be done.

Amid all the thoughts of her husband's absence, there had been another absence too. Because Ronan was gone. Ronan hadn't even called. Grá wasn't sure if she had expected or even wanted him to.

Her body treaded water a little harder. It had opinions of its own.

She wondered if he had managed to find the Butchers and persuade them to sit for a photograph; if he had aimed the camera at her husband knowing what he had so recently done with his wife. She hated the power that gave him, but she forced herself to remember it was her own power that had brought the whole thing about—even if the sin was hideous, it had at least been her own.

183

Grá thought of her rebel sister, the final absence in the unholy trinity. She closed her green eyes and dunked her head below.

When she was ready to resurface, she felt something around her leg. It was just a weed, ankle-slicked. She kicked it off. When it stayed, she felt a flash of panic, then stemmed it at once. She would use her other foot to free herself.

She kicked again. The weed slicked around the other foot too.

Grá opened her eyes. The lake water was far filthier than she had expected. She squinted for other legs, for skin that was pale as ever. But the wall of shadows was eel black. She kicked out for a third time.

And surely by now the other two had noticed? They must have been worried? Must have seen the bubbles on the surface like a Morse code *SOS!* Unless, of course, they were deliberating whether or not to help—a flicker of grudges; a list of recent slights. Like an old friend acting odd with book club visits and no invite extended, or a mother with a new friend and a new kind of laughter in her eyes.

Oh, darling, you can't be a Butcher.

Grá felt her chest tighten; felt her limbs start to thrash.

You're a girl.

Flapping like the wings of a swan.

There has never been a girl Butcher.

"You all right?"

The air, when her lungs found it, tasted different entirely. Grá opened her eyes.

"Silly goose. I thought you said you could swim?"

The sun, ever witty, had finally emerged from the clouds. Grá tilted her head like she could swallow it in yellow gulps.

When they arrived back, the house was empty as a promise. The biscuits on the table had turned chewy. Úna declared herself "starving" and ate five in a row, swallowing noisily, until Grá told her to stop. Mrs. P glanced out the window and remarked on the garden—she had never seen it grow so wild. She was clearly lingering for the offer of tea, but Grá was desperate to draw a bath; to wash off the lake and everything else.

Later, over dinner—*no menu; no special tonight*—Úna recounted all the things she and Mrs. P had discussed on the walk. Like the government's promise to finally shut down the last ever Magdalene Laundry this year. Or that Irish swimmer Michelle Smith off to the Olympics this month. Or that journalist Veronica Guerin who was shot dead in Dublin. Apparently she had been working on a story about a group of gangsters—all men—so one of them had decided to try shutting her up.

Across the table, Grá shuddered. She had read the obituary, all right—mother of one; only four years younger than herself. Last Thursday afternoon there had been a national minute of silence. Grá wondered if, as the whole country fell hush, any of those men had heard their conscience at last.

"Did you know Mrs. P wanted to be a journalist?"

Of all the things Grá thought she would hear, this wasn't one. "Really?" Her voice, she noticed, had the trace of a smirk.

"She did a course and everything. Long before she was married. Even had some articles in the *Irish Times*."

Still Grá felt the instinct to laugh, to disbelieve. Or maybe it was more to do with hurt? That her friend had never shared these things?

That she had never thought to ask?

"Mam, why didn't Dad visit in June like he said he would?" Her daughter's question, though, quelled all the other questions.

"You knew about that?"

"I heard you," Úna said. "The night before he left."

Grá blushed. "I wouldn't worry, love—"

"Well then, why hasn't he come?"

Despite her instruction, Grá heard the beginnings of worry, all right. "It's just this BSE stuff," she tried. "The whole country has gone a little mad." Instantly, she regretted the joke.

"But he's definitely OK." The way Úna said it was less of a question than a statement. And yet, Grá knew her answer still needed to come instantly. It could be *Of course* or *Don't be silly* or even *Why wouldn't he be?*, though the last one would bring its own set of complications. A better mother would take the lie even further. *He already called—said he was coming in September instead.* But Grá knew she wasn't better. In fact, these days she knew she had gotten so much worse.

He's definitely OK.

You're a girl.

You know, I have a feeling that he isn't.

"Like I said, love, I really wouldn't worry." Grá looked at the clock. The minute's silence spilled into another and then another and then another.

Úna, eventually, had been persuaded up to bed. Still their bowls sat dirty and untouched. Grá thought back to the water, wondering if maybe she shouldn't have kicked; if maybe she should have just let Nature win.

But there was worried and there was pathetic, so eventually she forced herself to stand. She slipped a small square of paper from behind the noticeboard and dialled the number written across. As she counted them out, she could have sworn each ring was louder than the last. She pictured her daughter swallowing those biscuits one after the other after the other. For a second, she had thought Úna was trying to make herself sick. There were so many things she didn't want to pass down to her daughter, but that would be the very worst.

After the seventh ring, Grá sighed and hung up, annoyed and relieved in unequal measure. She took the bowls to the sink and let the water run until it was scalding to the touch. When the phone rang, her hands flinched in fright, spraying technicolour suds. She wiped them on her jeans and allowed herself one last question before she picked up. Because of the two men she knew would be at the end of this line, which one did she most want it to be?

It seemed, in that moment, the question that would decide everything.

"Hi there, I'm sorry I missed a call from this number. Who—"

In the silence her question played again. "Ronan? It's me." And then she added quickly to be sure: "It's Grá."

From behind, she could hear the bubbles fizzing in the sink. It sounded the same as static on a wire.

"Oh." When he spoke, there was no denying his surprise, though there were all sorts of surprises it could have been. "Great to hear from you. How have you been?"

She couldn't decide if platitudes meant one sort as opposed to another.

She told him she had been fine and he said he had too. She thought of his moods and the pills he sometimes took to help. But she couldn't linger. "I didn't know who to call. It's the Butchers—I'm sure they're grand, but I just wanted to check if you had heard anything?" Grá pictured him sprawled across his couch or maybe hunched in his darkroom, his face lit up by the red fuzzing light. She had asked him to describe the process to her, dipping his pictures blank into the liquid, then watching them emerge alive. It was a metamorphosis every time; a chrysalis into a butterfly; a change beyond recognition. "I'm sorry, I don't know why I phoned. I suppose if you hear anything just let me know. Otherwise best of luck with the exhibition—I hope you finally found that killer shot to pull it all together!" She was going to hang up—she really was—thinking now of the last time she saw him. The bedsheet had fallen below her breasts and she had left them there, cold and tender.

"Grá, wait."

Those two words brought more relief to her body than they should have. Which was ironic, given all the things they brought next.

"I'm sorry," he said. "It's just, I assumed you would have heard. I knew they were waiting for . . . Jesus, Grá." His tone had changed; there was breathing now and there was plenty. There was her name and then there was the Lord's name too. She realised she had never thought to ask Ronan a thing about religion; about whether he had any faith of his own.

"Grá." The way he said it, she knew to close her eyes. "They found a body." The darkness gave the picture a better backdrop to emerge. "One of the Butchers . . . Grá, I can't believe . . ." Feature by feature, rising out of the liquid. "I assumed you would already know."

But how could she tell him that what we believe and what we assume and what we know are never really the same?

As the night bled on, Grá watched the darkness rise up around her like a flood. From the back garden, she thought she heard barking, but she knew it was wishful thinking; knew there was little chance the orphaned cubs had managed to survive. Her body refused to move, whereas her restless mind began to wander, reaching for snapshots of the past to kill the time.

There was her in her wedding dress, grinning amidst the clumps of marigolds she had stuffed fat into jars. There was Cúch in her parents' kitchen the very first day she saw him, a dimple dug deep into each handsome cheek. And there was another image from another day, which proved—yet again, it seemed—she had been lying to herself all along. Because this wasn't the first time her husband had promised to come home during his travels, although the last time, the promise had been kept.

The nurse had warned them that the due date was rarely accurate, but that was the date he aimed for nonetheless. And sure enough, no sooner had he stepped in the door, her waters broke. It was a lake from her and of her and beneath her.

He had filled the bath like they had discussed and dialled the midwife's phone. Grá held his hand, the same hand that drew death every day. She heaved her pain into the water, an agony that was dulled, but fuck it was agony still.

Úna didn't linger, as if she knew there was only so long her father could stick around. The final push felt a lot like drowning—Grá's head rushed with the pressure and the gasping and the bubbles on the surface like a Morse code *SOS!*

When Úna screamed, Grá recognised nothing of herself.

Some time later, after the midwife had guided her through to the bedroom, Grá's vision finally returned. She found Cúch kneeling on the floor beside her, head bowed, muttering a silent prayer. When he lifted his face it was drenched. "You are a miracle," he told Grá. "I believe in you more than I have ever believed in anything."

After a moment, Úna screamed again. This time Grá recognised nothing of herself but love.

"Mam?" When Úna appeared now, she wore pyjamas and socks, her voice part concern, part croaky with sleep.

The kitchen had begun to lighten, which meant it was almost dawn.

"Mam," she tried again. "Will I make you a cup of tea?"

Grá opened her mouth.

They found a body.

"What about a biscuit?"

One of the Butchers . . .

"What about this?"

She looked down. Eight fingers were placed on her arm. She couldn't feel a single one.

Grá, I can't believe . . . I assumed you would already know . . .

But that was the worst bit, because of course deep down she had already known, and for some reason she had still thought that she could survive.

Eventually Úna had persuaded her up for a bath and Grá had wondered, too late: *Did I ever tell you, love, you were even born a special way?* But the longer she stood, the more she couldn't face the prospect of the water. Instead, she decided she might just never wash again. It could be a mourning ritual, plucked out of thin air, but didn't everyone love a good superstition? The stranger and dirtier the better?

The Curse of the Butcher's Widow.

She would spread the word far and wide; would let the dead cells gather around her like a shroud.

She hadn't thought to ask Ronan where the body was found; hadn't even thought to ask how the body was killed. She looked out the bathroom window. In the distance, a tractor beheaded the grass. The trees listed their branches to the left. Everything was the same—the fields the clouds the muck the ruts from the cart wheels down the hill.

Even as they approached, very slowly, they seemed to stay out of focus, the edges fuzzed like a dream or a memory. Grá counted the figures one at a time, then she counted them again. She craved every one of those awful biscuits.

Sure enough, there were only seven—seven pairs of shoulders burdened with the news they were about to give, thinking they were the first. Grá looked down on her flesh as if she had just remembered. She supposed she should at least meet her fate in clothes.

As she hurried to get dressed, she heard her daughter. "Mam, quick!" Grá fumbled the button on her skirt and ran down the stairs. Out in the driveway, there they were, standing solemn in an arc. And in the centre, there he was, looking up at her. "Hello, love."

Her heart stopped. Her head stopped seeing the world in snapshots. No, everything was clear and fluid again.

Her husband was alive.

Her husband was home.

It was the third day of July.

"Cúch!" She threw herself into his warmth and felt him flinch as if she had landed him a kick. "I'm sorry." She couldn't even begin to explain what for. But there would be time—so much time now—to make every kind of amends. When she eventually pulled away, she knew she was ready to start. "Let me do you some lunch." She knew she was ready, even, to attempt a joke. "Although you realise you're late, young man? Three days and counting?" She could have told him how many seconds, how many minutes, how many hours.

Cúch's face matched none of her laughter. It was only now that she noticed the bruises, yellow and black around his eyes. Grá thought again of rapeseed; of eels slithering in between legs. And then she checked the other faces where, sure enough, all six were battered too. She held her breath before she said the missing word. "Sol?"

CHAPTER ELEVEN
Davey

County Monaghan, July 1996

"Do you know what time the results are supposed to be in?" Davey sat sequestered on a stool at the O'Connell's bar, wrapping knives and forks in red paper napkins. The pub had started serving lunch—more than just packets of crisps or Scampi Fries. The locals deemed it fierce fancy altogether. Behind the bar, Faela was down on her hunkers trying to detach an empty keg that had got stuck. Apart from them, only a couple of regulars were propping the place up. It had only just gone eleven o'clock.

"If there's no word by three," Davey continued, "I'll nip down to the police station. It is definitely supposed to be today, isn't it?" He smoothed a napkin and swaddled the next cutlery pair like an infant babe, tucking it snug and tight around the corners.

Except for the grey mid-morning light that filtered in through the windows, O'Connell's looked much the same as it always did. There was no shattered glass or splintered wood; no banjaxed stools or dark spots of blood. In fact, the only trace of damage from the fight was the gap on the wall where the lucky hurl used to reside. Davey wondered what it meant for local luck. He wondered if they could get someone to whittle a replacement.

"They won't tell us everything, but at least we will know the cause of death. That should narrow it down, shouldn't it?"

All morning, Davey had been asking these unanswered questions. He had headed down to the cold store as soon as he woke. The perimeter of the site was still cordoned off with tendrils of yellow tape that made a smacking noise against the wind. The same Garda had been stationed there all week, a shortish lad with a moustache that looked almost definitely stuck on. Davey had plied him for details:

"Any witnesses come forward?"

"I heard the autopsy results are due today?"

"Do you have any inclination yourself?"

The Garda looked at him so blankly it was as if Davey were speaking in tongues.

"Got it!" It was Faela speaking now. She rolled the old keg out on its side, then showed Davey the fresh one that needed bringing in. He reversed the proceedings and manoeuvred the thing upright under the pump, its metal arse sounding a boxing-bell clang.

While Faela did the attachment, Davey recounted his own inclination. "I still think the Bull is the most likely suspect. After all, Sol's body was found in *his* shed. I haven't figured out *why*, but maybe he had beef with the Butchers, if you'll pardon the—"

"Davey, would you ever cop yourself on!"

He stopped. He couldn't tell if Faela was angry or just sick to death—he had been in here most mornings this week asking the very same things. But when she stood up, her face was softer. Her red hair was brushed shiny and smooth. "Look, Davey, I know what you saw in that cold store must have been *horrific.*" She swiped her hand through the air as if underlining the word. "But in terms of who actually did it . . ." He noticed her nails were painted bright pink. "I don't understand why you care so much?"

In the days following the O'Connell's brawl, Davey had wandered around in a daze. Each night he lay awake until morning, then took himself off on a walk. And even when his ears had stopped ringing from the thunder of the fight, the reality of what he had wanted from that evening refused to go quiet. He had, very carefully, picked out what to wear. He had, very patiently, waited for Con. As soon as the Butchers had arrived, he had, very quickly, melted. And he had peeled his eyes for the moment he and Con could slip away and do . . . what—something? Everything? More than a confused fumble in a byre or a brief peck on the lips, that was for sure. So even if things had gone horribly wrong (Davey could remember the terror of the crush, the wet sound of knuckles pounding flesh), surely he could no longer ignore the new inclination he had about himself?

Until one morning when he was out walking, struggling with all these unanswered questions, he passed the disused cold store and noticed its door was left ajar. Davey entered and saw the boots set neatly to the side, then he saw the hook and the feet and the two holes in the flesh. So regardless of how *horrific* it was, Davey was trying to stay focused on that image—everything else was another story entirely. And unlike the ancient myths, this one was happening right here and now, and it left Davey completely terrified.

"Well, what's the craic?" The next question came from the doorway of the pub where the backdrop of sunlight meant the figure was pure silhouette. Only as it approached could Davey make out the hulk of muscle and county colours—the GAA jersey stretched two sizes tight in white and blue.

"Turlough!"

There was a wee chain around the stranger's neck and a wee sneer around his mouth. He gestured towards the cutlery pile. "Looks like you two lovebirds have been busy." Faela came to meet him, pressing her pink mouth against his. Davey noticed one of the napkins had come undone.

Eventually the couple pulled apart and Faela made the introductions. "Davey was just passing. Saved me Trojan's work, so he did!"

Davey noticed the classical reference. *Trojan's work*. He wondered if she meant it as a kindness or maybe even a sort of apology.

But then Faela introduced something else. "We were just talking about the body that they found."

"I heard the autopsy's due." Turlough let his sneer return. "Though frankly, who gives a shite how it happened."

Despite himself, Davey knew better than to bite so easily. "I was just telling Faela, actually, I reckon the prime suspect is the Bull. Given where the body was found—you have to admit it doesn't look good."

Turlough's laughter was so forced it didn't really sound like laughter at all. Davey suddenly realised he looked sort of familiar. "Do you honestly think Goldsmith could be bothered with those gypos right now? And him busy trying to keep this country afloat?"

"Ah, another loyal follower." This time it was Davey who forced out a laugh. "Tell me, Turlough, why *is* everyone so devoted to that guy? He's clearly crooked as fuck—do you really think he cares about anyone other than himself?"

"Do you really think the prime suspect isn't your da?"

Davey had been on a bit of a roll, then suddenly he wasn't. He leaned back and found the edge of the stool for support. He looked at his pile. He thought Faela had said the new menu was mostly toasted sandwiches, so why did they even need knives and forks for that?

Of course, amid Davey's focus, his endless unanswered questions, he had thought of his da, all right. In the chaos of the fight they had got separated, every man for himself, the tidal wave of violence and hatred hurling them every which way. When he finally fled O'Connell's, the last thing Davey saw was Fionn standing on a stool, shouting like a maniac, his face blotched red and his old aggression wild alive. So despite the fact that, recently, Davey had begun to think that maybe—just maybe—his father was a changed man, if he was connected to Sol's death, that destroyed everything again. Davey placed his hands in his lap and spread his fingers wide. It was another reason he cared so much about finding the truth.

Faela had told him to grab a table while she fixed him some lunch for his troubles. Davey was about to protest, then realised he was starved; requested a pint to wash it all down. He picked a spot in the corner and watched as Turlough took his stool at the bar, then produced what looked like a mobile phone from his pocket. Davey wondered who the hell had bought him one of those; wondered what the hell he even needed it for.

After he hoovered his grub, Davey would head down the station and see if there had been any word yet from the morgue. Then he would phone the *Anglo-Celt*—it was a joke there still hadn't been any news coverage of the case. He thought of that dead journalist, Veronica Guerin. He thought of that photographer lad wanting to capture the Butchers "as they truly were."

He knew that, all things considered, "capture" was a terrible choice of verb.

But that only led him back to considering who *would* want to capture the Butchers, literally like? Who the hell would do such a fucked-up thing? Not to mention the issue of *how*— Davey wished he had taken a closer look at the pulley system. He assumed the meat hook had been sent off to a lab. "Tell me, Faela, roughly how much does a dead body weigh?"

Faela's tray bore a pint, a dish of condiment sachets, and a ham and cheese toastie on white. Although, Davey saw that "toastie" was a bit of a stretch—the bread looked more wet than it did particularly browned. "As in, would you need two people to lever it, or could you do it yourself?"

Faela placed down the glass and the plate, but kept hold of the sauces. "Davey," she said, "after this, would you not go home and have a rest?" He realised she hadn't brought any cutlery. "Have you been sleeping?" When he didn't answer, she turned, taking the sachets with her.

The cheese, at least, was faintly pungent. The ham was salty and strong—apparently the pork farmers were having a field day at the moment. Without a napkin, the butter leaked yellow down Davey's chin. He gulped the drink and glanced at the bar where Turlough had finished with the phone and was reaching across to place his hand on Faela's pale cheek. Her eyelids batted like one of those American actresses from the films Davey's mother always played on repeat.

And now Davey found himself trying to remember—it had been only a few short months ago—if he had ever placed a hand on Faela's cheek quite like that. And if so, had the story really changed so completely since then?

And was it too late now to change it back?

Davey drained the pint and wiped his mouth with his sleeve. Enough of that—he had to stay focused; had to concentrate on other questions instead. He was about to stand up when the joke arrived from a jostle of men at a table in the opposite corner.

"What do you call a Butcher with a big cock?"

"I don't know, what?"

"Hung!"

The punchline was delivered loud enough for the entire pub's benefit. The sniggers around the room responded in spades. It was only a bit of messing, a bit of rudeness, but it was enough to let Davey know he wasn't the only one in here with the dead body on his mind. So he decided he would order another drink and stay put a bit longer; would wait for the tongues around him to get a bit looser, just in case there were any new versions of the story that might be worth listening to.

"I heard the corpse was castrated.'

"I heard it was stuck up on a pole like a fucking scarecrow."

"Well, yous have it wrong—I heard your man was stripped down to his jocks and crucified like Our Lord."

Hours later and Davey had barely moved except to order more drinks and take a see-through piss. His head was finally feeling a bit less wired. The questions, at least for now, had eased right off. And the conversation around him had moved on from the dead Butcher—beef sales were way down; slaughter season was looming and prices per kilo were shite. The word "boom" hadn't been uttered in a while. Beneath the grumbling came the musical clink of pocket change as the men struggled to count out the cost of another pint. Davey considered his own prospects. He had the munchies. What about another toastie? With some ketchup this time, pretty please? He looked up at the bar to catch Faela's eye—maybe he would have a go at a whiskey—but she was busy, blushing as her new boyfriend whispered something in her ear. "Behave yourself, Turlough Hynes!"

Davey tried to roll his eyes, but found they were already swimming a bit in his head, so he only moved them to Turlough and thought of all the meathead lads from school. He wondered if their end-of-exam rave had been a success; wondered if the Pez dispensers of pills had managed to lose them all their minds. But that only made the questions start up again, because hadn't that been the Saturday after the exams? The very same night as the brawl in here? So what about a version where a gang of yoked-up eighteen-year-olds find an old man in the woods? A celebration prank gone very very wrong?

Slaughter season.

Davey closed his eyes. He thought of Sol's kindness back at the Butchers' camp.

A tragedy for any man.

God knows my missis would be beyond cure.

When he opened his eyes, Davey's vision was beyond blurry. He used the TV above the bar to bring his focus back. Although it took a couple more blinks to make sense of the strange image that was playing on the screen; the orange blaze that was leaping hot across. Davey's first thought was that it was probably something to do with the annual bonfires they would be lighting up north next week. It was an old Loyalist tradition, a series of ritual infernos piled high to mark the eleventh night. But when the camera zoomed in, Davey saw amidst the flames there were arms and legs; there were tails and there were definitely eyes. So his second thought was a different ritual altogether—the ancient Greeks burning their animals on altars. *A pyre.* A sacrifice to their sinister gods.

The camera panned away to a reporter standing downwind of the smoke, trying very hard not to breathe. Davey squinted at the caption beneath: *Widespread destruction of English herds.* His third thought was the Bible and the fucking apocalypse— pure Judgement Day fire-and-brimstone stuff. He knew at this rate Ireland would probably be next: the green fields scorched black; the muck strewn with ashes and bones.

"Davey—there you are."

When he looked down from the screen, the picture in front of him wasn't much more appealing. "What are *you* . . . ?" He tried to speak and heard the slur in his words. He stopped and swallowed, then went again. "What are *you* doing here?"

The second time wasn't much better. The corners of his mouth were clagged together. He reached for his glass and swilled the last of the liquid.

"Faela called me." His father took the opposite stool. "She said . . . she was a little worried."

Davey opened his gullet and downed the warm mouthful in one.

Fionn sighed. "Be careful with that stuff, lad. God knows, you don't want to end up like me."

When Davey heard this, he went to meet his father's eyes, to tell him that they were nothing alike, but his vision had gone blurry again. He could just make out Fionn's stubbled face, the grey flecked with bits of copper. He thought of embers; of tiny sparks that, very easily, could catch light.

And then Davey had another thought and he didn't give a flying fuck whether he slurred this time or not. "Tell me, Fionn," he said, leaning forward, "was it you?"

"What?"

"Are you the one who murdered the Butcher? After I lost you the other night, did you go berserk and beat the living daylights out of your man Sol?" Even as he told it, Davey knew this version of the story wasn't the most eloquent, the most complete, but he also knew it had just enough pieces to hold together. "Did you drag him to the cold store and hang him up by his poor wrinkled feet? Because for some reason your beloved Fergus Hynes said he would give you a bit of cash for it?" He didn't know what answer he had been hoping for, but by the time the story was finished, he saw Fionn's pale face was burning and Davey knew that he had it.

He knew there could be no going back.

"Good afternoon, everyone!"

And now the pub door was swinging open and three men, one at a time, were stepping inside. The room took a moment, then fell hush. Someone switched off the television, though the man suddenly standing before them was a fairly regular appearance on the news. "So sorry to disturb." The Bull was definitely better looking in real life. His face was tanned and cleanly shaved. He wore a three-piece suit with a Windsor-knotted tie, and a silk square peeked perfectly from the pocket. Behind him was the Garda with the awful moustache, who removed his hat and placed it over his chest. The third man had black hair with a grey clump at the front. Davey glanced back at Turlough and realised it was true that a lot could be read from the way a father teaches his son to carry himself.

"For those of you who don't know me, my name is Eoin Goldsmith. I am . . . I do a little bit of work on beef." The hush gave way to a rumble of laughter, the room already putty in the baron's hands. "I won't keep you long, only it was brought to my attention that some O'Connell's punters have been making a few *insinuations*. So I just wanted to pop by and clear things up, if that's all right?"

Beneath his breath, Davey snorted. Even if you hadn't already known, there was no doubt this lad spent time in the company of politicians. The euphemisms and charisma; the faux concern; the exceptional polish of the brogues and the emerald green of the pocket square.

"Over the weekend, a discovery was made in a former facility of mine. No one, let me tell you, was more surprised than me. But I am *all* about honesty, so I have been assisting the Gardaí with their investigations, and now they have some important news to share."

If there had been fidgeting before, there wasn't a trace of it any more. Davey wondered if the men had placed any bets on the cause of death. It would be a way at least to win back a bit of much-needed cash; a way to scab the price of the next round of pints.

The Garda didn't step forward so much as the Bull stepped back. By contrast, the Garda clearly detested the spotlight. "We got the autopsy results," he stammered, still clutching his hat over the left side of his chest. Davey wondered if it was a reflex or something they had been taught in training, and if so, was it out of self-defence or respect? "The heart," the Garda said, as if he had overheard Davey's thoughts. "It was a heart attack. Natural causes, like. Nothing more." As soon as the verdict was delivered, he took a step back, his face coated in a thin film of sweat.

"Well, isn't that a relief?" When the Bull clapped his hands, they all jumped. He resumed his position centre stage. "God knows we have enough to be worrying about at present. Lovely lady?" Next he cocked his eyebrows high and far. It took Faela more than a moment to return the favour. "How about a pint for everyone on me? My friend Fergus here will settle up." And then the Bull cast his clasped hands away as if releasing a pigeon or a snow-white dove. Davey traced the line of invisible flight, thinking of *hubris* and Icarus and soaring high enough to be among the gods.

When he looked back, the Bull was already halfway out the door. Davey had expected a queue to touch his cloth; a line around the block to kiss his exceptionally polished feet.

"Mr. Goldsmith." But of all of them, Davey was the one who wasn't finished with him just yet. He stood up and watched the Bull pause mid-step.

Fionn reached out a hand, warning his son, but Davey brushed it off. "What about what they did to him *after* he died?"

If the room had relaxed, it suddenly tensed again. Davey ran his tongue along his teeth. His feet were planted in one spot, but his body felt as if it were swaying in little circles.

The Bull's smile had the distinct look of a grimace. "Ah yes, you must be referring to the rumour about the *position* of the corpse. I did hear—"

"It's not a rumour," Davey said. "I saw it."

Slowly the smile became a squint. The Bull glanced down to Davey's right. "Of course," he said. "Young Mr. McCready. I believe it was *you* who had the misfortune of having to phone the police. We all owe you a *great deal* for that."

Even through the fog in his head, Davey could hear the threat in the tone; could feel his father's agitation next to him. But he was nearly finished. "Even if it *was* a heart attack, it's still defamat—*desecration* of a corpse. It's still a crime. Surely you can't just leave it at that?"

Of all the people, though, it was the Garda who delivered the final blow. "The body has been returned to the family," he said. "They have agreed there will be no further investigation." He placed his hat on his head and disappeared smartly out the door.

And Fergus Hynes disappeared too—no word of farewell to his son—whereas the Bull chose to linger a moment more. He gave a sigh, his face relaxing for the first time all night; his eyes

filling up with pure regret. "Look," he said, "we may not understand these strange men—may not *agree* with their ancient
traditions. But whatever *rituals* they choose to perform on their
dead, ultimately we must respect." He waited until the insinu-
ation had worked its way across the room; until one version of
events had been set down for good. Then he left, and Davey
knew the story would never be told another way again.

When they made it back to the farm, Fionn helped him upstairs
and on to his bed. Davey lay flat on his back and watched the
room reeling. He thought a bit about the gods and how a man
decides what it is he truly believes. He thought about loving a
man who thinks it is acceptable to defile another man's body.

He thought a bit about loving another man.

Hours later he woke and the dusk had settled around him.
His head had settled a bit too. His mouth was dry and foul
so, very slowly, he stood up and crossed to the bathroom for a
drink. On his way back to his room he heard his name.

He found his mother sitting up in her bed, her fingers
fanned regal across the blanket. "You look tired, love." As ever,
she went straight to the point. "I know it's been a mad few
days—an awful lot has gone on."

Davey nodded, but he didn't speak just yet. Instead he
took a step towards the window. In the yard below, Blackfoot
was sprawled and chewing something large between her paws.
Davey couldn't see whether it was a bone or something else.
He realised he was hungry.

But his mother went on. "He was terrified when Faela called
and said you were drunk. He blames himself, you know?" She

went quieter then: "He blames himself more than we ever could. All I ask is that you try to remember that sometimes."

Davey took another step. Beyond the dog, he saw the blue Fiesta parked up. In the half-light, it looked as if the tyres had been freshly pumped. He wondered why his father even bothered keeping it any more.

"Well, are you just going to stand there all night or are you going to talk to your dying mother?"

This time Davey didn't move. He closed his eyes as if that would block out the words, though the sound of "dying" still echoed through the room. And the sound of "talk" lingered too, because he knew his mother wasn't looking for idle chat or gossip from the pub. No, he knew she was looking for so much more.

So Davey thought of talking to his dying mother about the Butchers and how the Bull had just alleged that *they* were the ones responsible for hooking Sol's body up; he wanted to ask how much she knew about their ancient traditions and whether it even mattered if it was true. He thought of talking about his father and how really, Davey struggled to let him in for fear that Fionn might just not like what he found there; how he would try a little harder, if only for her sake. The longer he stood there, though, the more Davey realised he wanted to talk to his dying mother about something else—about a certain inclination. He wanted to talk, finally, about the truth. He opened his eyes and turned around, moved to the bed and sat beside her. His body felt the generosity of the mattress's give.

Davey began at the very beginning and told the story of himself, of the kind of man he had become. Or really, he suspected, the kind of man he had always been. He told the story of Con and how he was the spark that had finally brought the whole thing blazing to life. He told her the burning inside him didn't feel like shame any more.

When he was finished, Davey felt lighter, emptied out. Although the bedroom felt emptied too—there were no words of approval or acceptance; no tears of shock or shame or savage disappointment. Davey looked at his mother and wondered if she had even been listening or if maybe her poor brain had decided to glitch at the perfectly imperfect moment.

He wondered if stories could be passed down through generations without ever being told aloud.

"You had better call the doctors." When she finally gripped his hand, Davey was filled again, this time with fear; with the thing he had been dreading now for so long. He wondered if his father was out in the field or waiting outside the door; if he had somehow managed to overhear everything.

"Tell them my headache is gone." Davey's mother moved his hand up to the side of her face. "Tell them," she smiled, "my son is after getting me cured." She let her skull rest against his palm as she closed her green eyes. Davey felt her pulse and her warmth and her relief.

CHAPTER TWELVE
Úna

County Cavan, July 1996

Ten o'clock sharp and Úna was waiting for her mam by the front door so they could finally set off for Mrs. P's. It was about a forty-minute walk, depending on the weather and the traffic and the occasional flock of sheep clogging the road like a cotton-wool stopper in a bottle neck. Since the Butchers' return, the trip had become an almost daily pilgrimage. Úna wasn't complaining—without school, it was nice to have a reason to get them up each morning and breakfasted and dressed. Not that her mam joined her for porridge; Úna had noticed her eating less than ever these days. She had noticed her mam's friend Ronan vanishing without a trace.

Being honest, the visits to Mrs. P were also kind of nice because they were an excuse to escape the tension of the house. With her father home, the whole place was eggshells, hurried voices behind doors and under breaths. He had bruises on his face and all down one side of his body, but he refused to say how or why. He refused, despite his wife's pleas, to see a doctor.

As it happened, over breakfast this morning, Úna had heard a different kind of doctor on the radio. He was talking about the BSE, but also about other animal diseases. There was one called scrapie, which was for sheep and which also sent them mad. There was one, unimaginatively, called foot-and-mouth. He tried to explain how some of the conditions were genetic—passed down from a parent animal, which meant the offspring was doomed to be born wonky from the start.

Úna sighed. What was taking her mam so long? She turned to inspect herself in the mirror while she waited; saw the mousy hair that had been passed down from her father and the green eyes that had been passed down from her mam. She sometimes wondered about the bits she couldn't see—like whether they were her mother's kidneys or her father's lungs or maybe one of each. It was the heart she wondered about the most.

But then the doctor had tried to explain how, with some of the diseases, genetics were only part of the story. Because an animal could be born one way and then, over time, it could be changed—it wasn't just about Nature any more, it was about "Man intervening and altering things."

"Sorry, love." There was a clatter on the stair. Her mam was red around the eyes. "Have you got everything?"

Úna took one last look in the mirror, shoved her hair behind her ears, then vanished out the door.

Back before she was a widow, Mrs. P had always welcomed them to her cottage with a smile, hurrying them inside with gossip and plates of homemade treats, still warm. These days they tended to just slip in quietly, then spend an hour nursing milky tea and silences. Truth be told, Úna didn't know which one made her stomach the more sour.

But this morning there was nothing quiet about the welcome whatsoever. "Come in, come in!" Mrs. P ushered them
with hands covered in dark smears, jet black with a glossy
sheen. Úna frowned, then thought of treacle or molasses and
decided the widow must have finally gone back to her recipe
book. Flapjacks were an easy place to start.

The kitchen table was so covered in newspaper you couldn't
even see a sliver of wood, headlines and articles criss-crossing
to form a black-and-white tapestry. Úna spotted a picture of
the Bull, which took up half a broadsheet front page. These
days, he seemed to be the only one still smiling.

"You'll have to excuse the mess." Mrs. P, on the other hand,
was busy wiping her forehead with the back of her wrist. "I've
been hard at it all morning."

Úna glanced at the oven, but the light was off. She inhaled. The kitchen smelled strange, but not particularly
sweet. So what was it Mrs. P had been "hard at"? Next Úna
remembered her revelation from the lake—that she used to
be a journalist—so maybe the newspapers had something to
do with that?

When Úna found the boots, one of them was shiny and
the other one was not. She knew both of them had once belonged to Sol.

"I thought I'd be finished by the time you arrived, but they
were absolutely filthy." Mrs. P picked up a little pot and a
hard-bristled brush. "Grá, would you ever be a saint and get
things going with the tea?"

Úna's mam, though, didn't move, only stared in shock.
Around them, the strange smell finally made sense. The shoe

polish gave off a sharp and headachy smell like toilet bleach or disinfectant for a wound.

"I could have sworn he had another pair somewhere in a bigger size—did you know that feet shrink with old age?" Mrs. P began to scrub at the tip of the toe. "I might try the attic later on."

Finally Úna's mam took a deep breath and replaced her shock with sympathy. "Love, I . . . I don't think he'll be needing his boots any more." She had already warned Úna that grief went through many phases; many forms. "You do remember that Sol . . . I'm so sorry, but Sol is gone."

On the day of the funeral, it seemed as if Mrs. P was going through her silent phase. She had barely uttered a word; had barely shed a tear as she watched her husband's body being fed back down into the earth. The Butchers had each placed a hand on the wicker box, guiding it all the way—three men on either side and Úna's father weeping wetly at the head.

It was only afterwards at the house, scoffing sandwiches and wholemeal scones, that the widow had finally come back to life. She said that heart disease had always been in Sol's family—he had been complaining about chest pains just this Christmas—but she said that didn't really explain about the rest. "I mean the *holes* . . ." She had faltered. "The ones in his feet. I found them when I was doing his final bath." Her whole body had started to shake. "The water . . . it just poured straight through." Before she collapsed to the armchair with both hands pressed against her mouth.

Úna's own mouth had gone slack as she watched the other mourners rush in with soothing words and whiskey nips. She had waited for Mrs. P to sit up and apologise for her muddled head. But apparently what she was saying wasn't muddled at all, it was true, and no one could offer any explanation—not that afternoon nor in the days and weeks ever since. It was the thing Úna heard her parents arguing about the most, anxious whispers through the bedroom walls.

"Cúch, what *happened* to him?"

"I don't know."

"So go back and find out!"

"We've been through this; I can't."

"Why do you always have to be so set in your ways?"

"Grá, I told you—if the Gardaí returned the body, there were to be no more questions—that was the deal. Plus, Wyn's son is a doctor and he said it was definitely a heart attack. The rest . . . We just have to leave it be."

"Of course I *remember*." Back in the cottage kitchen, the noise of the bristles had ceased. "But now that the Butchers need to appoint an eighth, I would like for Sol's replacement to wear his boots." Here Mrs. P held the left foot up to inspect her handiwork. Úna thought how strange it was that shoes had tongues. "My husband may be 'gone,' as you so *delicately* put it, but the old rituals have to carry on."

"And I'm sure they will . . ." And now Úna thought how strange it was to see her mam choosing her words so carefully. "But you don't need to worry about all that, Aoife. The most important thing for you is to get some rest and just—"

"Just *what*?" The boot slammed down on the table, full-force. Úna had never heard the old woman raise her voice in her life. She had also never heard her first name—had never even considered the fact of her having one. "Just spend my time baking cakes you don't even eat? Imagining all the ways they might have torn shreds from my husband's limbs? No, I would prefer to do something useful, thank you very much." The bristles resumed their agitated rhythm. "You do *remember* it is our faith too?"

When she had finally finished her task, Mrs. P went upstairs to scrub the black from her fingernails. Úna's mam went outside to shove the dirty newspapers in the bin. Úna was left behind to do the tea. As the kettle boiled, she considered all that Mrs. P had just said. Or really, this new woman "Aoife" who polished old boots and shouted at old friends.

All the ways they might have torn shreds from my husband's limbs . . .

Úna tried to think who "they" could even mean? Tried to think if it could be the same "they" who had bruised her father's face?

You do remember *it is our faith too?*

But Mrs. P had said another thing, which Úna didn't need to try to think about.

Now that the Butchers need to appoint an eighth . . .

She remembered Wyn's son and wondered if being a doctor made you better with knives and blood? She wondered if a Butcher's child was statistically more likely to be a boy or a girl?

I would like for Sol's replacement to wear his boots.

She looked at the pair drying side by side by the radiator. The unknotted laces lay long like four mouse tails. She leaned back and peered through to the hallway; the coast was clear.

She took off her shoes and socks, then, one at a time, she stepped her two feet in.

Úna flexed her toes into the empty space until the heat began to rise. It moved up through her bones and past her calves; past her hips and her trouser crotch. By the time it had reached all the way to her chest, where the breasts she so hated had started to sprout, she had answered one of her questions at least. Because if the doctor on the radio was right, then not everything had to be defined by Nature. Not everything was to do with genetics—no, Man could intervene and alter things.

Úna closed her eyes and inhaled, letting the realisation sink fully in.

You could be born one way and then you could be changed.

At dinner that evening, her feet were bare again, but her body felt hotter than ever. On the table sat three steaks—they had eaten from the freezer stash most evenings since her father's return. *What's the special tonight? More beef, love!* At this rate they would run out very soon. Úna wondered if the Butchers had brought back any fresh cuts of meat from their travels or just a body with some inexplicable cuts below the toes.

She had passed the afternoon in the bathroom while her father was out and her mother was in the garden. Úna had stared at herself in the mirror, prodding and poking and racking her brains. Every time she pressed the new flesh on her chest, she watched it bounce right back.

She paused. It wasn't right at all.

But then she had remembered the other morning when she spied her father changing the bandages on his torso, his left arm up to the sky, the fabric looping round and round like a mummy's wrap. So Úna had returned to her bedroom and searched her drawer for a pair of tights, then stretched them taut. She saw a ladder from one of the heels climbing up the leg. At first she flinched when she pulled the material flat across her nipples, but the pain only made her pull harder again. She looped slowly and patiently; tied a triple knot at the end and checked the mirror.

She smiled. The first half of her plan was complete.

Now, sitting at the kitchen table, she could feel the itch of the denier chafing her skin. She lowered her eyes, marvelling at the uninterrupted view to her lap. She cut another mouthful of steak, far too big, but she ate it all in one go anyway. The sound of her chewing filled her head. Neither of her parents had spoken a word. Her mother wasn't usually one for wine, but tonight she kept topping herself up until the bottle was nearly empty. Eventually it was Úna's father who risked the silence. "I met with some of the others earlier," he said. "We took your advice—a couple of the younger lads are headed back to the borderlands tomorrow to see if they can find out anything more."

Úna saw her mother lower her glass. "Oh?"

"I mean, about what they . . . About what happened to Sol. After his heart attack."

Next Úna saw her mother's thin face warring—all the things it wanted to say; all the things it wanted to ask or even demand. "Who will go?"

"Con volunteered straight away. Mik said he was happy to keep him company. I just . . . We're just worried it might be dangerous—"

"They'll be fine." Her mam cut in with the assurance, as if she could possibly know. "And anyway, you owe it to Mrs. P. When we saw her earlier . . . Oh, Cúch, she's in a terrible state. Some answers might at least bring her a bit of peace." Then she downed her glass in one before she softened, just an inch. "You said you took my advice?"

Úna's father nodded in reply, trying to see what the question was really asking, while Úna saw that he had barely touched his steak. She prayed her mother hadn't noticed. But of course, Úna didn't need prayers any more, because it was time for the second half of her plan to come to pass. She excused herself to the bathroom, then went softly with the stairs. She had stolen the small scissors from the drawer earlier, while her mam was busy in the garden. It reminded her of stealing knives all those months ago for the mouse.

In the bathroom, she looked in the mirror. Her eyelashes were very long. If she had had the time, she might have given them a trim as well. She took the first lock of hair in her fingers and realised the word was a perfect fit. *Lock.* Because it trapped you into things you might want to escape. She snipped smoothly and straightly like her mam had taught her. The strand fell to the sink in a single coil. She kept going, the blade cold against her scalp, but she knew that meant she was getting everything right at the root. She thought of the back garden and how scraggy it had grown. She thought of her mother out there on her hands and knees trying to see what could be saved.

When Úna was finished, she placed the scissors back in her pocket, lifted her T-shirt, and readjusted the tights. Already they had begun to dig a rut across her chest like a line drawn in red pen. She didn't bother to step softly down the stairs and her mam didn't bother to say a thing when she saw her, only waited for her husband to turn and follow her gaze. It took him a moment—and a bit of pain—to manoeuvre himself around. Úna wondered if tights or bandages were better for fixing a body; for intervening and altering things.

"Dad, I've made a plan." When she spoke, she pitched her voice low; felt the stray hairs down her back like a fur. She realised she had never thought to check if the mouse was a female or a male. "Now that Sol is dead, I know you will need to find someone new before you can head back on the road, so I am putting myself forward as a replacement Butcher." Here she paused and nodded to her mother, both in acknowledgement and apology. "Don't worry, Mam told me the rules. But as you can see, I have decided to change." She rolled her shoulders tall and took a final breath. She was ready. "I have decided I don't need to be a girl anymore."

When her mother's tears began, Úna thought of her disappearing under the surface of the lake the other day. When her father stood up, she thought he really was a giant. She smiled at him. Maybe they would let her have a glass of wine to celebrate. Either way, she really was ready.

"Úna, the reason the men and I met up this afternoon was to discuss the future of the group. Between Sol and everything . . . It's not safe for us out there . . ." He gave a little cough to clear his throat and Úna realised it must have been gristle—that was why he hadn't touched his dinner—he must have been served a chewier piece of meat. "And now the farmers are saying they can't use us any more. The government's bringing in this new monitoring system—some 'modern' technology to trace every animal from birth to slaughterhouse . . ." His throat caught again. He coughed his words up. "So we have decided, Úna— trust me, it has been a very difficult decision—but the Butchers have decided to disband."

By the time her father was finished, the heat from Úna's body had vanished entirely. He stepped forward and held out his arms, a consolation offering of flesh and warmth and pure regret. But already she had turned away from him, from his words, and started for the front door. She made sure not to look in any mirror as she went sprinting out.

Habit—or was it tradition?—wanted to lead her left towards Mrs. P's, but Úna broke with all of that and turned right down the road instead. She ran, pumping her arms and legs, and didn't check behind—she knew her parents wouldn't be following. What she didn't know was whether that made her hate them any more or less.

The light was fading but not quite gone, the magpies flitting branch to branch, swallowing late-evening bugs they caught on the wing. The tarmac held the residual warmth of the afternoon's sunshine. Úna suddenly remembered she wasn't wearing anything on her feet.

A motorbike zoomed past, too close, so she veered a little nearer to the ditch. A van driver honked his horn and shouted something out his window about her arse. Úna felt the tights chafe a bit deeper; felt her limbs move a bit faster as the whip of the wind kept the worst of the moisture from her eyes.

She saw the turn for the playground and followed it, the path a slightly different texture underfoot. Back in her home-schooling days, her mam had taken her here for "PE" classes once a week. Apart from a dented slide, some monkey bars, and two rusty swings, there wasn't much to speak of. Úna had loved to turn the swing in a circle, winding the chains tighter and tighter, then let go with her head thrown back and spin.

When she spotted Car McGrath on one of the swings, the first thing she noticed was the state of his hair. It had gone gaudy over the summer, big orange blotches from spraying too much cheap and nasty bleach. The second thing she noticed was his dinner. Úna couldn't believe McDonald's was brazen enough to still be selling burgers. She couldn't believe anyone was stupid enough to still be buying them.

Her pace faltered until it stopped. Her chest felt as if it was on fire, especially where the bright red line ran straight through her heart.

It must have been her panting that gave her away. "Freak?" Car's voice was an explosion through the dusk. "Oh my God, is that really you?"

Úna flicked her eyes around. They were completely alone.

For as long as she could remember, she had hated the "f" word—had yearned for Car and his gang to call her by her real name. This evening, though, she realised that maybe it was better after all. Because freaks could be boys or girls, which meant maybe freaks could decide for themselves.

"Is it a new ritual?" Car continued. "The Baldy Butchers?" He sniggered, pleased with his alliteration, his shoulders shaking, which made the chains above him jangle like coins. But

Úna knew that he had it wrong—that, apparently, the Butchers didn't even exist any more.

A stitch stabbed her side. She needed to sit.

As she approached the other swing, she heard the chains go still. She could sense Car's eyes tracking her every move. It felt good to take the weight off her blackened feet; to focus on steadying her breath. She shifted the scissors in her pocket so they didn't jut into her ribs. She noticed the smell. "Can I have a bite?"

Car's eyes now tracked their way down to the burger in his hand as if trying to remember how it had found its way there. Tentatively, he held it out. His teeth had left little scalloped ridges in the bun.

The first mouthful was so much sweeter than Úna expected, like a spoonful of sugar had been sprinkled over the top of the patty. Her next bite had a bit more ketchup, a sting of pickle, and a plastic flub of cheese. She wondered if she would be able to taste the madness straight away; if it would work its way down to her stomach or go directly to her head. When she had finished, she wiped her hands on her thighs.

"Wow!" This time Car's laughter was a much kinder variety. "I was *not* expecting that."

Úna felt a wash of anxiety. "I'm sorry," she said. "I'll buy you another one when—"

"Don't worry. Sure it was only an excuse to get me out of the gaff." It wasn't just Car's laughter that was different now, it was his voice as well—it sounded more normal; natural. Úna supposed, with none of his gang around to watch, there was no need to keep the bravado up. "I eat my dinner here most evenings—to avoid the old pair, like. Although it gets pretty boring. What about you, why are you here?"

Úna heard the question and thought it also sounded pretty normal, natural, as if Car were genuinely interested in the reasons behind her impromptu arrival. But she also heard everything her father had just said.

A very difficult decision . . .

The Butchers have decided to disband.

She didn't even know where to start.

"Did you cut it yourself?"

She also didn't know how to answer that.

"It reminds me of your one Demi Moore," Car continued, "from the film *Ghost*. Have you seen it?"

This time Úna managed a vague shake of her head.

"Ah, no way? It's an absolute belter!" The chains gave music to Car's delight. "You've heard about the famous scene at least? The one where they get fierce kinky with the clay?"

Eventually, Úna forced herself to reply. She said that no, she hadn't heard about the famous scene. In fact, she didn't really know much about films because her family didn't own a television. Car couldn't believe it—what did she *do* with her days? She told him about listening to the radio and helping with the dinner; about already finishing their summer homework. She didn't tell him about playing with the Lego men.

It felt good to talk about normal things—to distract herself from her father and his words; to distract herself even from the fact that it was Car McGrath she was talking to. Car hadn't started their summer homework. Truth be told, he was considering not going back to school at all. He said the teachers picked on him because his brother had been such a wee shit.

"Can you believe the gossip, though?" Here he brightened again. "It's been confirmed—Feary and Donoghue are definitely riding."

Úna pictured her Civics teacher holding up portraits of politicians. "What, did someone catch them in the Art room getting fierce kinky with the clay?"

This time Car's laughter was a full eruption. "Wow, Úna. You really are *full* of surprises tonight."

The sound of her name made her cheeks go warm.

"And you are also kind of . . . cute when you blush." Car stumbled over the compliment. His voice sounded different again—less sure of itself, suddenly. "Although you do have a bit of ketchup on your mouth."

And then his hand reached out, crossing the gap between them and landing on her face. Úna froze. Car rubbed, very gently, his thumb against the corner of her lip. Úna hated it at first and then, just for a moment, she didn't hate it as much. She thought that, actually, it felt sort of nice.

But the moment didn't last, because even if her body was frozen, her mind had started to reel. This was Car McGrath, for goodness' sake—he had made her life a misery for an entire year—it didn't make any sense! She turned away, gripping the chain to steady herself. The spinning in her head made her think of the burger and the madness and if maybe it could get to work even quicker than she realised.

"Hey, are you all right?" Car slinked down from his swing and walked around to stand in front of hers.

The Butchers have decided to disband.

No, she wasn't all right.

The ones in his feet. I found them when I was doing his final bath.

No, nothing made sense any more.

"Úna, I was thinking . . ."

She closed her eyes. Her brain was speeding so fast she wondered if it might burst out of her skull. She wondered, for a split-second, if Demi Moore from *Ghost* was pretty.

"Can we forget about before?"

She felt Car's hand again, cupping her chin and tilting her face up towards his.

"Can we maybe start again?"

But out of everything, that was the bit that made the least sense of all. Because could you really just click your greasy fingers and forget about the past? Just go from being enemies to friends? From a group of Butchers to any other group of men?

Trust me, it has been a difficult decision . . .

Could you just erase everything you'd spent your whole life believing in?

"No."

Whether he had heard or not, still Car leaned in to kiss her. Úna could feel the weight of his body; could smell the salt on his breath. "Please stop."

It's not safe . . .

"Leave me alone."

"It's OK," Car whispered.

They can't use us . . .

"Don't be shy."

Trust me . . .

"I said get off me now!"

By the time she had opened her eyes, Úna was standing behind Car and his hand was no longer touching her face. Instead, it was her arm that was wrapped around his body, her muscles strained taut with the grip, the control.

"What the hell?" Car's neck twisted back to look at her. The sinews were the twirled chains of a swing. "I thought you wanted . . ." His words were a breathless mix of confusion and hurt. "Most girls would . . ." But then his breath stopped and his words turned to something else entirely. "What the fuck is that?" It took Úna a moment to recognise it as fear.

She followed his eyes to where her other arm was bent inwards, pressing the scissors up against his throat. She felt Car's limbs start to shake. She thought of a roll of gaffer tape to hold his body in place.

"I *asked* you to stop." When she spoke, she didn't try to pitch her voice low like earlier. In contrast to Car's quivering, she felt strangely calm. The only thing that moved were her fingers as she rotated the scissors a full turn away from Car then back to his neck.

"I *told* you to leave me alone."

The metal of the blade caught the glimmer of a nearby streetlamp. The skin of Car's throat stretched taut and white and ready. "Úna, please." His voice cracked in two.

She rotated the scissors a second time.

"Úna, I'm sorry." His eyes and nose started to leak.

She did the third and final turn. She was ready.

"Car!"

The voice came from across the playground and the pair sprang apart in unison, though not before the edge of the blade had nicked the skin under Car's jaw. Úna watched him touch his hand to the cut, then stare at the blood on his finger as if, once again, trying to figure out how it had found its way there.

"Oh my God," another voice was calling now, "is that *cowgirl*?"

"Fuck me, I think it is."

"Yeehaw!"

Úna kept her gaze on Car. He wiped the red smear on his jeans and wiped his face with the crook of his arm. When he met her eyes one last time, there was an expression there she had never seen before.

"All right . . . faggots?" He flung the question over his shoulder, a brief stumble before he was pure bravado again. "Anybody hungry?"

"What?"

"But isn't that—"

Yes, Úna wanted to say, *I am suddenly famished.*

"Well, whatever about you pussies, I would murder a milkshake. Hurry up before the bloody place shuts." Car swaggered off past his friends, ignoring their bafflement and leading the way towards the village.

Úna stood in the dirt and listened until their outrage had faded into the night. Once she was alone, she knew she should find a bush and use two fingers down her throat to make herself sick. Instead, her body didn't move, too busy trying to make sense of what had just occurred; what she had just done or maybe even just achieved.

Eventually she placed the scissors back into her pocket and checked the moon. It was very full. She checked her head, which was no longer racing. It was very still.

INTERLUDE

New York, January 2018
"When you first got famous, it was hard to believe it was really you." If she had grown a little hostile before, it seems Úna is all smiles again, now that they have established they know each other—or, more precisely, knew each other way back in a former life. "I read about your debut exhibition in Dublin. Then the one in London a few years later. You said in an interview you didn't get on with your parents, but the dual nationality thing ended up serving you nicely, hey?"

Despite having finally placed her, though, it is her sass that makes it difficult to reconcile. Úna? The same scrawny child who hovered awkwardly down the back of that County Cavan kitchen? Instead, when he looks at her now it is still her mother that he sees—the brilliant stare; the lilting tone; the occasional delight in watching his discomfort squirm.

Even after so long, Ronan can recall the calming effect Grá had on him that summer, especially towards the end of the project when he was using a fair bit, trying to stave off the worst of the depression. He can remember being so manic, so utterly desperate to get that perfect final shot, he didn't allow himself to sleep for days.

"And then I was over here visiting my cousin when I read they were doing a retrospective of your work. And thank God

I came! Because otherwise I would never have known about it. The photograph, I mean. *The Butcher.*"

For some reason, the effect of this is the opposite of calming. Ronan realises the irony—after his initial disappointment that the unknown picture hadn't attracted any attention.

Whereas Úna now is all attention. "I think it's an incredible shot."

He looks at her, resisting.

"No, I mean it. Staggering."

"I appreciate that."

"A proper masterpiece, like. Which then begs the question, of course, why you never displayed it to the public until now?"

The waitress produces the check on a silver platter; a couple of complimentary mints. Ronan is tempted to grab one and shove it in his gob, to render it out of action. Then again, when it comes to photography, he can always manage a bullshit answer. "It just didn't feel right, you know. *Exploiting* his tragedy. Taking advantage . . . *Benefiting* from the poor guy's misfortune."

But Úna isn't easily fooled. "Surely that tension's sort of at the heart of the profession? I've heard war photographers talk about it—whether to just document or intervene. And really, what do you have to feel bad about—you only took the bloody thing, am I right?" The final question isn't really a question and yet, because of what comes next, it seems to linger between them. Úna yanks a band from her wrist, flicks out her hair and scrapes it violently from her neck. She ties it up, twisting once, twice, three times, until it forms a tail at the back of her skull. She looks more masculine this way, somehow; more beautiful.

"It *was* a tragedy, though, you're right." When she sighs, she also looks more innocent—he would recognise her a mile off. "I mean, Sol's passing. Poor Aoife—his wife—when she discovered how he was found, she never really recovered. The total debasement, you know?" She licks her finger and presses it to a spare crumb on the table; raises the pie remains to her lips. "Then all those rumours started doing the rounds—saying it was the Butchers who had hooked his body up; that it was one of their *rituals*—have you ever heard something so absurd? But people honestly believed it. Or at least, believed it enough to stop inviting the Butchers to their homes. After hundreds of years—just turned their fucking backs."

By now, the knot in Ronan's stomach has begun to turn. He glances away and finds the waitress on the side. She is scrolling through her phone, clicking little hearts beneath little images of lives far more beautiful than this. And suddenly Ronan is reminded of one more image. He almost laughs—how did he not think of it before? It was the very last time he saw her, out in her back garden one May Day afternoon. Her hair was wild and her green eyes were wilder as she flung frozen meat from her family's shed, roaring like some feral animal.

He smiles as he realises, two decades too late—*that* was the magic shot he needed all along—the one that would have pulled his whole collection together.

Ronan reaches deep into his pocket, folds the dollars and drops them on the silver plate. "Come on," he says, standing up. "There's something I need to show you." With one hand he grabs the mints and with the other hand he grabs hers, expecting the skin to be smooth. Instead it is tough, calloused hard like leather.

CHAPTER THIRTEEN
Grá

County Cavan, August 1996

For the entire journey, she kept returning to that same awful phrase.

Death rattle.

She wondered if there was an equivalent for birth. And if so, which one of them hurt the most.

The bus shuddered something violent, the suspension and the chassis barely clinging on, the windows threatening to shatter and let the silage stench come suffocating in. The fact that the service ran only twice a day suddenly didn't seem such a farce—it was all the vehicle could do to hold its bones together.

Grá held her daughter's hand so tightly. She thought of it again.

Birth rattle.

She tried very hard not to shut her eyes.

The driver did the best he could, shunting the gears and swerving the potholes; braking just in time to avoid the downy thump of death-wish hares darting across the road. More than once, they passed a victim who hadn't quite timed its escape. A tongue flopped out pink. An intestine spilled purple like a rope.

Grá glanced at Úna, the scrags of hair lopped uneven round her face. She had almost offered to tidy it up; almost suggested a hat. Instead, she had assured her daughter she was as beautiful as ever.

She had overheard her husband doing the very same.

And she had told her daughter that the trip to town was on account of her imminent birthday. Unlucky thirteen—a teenager at last! But of course, the journey was so much more than that—an apology and a peace offering and a desperate attempt to compensate for the heartache of last week.

I am putting myself forward as a replacement Butcher.

I have decided I don't need to be a girl any more.

Grá clutched the fingers tighter than ever.

As it happened, in the last few days, Úna seemed almost back to her unusual self—all smiles and games and questions plucked out of thick air. But Grá knew better than to believe in what the outside showed. Hadn't she spent an entire lifetime appearing happy? Appearing, all things considered, content?

Eventually the potholes began to shrink. They passed some traffic lights and a couple of petrol stations. In the distance, a row of taller buildings rose up, off-white; a grey-black cross atop a Gothic spire. But tallest of all were the yellow cranes from the various building sites that rimmed the edge of the town—construction was under way, modernity overspilling one concrete block at a time. Grá wondered about living right on the frontline where Man and Nature met. She wondered if all borders led, eventually, to war. She thanked the driver as they alighted and wondered, if that was the case, who would win this one in the end.

It was only a Tuesday morning, so she knew that Main Street could have been a whole lot busier, but for them the bustle was more than enough. A busker strummed some acoustic Boyzone. A group of Americans boarded a pleather coach. Something slicked to her ankle. Grá flinched. The plastic bag flew away in a single kick.

When they reached the charity shop she told Úna that she could choose anything she liked. It was mustier here and quieter—a muffled home away from home. Grá noticed there were only women in the place, so she imagined a world where men got to use and read things first and women could only use and read them after. She fingered the spine-break of an ancient paperback, trying to imagine things any other way.

She stared at the shelves of chipped knick-knacks, the rows of natty jackets, the faded posters in their frames. There was the Virgin Mary and an old map of Ulster. There was Audrey Hepburn in *Breakfast at Tiffany's*. Immediately Grá thought of Lena's love of the old classics, then tried to push her out of her mind. Instead she thought how strange it was to imagine Hepburn, the beautiful idol, now lying six feet under.

"I've found it, I've found it!" It wasn't long until Úna came sprinting back. "The lady at the till promises it still works. She said it just needs a new roll of film."

Grá heard the joy in her daughter's voice and saw the glow in her daughter's face. Eventually, she really would be back to herself. But for now, Grá was distracted by something else, so she placed her hand on the rail. The wheels skidded, threatening to go flying; to send her collapsing to the floor. And she would lie amidst the moth-eaten jumpers for a very long time, wondering how on earth she could have been such a fool. Because for all she knew, her sister could have passed away. For all her idolising, Lena could have already been dead for years, lying six feet under the blackened earth.

Two hours and a sticky bun later, it was time to be heading home. Úna had chosen a Polaroid camera. The irony was almost enough to make Grá smile. They were around the corner from the bus stop with twenty minutes to spare when Úna pointed out House of Blooms. A sign in the window announced, "JUST OPENED."

"Let's go."

"Úna, wait."

But already the bells above the door were tinkling.

Inside, the air was moist and sweet. There were freesias and gerbera, purple irises streaked with a yellow so bright they must have nicked it from the sunflowers in the next bucket along. There were things Grá had seen and grown before—great clutches of stock with their heady, synthetic scent—and then there were other things, the magnolia petals thick like expensive paper meant only for fountain-pen ink.

"Can I help you?" The woman appeared from the back, a bundle of foliage swaddled in her arms. She wore red glasses looped on a chain.

"Just browsing, thanks."

"Take your time. You'll see I over-ordered—I wanted to start with a bang, but I'll be out of business by the end of the week if I let all this go to wilt."

Grá felt the ghost of a sales pitch lurking, and yet she was curious. "You're the owner?"

"That's me." The woman placed the leaves on the counter and started ripping off the brown bits. "I moved home from Dublin last month. I wanted—"

"I think Mrs. P would like these." Over on the side, Úna was staring at a swathe of blue nigellas.

"Miss Jekyll," both women said at once.

Grá looked at the stranger.

"I'm Helen," she said.

"I'm Grá. And this is my . . . this is Úna."

The bells above the door were tinkling again.

On the journey back they sat right up the front, which meant the rattle was a little better. It also meant they were a little closer to the driver's radio. The afternoon chat show was a panel of experts, all of them men, all in possession of Dublin accents. Grá held the flowers across her lap, while Úna dozed against the glass.

Grá felt exhausted herself—it was the reason she rarely made the journey into town. Long walks through borderland fields were one thing, but this required a different breed of energy. When she was just nodding off, though, she heard the announcement and she was wide awake again. She leaned forward from her seat to catch each ominous letter in turn.

M-B-M.

It had just been confirmed—the source of BSE in Ireland had been the meat and bone meal all along. Grá's rattle came back now worse than ever, the death and birth variety both.

Because she was seething—hadn't they outlawed that stuff years ago? Hadn't they realised it was unnatural, feeding cattle on bits of other cattle? Turning the poor things into cannibals?

But the men on the radio tried to explain that "natural" hadn't really come into it—MBM was just a lot cheaper to produce. So somebody (the authorities were launching an investigation into who) had obviously decided to ignore the law and start making it again on the sly—it was just money, the "modern" priority. Grá looked down to her lap where the flowers lay and her empty purse sat nestled beneath. One of the men made a witty remark and the others laughed. Then they finished up—it was time for a bit of music, some American crowd called the Fugees. She recognised it: "Killing Me Softly."

When they got home there was no sign of Cúch and there was no denying Grá's sense of relief. She knew it was an unnatural thing to feel. Her mouth was dry. She should have ordered a drink in the café—a glass of water wouldn't have hurt.

"Thanks for today."

She felt the wet kiss on her cheek, but by the time she had turned Úna was already halfway up the stairs.

"You sure you're all right, pet?"

Úna rolled her eyes. "Mam, I'm *fine*." Grá supposed it was a good sign. "I'm going to study the instructions." She held up the bag with the Polaroid.

Grá watched her go, then looked down. It took a couple of moments to realise the pool of water was from the stems. She knew they were meant to be a gift, but she decided she would put them in a vase for now. It seemed a shame to leave them wrapped in their paper shroud. She ran the tap and fetched the scissors from the drawer, and it was only at the last minute she noticed it. The drop of blood had hardened to black. Her daughter must have cut herself too close.

I am putting myself forward as a replacement Butcher.

I have decided I don't need to be a girl any more.

Quickly Grá ran the blade under the water, desperate to wash away any trace of that awful evening. She remembered the hairs she had found in the upstairs sink and her hurry to wash them down the drain too. But now she realised she should have kept some of it—should have coiled it up and put it in a locket next to her heart.

She realised she shouldn't have married a Butcher.

She shouldn't have slept with Ronan.

She shouldn't have become such an unnatural mother; such an unnatural wife.

She placed her hand on her mouth to catch the sob. The gush from the tap almost drowned it out. And the din was so loud she nearly missed the doorbell. She turned off the water and dried her hands on her jeans. She still hadn't drunk a single thing.

She wondered if Mrs. P had somehow smelled the flowers and known to drop in. She hadn't really been around to the house since Sol's death. Grá hadn't really invited her. Part of Grá believed it was just easier for them to go visit the widow, but another part knew it was more complex than that; it was more, really, to do with shame.

Here is my home with my husband and child.

Here are the things I have that you don't.
Here are the things I have that I don't deserve.

"Grá?"

But the woman on the doorstep wasn't her friend; she was so much more. Or maybe, after all these years, so much less. And there was much less of her now—her body had shrunk, her hair had thinned out—yet it was definitely her, here, as if it were the most natural thing in the world.

"Lena."

Her sister checked over her shoulder to where a small blue car sat crooked-parked in the drive. "Actually, it's Eileen now."

Her guest moved through the hallway slowly, inspecting the rug, the hall table, the wooden banister that led upstairs. Grá wondered whether to call Úna down; whether she had taken her first photograph yet, watching the colours surfacing like a bruise. Back in the kitchen, she used the kettle as an excuse to cross to the other side. The flowers lay splayed across the worktop. But when she turned, Lena—had she really said Eileen?—wasn't there.

Grá's heart leapt.

"It's lovely." Her sister appeared in the doorway.

"Thank you." Grá's heart just about settled. "My husband inherited it." But then she cut straight to the big question. "How the hell did you manage to find it?" She didn't have time to wonder why she had said "it" and not "me."

"The Butchers." It was only now that Grá noticed Lena was wearing lipstick. It seemed her instinct for glamour hadn't shrunk a bit. "I realised if I spoke to them I could ask if they knew what had become of our family. So I planted the seed with my husband and son, and eventually they invited the Butchers round. Then I got the old lad alone—Sol, is that his name?—and I showed him your photograph. I wasn't surprised when he knew exactly where you were. I assumed there aren't that many families left."

For all the delight of the coincidence, the deep ache at the mention of Sol, there was one detail of the story Grá noticed most. *Your photograph.* She turned back to the counter and closed her eyes. Her sister had disappeared twenty-five years ago. Her sister had carried her image with her all that time.

When the kettle was boiled, they descended to the kitchen chairs clutching their cups. The table was still a solid divide between them. Grá remembered Lena once complaining to their parents about the endless stream of tea.

Can't we have coffee for once?

This isn't the bloody 1900s.

It was one of the first signs, maybe, of rebellion.

Grá wanted to voice the memory, but it seemed such a silly place to start. Or maybe in a way, too loaded a place. So instead, they sat in silence and held their cups and started nothing at all.

"Did you hear about that clock on the River Liffey?" It was Lena who finally took the plunge. It wasn't a silly place, exactly, just an odd one. "Counting down to the Millennium? I was listening on the way over—apparently it broke again. The algae keeps playing havoc with the tech."

"Can they fix it?" Grá tried.

"I hope so—otherwise we'll be late."

"For a very important date."

The look between them was more shock than smile.

"So do you live near it, then?" Grá moved on.

"What?"

"The clock?"

"God, no. We're in Monaghan—Fionn's family farm. Although he has sold off most of the acres by now, so we're barely a farm at all, we're—What's so bloody funny?"

Grá had tried to keep her laughter quiet, but the toll of the day had sapped every trace of restraint. "You live on a farm?" she said. "In Monaghan?"

"Yes."

"All this time?"

"Yes." This one had a trace of irritation. And then: "Why?"

But Grá couldn't answer, because she had doubled over with laughter.

Here are the things I have that you don't.

Here are the things you didn't have after all.

"Grá, I wrote," Lena was sighing now. "And I tried to call, but they must have changed the number. I assumed you were just too raging with me to bother to reply."

Grá stopped her laughter. Even if she didn't any more, she knew she had once deserved so much better. "I didn't get anything. Do you have any idea . . . ?" But she also stopped her anger. It was far too late in the day to be climbing mountains.

Despite her frailty, her sister was willing to try. "Grá, I'm sorry," she said. "I know it was selfish to leave, but I—"

"Are you still with him, then?" Grá cut her off with a more gossipy tone. It was the best that she could manage.

Lena waited, as if deciding whether to protest the evasion. "Just about." But then it was her turn to laugh. "Sure, you know what men are like. Drive you up the bloody wall!"

And Grá could tell her sister was evading too—covering up for so much else. She couldn't decide if that made her feel better or worse. "You mentioned a son—do you have any other children?"

"No, just Davey. An absolute pet. Mind you, he gets his Leaving Cert results next week, so all being well he's about to leave me far behind. And what about you? I didn't have long with Sol, so he didn't give me much beyond your address. And of course, who you had ended up marrying."

"Were you surprised?" For some reason, Grá suddenly felt that the answer mattered.

Still Lena's tea lay untouched. "You know, in a strange way I think I had a suspicion."

Grá nodded, unsure if she believed. "Although the Butchers have just announced they're shutting down."

"What?"

"I know."

"After all this time?"

"I know."

"Such a shame."

"I know." Even on the third attempt, it didn't sound convincing.

"So what happens next?"

Grá blinked. It was the biggest question of all.

The air around them had grown muggy. She wanted to check the nigellas—the blue would be streaking browner by the minute. She would have to try to resurrect them with a drink of water—them and her both.

She didn't even begin to try explaining that Sol was dead.

"I was in town earlier," she offered instead. "We rarely go in, but I met this woman who had just opened a florist's. She moved back from Dublin and started it by herself." Grá stopped. She wasn't sure where the strange anecdote had come from.

She wasn't sure her sister found it strange. "You could do that," Lena said.

"What?"

Lena nodded. "Why not?"

"Don't be daft." And yet, it was the first time all day Grá's chest hadn't rattled a bit.

After a while, she filled the kettle again and rummaged in the depths of the cupboards. When she pulled out the jar, she saw the coffee granules had caked together, but she chipped some free and placed them, watered, before her sister.

They laughed the same laugh at the same time.

Slowly, their conversation grew a little easier—not so much a very important date as just a couple of women having a chat. They discussed childhood holidays to Connemara—how a daring Lena had managed to teach a timid Grá how to swim in the sea. They discussed that new play everyone was talking about—*The Beauty Queen of Leenane*—and the new Domestic Violence Bill that had come in. It meant a wife could finally take out a barring order against a husband for assault. For the first time, Lena became a little hesitant. Grá let the conversation move on. They discussed the revelation about the MBM, wondering who would stoop so low as to still be making and selling such muck, even when they knew the horrendous consequences. They discussed where they would go on their holidays if they ever won the lotto. Grá surprised herself by saying "Japan." She pictured the cherry blossom in full bloom—it was supposed to take your breath away. She pictured standing in the middle of Tokyo with eight million people racing by.

But despite their best efforts—despite how their various topics ranged far and wide—still they couldn't seem to get beyond exactly where they were. Or really, beyond *what* they were—two women who had long ago made two very different choices; two lives defined by a thing called "love," or was it just "men," or just a desire for escape?

And did they, after everything, feel free?

"Grá, I'm sick."

When Grá looked up at her sister's sunken face, she saw that the remark made perfect sense. "Oh?"

"Brain tumour," she said. "They got it out, but apparently it'll come back soon enough. In the meantime I take these wretched drugs that are supposed to stop me having fits, but they leave me . . . I get terrible . . ."

As she listened, Grá knew she was supposed to be feeling shock or devastation. Or maybe confusion—a brain tumour at forty-six?—surely that couldn't be right. But instead she felt a strange relief that *that* was the reason their reunion had been so awkward; the reason it wasn't living up to all those years of fantasy. Her sister was sick. The wretched drugs left her . . . She got terrible . . .

Grá felt an urge to ask what words came next.

"And my husband keeps mentioning some fancy clinic down in Dublin, but the doctors haven't heard of it, so I suspect it's a bit of wishful thinking on his behalf. Anyway, I thought I better let you know—5 per cent of brain tumours are hereditary, apparently—so just in case the bloody thing runs in our family."

Grá tried to absorb the information, the grim statistic, the weight of the words "our family," but then she heard the sound of the front door opening and the almost-birthday girl rushing down the stairs. "Dad, Dad, look what I got in town!"

Grá and Lena stood up. Úna panted as she pulled Cúch into the kitchen by his hand, his bruise still a gaudy sunflower yellow. Everyone froze. Grá glanced from one face to the next and thought of the saying about your whole life flashing before your eyes. This scene was very still.

A photograph.

A Polaroid.

A family portrait.

"Who are you?"

"Úna, this is my sister. Her name is Lena. We haven't . . . We fell out of touch a long time ago, but this afternoon she rang the doorbell and, well, here we are."

Grá watched as her daughter took in the information, piece by shaky piece. She watched as her sister took in her daughter, hair by uneven hair.

She couldn't bring herself to watch her husband.

And even despite their closeness, despite the jokes and the secret rituals that were theirs and theirs alone, at first Grá couldn't understand her daughter's response. "You told me it made us more *special*?"

"What's that, love?"

"Being only children. Having no siblings. Why did you lie?"

She had no idea where to begin. But fortunately she had forgotten that that was what older sisters were for.

"I'm afraid that's my fault, pet." Slowly Lena's frail body folded itself downwards until she was the same height as her niece. "When I was a bit younger I took a notion to annoy our parents by running away with a non-believer. And it worked! But do you want to know the truth?" Here Lena grimaced, though it was impossible to know if the pain was to do with her illness or her confession. "I realise now that I should have run back."

"How long is the drive?"

Lena fumbled her keys around the lock, drawing little scratches into the blue paint. "Only an hour, but I need to be home before the boys. They'll go mad if they catch me—I'm not supposed to drive."

"Why not?"

"I was going to write, but I had to see you. Then I looked into getting the bus. Until eventually I thought, What the hell. And sure, didn't I make it in one piece?"

"Lena, I can give you a lift."

"If you think I'm going to start letting my little sister boss me around after all these years, you can think again!"

Around them the afternoon had gone golden, sepia hues like a vintage film reel. Smiling, Grá let the matter drop and realised she had far more important things to clear up, because—talk about mad!—they had forgotten to swap details all over again. "Wait, you never told me—" But when she saw Lena rubbing her temples, ready to depart, Grá realised something else. This would be the last time. So she changed her question. "Your holiday destination?" she improvised. "If you won the lotto?"

Lena blinked. Green eyes and childhood holidays—those were the things they would always share. The rest might have disappeared, might have been rescued from drowning too late, but they would always, at least, have those.

"Hollywood Boulevard." Lena didn't even need a moment to deliberate. "The Chinese Theatre with the handprints out the front—I'd use my winnings to buy a slab of my own. At least then I would know I had left some kind of mark on the world."

Grá stood outside the house long after the sound of the engine had evaporated. She wrapped her arms around her body even though it wasn't cold. In the distance, she saw the starlings approach, then begin their show, throwing black shapes against the sky. A murmuration, swooping and redoubling, perfectly synchronised.

Beyond them she saw the coast of Connemara where a rental cottage crumbled to the sea; saw two girls scratching each other's names with sticks into the wet grey sand. She saw a bottle and a piece of paper, which, without a clue of what to write, she had just left blank and thrown into the sea.

"Grá." He stopped a few inches behind her, always that little bit out of reach.

She spoke quickly. "I should have told you." She wanted to get in there first. "I should have admitted I had a sister, but—"

"I already knew."

She nodded. "Lena spoke to Sol."

"No, Grá, I've always known."

Her breath caught. "And you didn't mind?"

"Of course not."

"And if I had stopped believing too?" It was a stupid question. There were things that could and could not be undone.

The starlings were above them now, their movements more like liquid than something airborne; their swell and flow like great crashing tidal waves.

"Cúch, we need to talk." She dropped her arms to her side. "Things can't stay so fixed—there has to be a change." She heard him step closer, but it was still important that she didn't turn around. "Úna is the priority, of course, but I need . . . I don't think I can go on unless I have something of my own this time." She didn't realise she was crying until she tasted the sea on her lips. She wondered if she would ever not be thirsty again. "Lena had this daft suggestion . . ." She closed her eyes. "Cúch, she's dying."

When she opened her eyes, her husband had walked around so now they were face to face. The swelling meant that one of his dimples dug deeper than the other. "Grá," he said, "I understand."

She wondered what words she would write if she had that bottle and that piece of paper now.

"Grá, I don't know the answer, but I do know we will find a way."

She wondered if she would stand on the shore of the Atlantic for ever, waiting, somehow certain a bottle would wash up bearing a reply. She wondered if that was the definition of love or faith or maybe both.

"Grá?"

But for now, all she had were the same words her husband had given her thirteen years ago, the first time they had made a brand-new life together. "I believe in you," she said. "More than I have ever believed in anything." Hearing them now, second-hand, they almost sounded natural; almost sounded true.

CHAPTER FOURTEEN
Davey

County Monaghan, August 1996

"The headlines this morning: across the country, fifty-nine thousand students are anxiously awaiting their Leaving Certificate results. The Department of Education has reported a significant increase in the number of As awarded for Maths and Science, but a significant decrease in the number of As awarded for Irish."

Davey woke then unwoke then woke again completely, the world slowly resolving itself into shapes. His room was so neat it almost appeared empty; almost as if he had tempted fate and gone ahead and packed his bags. He had hooked his outfit for the day off the side of the wardrobe, the limbs sagging from where they hung. The pale green shirt looked as if he were off on a date, not just down to the school to collect a small brown envelope.

"Of course, most newspapers are leading with the story that this year's cohort will be the first to avail of completely free third-level education. According to politicians, the abolishment of university fees will generate a highly educated workforce which will further the country's transition into a major global economy."

Davey pulled himself up and into the shower, praying the immersion had been switched on. He closed his eyes and reached downwards, even though a wank seemed out of the question this morning. He was far too nervous about the day ahead; about everything that was finally at stake.

But he knew there was more to it than that, because any urge or desire still meant thinking about Con. And thinking about Con also meant thinking about Sol and the terrible harm the Butchers had, apparently, inflicted on his body. Since the Bull's declaration there hadn't been another word about the case, or indeed about the Butchers. Davey sometimes wondered if the whole thing hadn't been a terrible dream.

"Meanwhile in farming, another blow as the first suspected case of CJD—the human variant of BSE—has just been reported in a young woman in County Clare."

Once dressed and doused in Lynx, Davey descended to the smell of bacon. His mother was by the hob, the table set for one. He couldn't remember the last time he had seen her up so early. "Morning," she called over the hiss of the pan. "I thought it better you didn't head down on an empty gut." Even though the window had been cracked, for an ugly second Davey thought of getting changed. The fried smell would ruin his shirt.

When the rinds were crisped, his mother used tongs to pick them up and drape them across two sheets of kitchen roll. Davey's chest twanged. He knew she was only doing it like that because it was the way he preferred. "Your father's in a flap," she said. "Apparently the inspectors are testing the herd for BSE this morning. Though if you ask me, a diagnosis wouldn't be so bad—not if it meant cashing in on the government compensation." She arranged the bacon on one slice of buttered bread and matched the other on top, a jigsaw fit. "Either way, I'm going to cook the three of us a celebration lunch when you get home. Your father suggested we defrost the first of the Butchers' cuts." She pressed down hard; the butter dripped brown. "What a special day. Is it noon the envelopes are arriving?"

Davey knew the first bite would be pure filth and delicious; he knew, after that, he wouldn't be able to swallow a thing.

When he arrived to the school, the car park was deserted. The bins, for once, weren't spewing their guts. The walls had been sopped clean of their usual graffiti, leaving just a few faded scrawls.

Outside reception, two mammies sat fretting on a bench. They had probably come straight from lighting a final candle in St. Michael's on their sons' behalf. Davey tried to catch their eyes, then wondered why the hell he was the one doing the reassuring. He could still taste salt and fat at the back of his tongue.

The hush inside the corridor was vaguely church-like itself. There were the cheap lino floors and the dead windowsill flies. There was the trophy cabinet and the cork noticeboards crumbling damp around the edges. The details, though, weren't as familiar to Davey as they should have been—it had been only a couple of months, but more had changed in that time than he could possibly say.

He looked down at himself. He smelled his shirt. He was so relieved not to be in uniform.

And yet next to the relief there was also the fear of encountering his meathead classmates once again; of them taking one look and seeing everything the summer had finally revealed. He thought of the mammies outside and how they would probably light a candle just for him, hoping that God could cure him of his terrible disease.

As he walked, he passed faded projects about 1916 and the anti-British cause. He spotted essays about the Famine—the crops that had failed and the millions who had died or gone on boats far away. One poster showed emaciated people swallowing black fistfuls of dirt. Another simply spelled out the words *Our Holocaust.*

As far as Davey could remember, his History exam had gone OK. English had focused on Patrick Kavanagh—a Monaghan man himself. Davey had written an essay about "The Great Hunger" and concluded, more than anything, his own poetic talent wasn't actually up to much. Then there had been the final Classics exam, which should have been a walk in the park, but instead Davey had spent the afternoon in a tangle of nerves. He thought of poor Prometheus chained to a rock. He thought of the irony of missing the grade and being chained for ever here.

Without the rows of desks, the assembly hall was a vast and hollow thing, an echo chamber of congratulation and commiseration. Three tables had been lined up on the stage, the all-important envelopes stashed in cardboard boxes. Above them, Jesus watched down in anguish, crucified.

Across the floor a few clusters were straggled, teachers and former students both, though without their uniforms and suits it was hard to tell one type of man from the next. Some held open envelopes, thinking: *What happens now?* And: *What about not needing to bother with college? What about a fucking "boom"?* But for the most part, the faces didn't give much away—no sign of delight or disappointment; of a significant increase in As or Bs. Instead, their jaws were steeled and their eyes were glazed, because they were now officially men of place, here where no trace of emotion was ever betrayed.

Davey cast around for Mr. Fitz, but couldn't see him anywhere.

The walk to the stage felt a mile or more. The teacher rifled through the half-empty box, front to back. She must have missed it. She tried again, back to front, going slower this time to be sure. Davey thought of all the productions he had seen put on here down the years. *Juno and the Paycock. Dancing at Lughnasa.* He saw the spotlights above and the darkness of the wings either side.

When she handed over his script, Davey thought the teacher called him a "bastard." He looked up. "What did you say?" She repeated something about a *plaster*; something about bodies and pain and how it was often easier to just grab a hold and rip it off. And Davey wanted to ask if she had heard about the body of a Butcher that had been found strung up recently; if she thought you could crave the touch of someone so much it caused you actual pain. But now he was unpicking the gum of the lip and removing the document, its neat column of As swimming before him, the hot sting of tears sending him blind down the back staircase, past the props cupboard and the costume rail, the sequins shimmering with all the possibilities of who he might just be able to become.

The playground was busier now, lads gathered with hands in their pockets like a congregation after a funeral. Some had found a ball and were taking it in turns to do elaborate keepie-uppies, counting and competing, because at least this was a test in which they actually stood a chance.

Can you believe the fucking Krauts won the Euros?

Did you hear they're trying to reject Irish milk?

Don't worry—I've heard the Bull's sorting them out.

They sounded like their fathers, or at least how they thought their fathers were supposed to sound. Davey thought of the stage and them all stepping up to their roles. He thought how everything was just a cycle—crop rotation, field rotation—another new generation laying its claim, round and round in circles with hand-me-down jumpers and hand-me-down dreams.

For now, though, the lads didn't seem to be stepping anywhere at all. Instead they stood smoking fags and kneeing a flaccid football to the sky. For this afternoon and this afternoon only they were still boys—still pure possibility. They would linger until the gate was chained and locked.

Davey was checking around for Mr. Fitz one last time when he looked back at the gate and saw the visitor. He was facing the road, but Davey recognised him instantly; the broad shoulders and the suntanned neck. "Con?" His shout was too loud, but he couldn't stop himself. His joy was a gormless, graceless thing.

The Butcher didn't react straight away, so for a second Davey thought he had got it wrong. And even when Con did turn, his face was a little late. So that before the smile and twinkle—before the wash of warmth—there was the briefest moment of darkness around the eyes. "There you are," he greeted. "I was starting to worry I had missed you."

"Con," Davey repeated, slowing down. The closer he got, the shier he felt himself becoming. "What the hell are you doing here?" The *donk* of the football could be heard behind. Davey thought of a pig's bladder that might burst.

"I just . . ." It was Con's turn now to be shy. "I knew how much today meant to you."

One of the boys must have set a new record because a giant cheer came roaring next. Unless one of them had just announced that he had nailed his results and was off to the big smoke to study Law. Davey considered the odds. He considered, very carefully, Con's words.

"Well, don't just stand there, how did you get on?"

Davey handed over the envelope and watched as Con took out the page.

"Fucking hell," he pronounced. "You absolute nerd—congratulations!" And then, "I'm guessing you get your brains from your mam."

And just when Davey had managed to swallow his disbelief, the mention of his mother had him thrown again. He pictured her in the kitchen this morning—he hadn't seen her so well in months. He thought of her promise: *I'm going to cook the three of us a celebration lunch.* He thought of the olden days and her waiting out here to collect him in her bright blue car and her giant sunglasses.

"I thought I'd never see you again." He took a step closer, as if he needed to feel Con's body heat to be sure. There was so much he wanted to ask; so much that needed to be explained.

"Come on," the Butcher said. "I don't have very long."

Davey threw a final glance behind, but the football had been discarded, the men having kicked every last bit of life from the animal's skin.

They took the back lane where the rowan bushes had grown so big they choked each other's necks. The haws had swelled fat like tumours, the bittersweet berries clumped together in fists. But when they rounded the corner the world opened out. The hay had been cut and rolled into generous bales so that the fields looked like a blonde woman's head with her hair wrapped up in giant curlers. Davey took a deep breath. The second cut of silage always smelled more delicious than the first. He thought of the name "bitter-sweet"; of longing to get away from a place, but having to leave so much beauty behind.

Eventually they found a bale at the edge of the world that was big enough to shelter them from sight. Davey hadn't noticed Con's satchel until he set it down and took the bottle out. "It's hardly champagne," he said, turning the cap. "And it's probably gone warm."

"It's perfect!" The cider sprayed them both in a cheap, sticky douse.

Despite the initial theatrics, the booze was flat, but Davey took heavy pulls of it all the same. He returned the bottle to Con and wiped his mouth. He tried to hide his burp beneath his breath. After a few more goes, he felt his nerves begin to ease. They sat side by side, legs splayed, ogling the view. In the news they kept talking about "Nature hitting back." Staring at her now, only an eejit would take her on.

"So when does college start?" It wasn't until Con spoke that Davey remembered all over again what today was really about. The offers wouldn't arrive until Monday, but already he knew he would be given his first choice.

"September." He shifted where he sat. He could feel the hay poking the back of his head. It was like a feather piercing the cotton of a pillowcase, only this was all the feathers at once.

"You must be excited."

As if to contrast the current vista, Davey replied by describing the photographs he had seen in the university prospectus— the ancient stone buildings; the gargoyles licking up the black fumes of the city's traffic-teeming heart. "I'll wake every morning without the smell of shite for breakfast or the groans from the cattle getting milked." Davey stopped. He hoped he wasn't being offensive. He noticed, yet again, Con's neck.

Next he described the course itself—lectures on Latin and Greek; seminars devoted to Roman literature and thought— and Davey was so grateful to Con for just listening; for allowing his excitement to run away with him for once. "Then outside class I'll need to get a job, but I can see my friends after that. I hear the Dublin bars are deadly." Davey paused, then he dared himself a little further. "I hear there's a savage gay scene. Although I suppose compared to a flagon in a field anything is savage, what?"

He glanced to his right. He had gone too far. He wondered if he was already a little tipsy. A wasp buzzed in, greedy for a taste, so Davey tried to swat it away.

"Davey, I'm excited for you . . ." When Con finally spoke, his tone didn't really match his words. Davey thought of that shadow of darkness back at the gate. "It's just . . . Don't go pinning your hopes too much, OK?"

Davey frowned. "What do you mean? I got the points. They'll let me in, they just—"

"No no." Con did his own kind of swatting. "I mean about Dublin. Don't go thinking it's some promised land. They like to believe they're much more 'modern' down there, but last time I visited I got called a fag and had my nose broken in two places. This is still fucking Ireland we're talking about." To finish, Con made some emphatic hand gesture that knocked the bottle to its side. Straight away he righted it, but not before a pool of golden liquid flooded the grass.

Eventually Con sighed. "I'm sorry. I guess I'm just a bit jealous of your plans, that's all. Everything's such a mess."

Davey stared at the puddle. Very soon there would be ants.

"It's over, Davey. The Butchers have decided to give up."

Davey thought about reaching out his hand in sympathy. He wondered where exactly he would place it.

"I'm going to stay with my brother while I figure things out, but I just . . . I'm still so angry about what happened."

At this, though, Davey's hand stayed exactly where it was. "You mean what happened to Sol?"

Con nodded.

"You mean . . . it wasn't you?"

"What?"

"We were told it was a Butchers' tradition. A mourning ritual to hang a dead man by his feet." Davey was certain that this time he had gone too far. He thought how Con was close enough to break his nose in two places.

He thought how beautiful Con looked when he laughed.

And the sound alone was enough to confirm what Davey had always suspected. Con tossed his head back and there was more neck than ever. Davey wanted, so much, to place his lips upon that Adam's apple. Not Eve's; no, it had never been Eve's. But when he opened his mouth, something else came out: "I keep thinking about this bit in the *Iliad*. It's where Achilles cuts two holes in Hector's heels and threads through two leather belts. Then he ties the belts to his chariot and drags the body around in the dirt." Davey paused. He knew he should be asking what the Butchers planned to do next; should be apologising for even half believing the Bull's awful lies.

"Why did Achilles do that?"

"Grief," Davey said. "His cousin Patroclus had died, stabbed in the stomach by Hector. Or, more likely, Achilles and Patroclus had been lovers. So in his heartache, his despair, Achilles defiled Hector's body while his poor family had no choice but to watch."

Con shifted around so his head eclipsed the sun.

Davey shifted so they were the same. "Come with me to Dublin."

"I can't."

"I know."

"You'll be OK."

"I know," he said again, as if he had a clue about anything.

But when they finally kissed, Davey knew he was willing to learn; knew this was the real reason he would always remember today. Their tongues spelled goodbye in each other's mouths as their hands reached for each other's belts.

He was willing now to try everything.

When he finally got home, Davey stared around the mess of the yard as if he barely recognised it. The hose lay flaccid and unfurled. The rusted barrels were orange and full of recent rain. The blue Fiesta was nowhere to be seen—his father must have finally sold it on. Davey could feel a bit of a breeze, though he was sure his blush wouldn't have faded yet.

In the kitchen, a raw lump of meat sat on a plate in a pool of pinkish water. Two flies were showing an interest, buzzing away, then landing back again. Davey swallowed his guilt, which tasted of apples. The celebration lunch. At least, he supposed, nothing had actually been cooked.

His limbs were still a bit tender as he took the stairs, certain he was leaving a trail of hay in his wake. He checked his own room and then he checked hers. The bed was made. There were no empty cups on the side, only a Bible, the spine completely smooth, the red ribbon flopping out like a tongue.

In the distance he heard Blackfoot barking. She was an old and noble thing, more part of the farm than Davey himself had ever been.

On his way back through the kitchen the flies were gone.

Already the sky had faded a little further, the daylight dragging downwards as if it weighed a tonne. Inside the byre it was almost black. The smell was sweet oats and saddle soap. Over in the corner, next to his beloved cow, his father slouched in an anorak and wellie boots. Davey thought of that photographer from O'Connell's trying to capture things "as they truly are." It would have been a perfect picture.

He stopped in the doorway, scuffing his final step to make sure that he was heard. He glanced at Glassy, the giant brown birthmarks patterned all across her warm white flank. She didn't seem to pay his father much attention, but the feeling certainly wasn't mutual. The old man leaned so hard on the railing Davey wondered if he was drunk.

"How did you fare?" The words arrived loudly, though the head didn't turn around.

Davey took a step forward and felt tiny grains of meal crush to dust beneath his feet. "I'm sorry about lunch. I got held up."

"Never mind, lad. But tell me—are you happy?"

The question felt so profound it took Davey a moment to realise it was referring to his results. "I am." Then he remembered— *Your father suggested we defrost the first of the Butchers' cuts*—so he tried something a bit more generous: "I'm really pleased, thank you."

He waited, not quite knowing what was supposed to happen next. The cow had started to chew, shunting her jaw in slow mechanical rotations. Eventually, his father pushed himself up and around. One glance told Davey he was more than sober. "Davey," he coughed. "Davey, lad, she's gone."

And for some reason, Davey's first thought was that his father was referring to one of the girls—a positive test from the BSE inspector, which meant the animal had been led away to the slaughterhouse.

"I was at the shops. She had sent me down to pick up some last-minute bits for the dessert." The smell of the place grew stronger, the pens around them strewn with clods of damp hay. Davey felt the little lines across his skin where the golden stalks had scratched. He looked up. The byre roof was close to falling in.

"She had a seizure. By the time I reached the hospital it was too late. Her brain . . . the doctors said they did everything they could."

Behind Davey's back, the sun had finally collapsed. In the darkness, the men's silence made much more sense, though Davey could have stood there for ever and still not known what to say—not in English or Irish; not in Latin or Ancient Greek. Instead, he could only picture Achilles dragging that corpse through the muck, the dust caking black and rancid into the wounds. He knew he would have done the very same to any man, any Butcher, if he thought it might ease the pain.

CHAPTER FIFTEEN
Úna

County Cavan, September 1996

It was hard to believe this day last year was her very first day of school. Úna could still remember the creases of her white shirt, fresh and stiff from the plastic packet; could still remember the swell of her gut, filled with porridge and delinquent butterflies. Amidst the anxiety, though, there had also been the buzz of possibilities. Of new friends and new beginnings. Of finding someone who would love to hear about her father and her Lego and her plan for the mouse.

And now?

Now her hair had grown back just enough to cover the tips of her ears. Úna had combed it down to be sure, grateful for the bit of warmth. Not that her classmates would care about that—they would only care about her weird new look, pointing and staring and calling the usual names.

Cowgirl got a haircut!

Úna rubbed the back of her neck. Without her ponytail, it felt exposed.

The Baldy Butchers.

Over the summer, she had tried to think about her playground encounter with Car McGrath. She still didn't fully

265

understand what had happened; what, in that moment, had come over her. When she made it home, she had brushed her teeth for hours, but the strangely sweet burger taste had stayed on her gums for days. She had returned the scissors to the kitchen drawer.

This morning, though, when her parents weren't looking, she had gone to the drawer and taken them back out; had hesitated, then placed them in the pocket of her uniform. Again, she didn't fully understand why, but as soon as she did it she felt better. She knew part of it was to do with protection—if he did decide to come to school today, there was no doubt Car McGrath would be out for revenge.

By now, Úna had reached the main door. Stepping inside, the noise was colossal, her classmates gabbing a million miles an hour, swapping summer stories and asking question after hurried question. Like who had gone on the most expensive holiday? Who had heard the village McDonald's was finally shutting down? Who had listened to that deadly new band called the Spice Girls?

I'm Scary.

I'm Sporty.

I'm Ginger.

I'm not allowed to listen to "bloody Brits."

Úna cleaved to the walls as she worked her way along the corridor. The bell would go shortly for Assembly, then double English where they were starting some new book called *A Portrait of the Artist as a Young Man*. As she reached the lockers, Úna found all the young men gathered together and her butterflies braced so hard they smacked into her ribs.

I'm Baby.

I'm Posh.

I'm in trouble now.

Up close, Úna saw that most of the boys' limbs had grown lanky over the break, white flashes of ankle and wrist poking out beneath their too-small uniforms. Meanwhile their faces bore flashes of pink where brand-new acne constellations had appeared. One or two bore the beginnings of stubble over their lips. It wasn't clear which of them spotted her first, but the elbows started nudging, and soon all the eyes were aimed in her direction. Car stopped whatever story he'd been telling— something about his big brother and a naggin of vodka. Úna saw his orange tufts had mostly faded. When he glanced over his shoulder, she saw the cut on his neck had mostly healed.

Their stares met, though Car was yet to actually turn around to face her.

What the hell?

In the silence, Úna remembered the last words he had said to her.

I thought you wanted . . .

Most girls would . . .

She still hadn't figured out how exactly he'd been planning to finish that sentence off. She still hadn't figured out why he'd thought she was suddenly like most girls.

What the fuck is that?

But at least Úna could feel the exact weight of the scissors in her pocket now; could remember the sensation of holding them against Car's throat. She thought of a Butcher standing over a cow, looking it in the eye and letting it know who was in control. She thought how most girls hadn't made Car Mc-Grath beg for mercy.

Úna, please . . .

Úna, I'm sorry . . .

"So the bird in the garage takes one look at my ID." When Car finally spoke, it had nothing to do with her. Instead, he had turned his head and resumed his story. "And she goes, 'But *you're* not Francis McGrath.'" "The other boys frowned in confusion, their eyes still trained on Úna, until the punch-line commanded their attention. "Turns out she was the one who had given him a wank at the GAA club the week before!"

Úna's shirt stuck to her back as she walked away. In her pocket, she had been clutching the scissors so hard she had managed to break skin. She stuck her finger in her mouth and tasted metal on her tongue. She knew she wasn't out of the woods just yet—Car had had the rest of the summer to plot his retribution, so there was a fair chance he was saving his elaborate plan for later, maybe in front of the whole school during Assembly or lunch break out in the yard.

She imagined a bottle of extra-strength bleach poured over her head until it burned blisters across her scalp.

She imagined a whole retinue of Big Macs forced down her throat until she choked to death.

But by the time the bell rang out at the end of the day, there had been no plan, no sign of revenge. In fact, no one had so much as pointed or laughed or called her a single name. Úna couldn't remember the last time she had eaten her sand-wiches without any interruption or had asked to go to the loo without a chorus of "yee haws."

So finally she understood what had occurred that summer night—finally she understood that the violence had brought her what she'd always wanted. She smiled. She suspected they wouldn't be bothering her any more. She closed her locker and headed for home. Already her gut felt different from this morning. The butterflies were gone—it seemed she had warned them off too. In their place, a new kind of power had begun to swell.

When she made it back to the house, her father was in the kitchen, the beginnings of dinner splayed out across the counter. The sound of his knife on the chopping board was a pneumatic drill. The new arrangement meant he was in charge of dinner on the days her mother went into town for her job. She read novels on the bus to pass the time—Úna liked when she brought home bits of the various storylines. Úna wondered if she had ever gone back to that book club she had seen advertised in the *Anglo-Celt*.

And Úna liked the stories her mam brought home from the various customers in the flower shop—the people who swapped their hard-earned cash for things they could have just grown out of the ground. There were the regulars and the special occasioners; the awkward-eyed who spent the least time and the most money. Her mam said she suspected those bouquets were meant for apologies or sordid affairs.

Her mam went a little awkward-eyed herself.

But most of all, Úna liked the energy that was slowly returning to her mother. She had started wearing earrings again; had started finishing some of her meals. Úna liked her father's energy, too—rushing around the kitchen, doing different things with different utensils, trying to find a new way, a new route to happiness.

Úna decided to leave him to it. She took the stairs up to her bedroom and closed the door. Glancing around at her own new arrangement, she was pleased—it looked so much more grown up. She had thrown all her Legos in the bin and peeled the faded map of Ireland from the wall. In its place hung a glamorous woman in a black dress smoking a long cigarette.

Breakfast at Tiffany's.

Her mam had brought it home as a present out of her first pay cheque last month. She had promised they could watch the film together once Úna had turned fifteen. For now, the other walls were blank. The whiteness looked nice, very clean, although it also looked kind of empty. Úna would have to figure out soon what she was going to put up there instead.

•

On Saturday night her parents announced that they were going to a restaurant on a "date." Úna insisted she didn't need to stay at Mrs. P's—she was more than capable of looking after herself. She was glad when her parents agreed, but after a while she was mostly bored. She blared the radio to fill the silence. The Spice Girls kept asking her to tell them what she really really wanted.

The following week, Car McGrath and the rest of her classmates were still avoiding her like the plague. The phrase made Úna think about the CJD. Another person over in England had died. Apparently the disease turned them depressed, then gave them strange hallucinations. The scientists were nowhere near finding a cure.

By Friday afternoon, Úna thought she might be having hallucinations of her own, because when she got back from school there was a white envelope on the hall table with her name and address written on the front. She tried to think if she had ever received a piece of post in her life. There had been the birthday cards last month, but they were delivered by hand so they didn't count. There was a giant thirteen-shaped one from her parents and a smaller pink one from Mrs. P. Úna knew, at the rate she was going, there was a fair chance there might never be a third.

Dear Úna,

My name is Davey McCready and I believe I am your first cousin. I didn't even know you existed until a few weeks ago. But then I met your mother at my mother's funeral and she told me everything. She seemed a lovely woman. She brought along the most beautiful wreath.

I am writing from Dublin where I just started a Classics degree. Do you know any ancient myths? My favourite is the Minotaur who was part man, part bull. If you haven't heard it, let me know and I'll explain.

Classical Studies was my favourite subject at school—what's yours? What do you want to be when you grow up? Have you ever visited Dublin? A friend once told me it's no promised land, but I suspect that he was lying.

Anyway, I'd love to hear all about you so I hope you'll reply when you get the chance.

Yours sincerely,
Your first cousin,
Davey McCready

After she had read them three times over, Úna knew all the words by heart. Her favourites were *first* and *ancient myths*. She also liked *promised* and *part bull*. What she didn't like was the final paragraph with its barrage of question marks. She thought again of a pneumatic drill, the relentless pounding in your skull. She had noticed before how some adults asked what you wanted to *do* when you grew up and others asked what you wanted to *be*. Úna wondered if the two questions meant the same thing, and if so, did that make it easier or harder to find an answer? Especially when you were suddenly having to start again from scratch?

"So you've finally found yourself a wee friend?" Her mother's earrings today were a pair of red swirls Úna couldn't remember seeing before.

She waited until she had her logic straight, then made her own enquiries: "You didn't tell me your sister died?"

Her mam let her smile go slack. "The death notice was in the paper a couple of weeks ago." She also anticipated what would follow. "I know you would have come with me to the funeral, but I needed . . . I decided I would go alone."

In the silence, Úna was aware she was supposed to say "sorry for your troubles" next, even if "sorry" made it sound like she had done something wrong. Then again, it did feel strange that her mam had lost someone so important while she, apparently, was gaining someone new.

"I spoke to Davey at the reception afterwards—he seemed a lovely lad. Another only child, as it happens, so he was very interested when I told him about you."

As Úna listened, she tried to match her mam's enthusiasm. She knew she should be "very interested" too. Because this was her very first bit of post; this was her very first cousin.

I'd love to hear all about you.

The problem was that, increasingly, Úna had realised she didn't have a clue at all about herself—who she was; what she wanted to do or be. She had discovered that holding a blade to a boy's neck could get you the things you wanted, but she didn't know what, for her, those things might be any more. Because everything had changed—everything that had defined her had vanished—or, technically, had been "disbanded." In fact, ever since the Butchers had "called it a day," she couldn't even figure out what she should be called. In the past, there had always been *special* and *believer*. There had even, for a brief moment, been *replacement Butcher*. There had been *freak* and *cowgirl*, but now none of those fit and she was just as blank as a bare bedroom wall.

Úna looked up at her mam's green eyes. Her pink cheeks had grown a little softer, no more bones jutting through the skin. Úna supposed she had started calling herself something new—*a florist*—so maybe Úna should try and do the same? Or she could be a photographer like Ronan or a journalist like Mrs. P before she became a wife who baked endless cakes or a widow called Aoife who polished dead men's boots?

I'm Scary.
I'm Sporty.
I decided I would go alone.

Úna folded the letter and put it back in the envelope. She turned it over and stared at the words on the front. She wanted to reach for the scissors and cut out her name; to stare through the gap and out the other side.

•

By the end of the week, there were far more than just letters arriving to the house. Úna was down in the kitchen setting seven knives and forks; folding seven napkins the fancy way. Her father had turned fifty so now the Butchers—the former Butchers—were travelling from all across the country to join him for Sunday lunch. It would be the first time the group had been together since the end. Úna suspected their feet were long past itchy. The age sounded impossibly old—half a century!—but when her father entered the kitchen he looked the same as ever. He wore a new chequered shirt. Last night, her mother had trimmed the back of his neck while Úna swallowed down a surprising pang of jealousy.

Now her mother was sweating into the oven, trying to manage the various bits of meat that were roasting there. There was a random assortment—a special menu made up of the very last of the freezer's stash. It felt strange to see her mam back wearing an apron—more and more recently it had been her father's job. Úna supposed that, just for today, he could be called a Butcher again.

She had felt guilty this morning without so much as a card to give him. Her mam had promised to pick one up for her in town, then forgot. Úna used to make them herself in Art class, but that felt a bit childish now. She supposed she could have just written him a letter.

She filled the jug from the tap. She hadn't replied to her cousin yet. Not for the first time today, she felt a growling in her stomach. She wondered if she was coming down with something (another animal disease? another plague?) or if something was coming over her. She thought of her aunt. Her mam hadn't actually said how she had died.

The doorbell rang to announce the first arrival, which was the Butcher they called Wyn. He was wind-faced and portly. "Úna, I'd barely recognise you!" She did her best to force a smile she didn't feel. Next to arrive were Mik and Farley, followed by the blondie lad named Con. He was the youngest of the group. Úna wondered if his name was short for anything or just a trick.

He was also one of the lads who had been sent back to the borderlands last month to try to discover the details of Sol's death. When they had returned, their findings had been whispered to Úna's mam, who was then tasked with delivering the news. Úna had accompanied her to Mrs. P's, but had waited in a separate room, which meant she didn't see the look in the widow's eyes when she first pictured her husband's body hanging upside down from a hook. She only heard the howl through the wall—the throaty, animal sound—and the sobs that followed after as if she were coughing an entire lake up from her lungs.

On the walk home, Úna had dared to ask her mam. "I thought you said some answers would finally bring her peace?"

"I did . . . Oh love, I was so naïve." Her mam's face looked as pale and drawn as the olden days. "Instead Aoife says her grief has only doubled."

"Why?"

"Because now she has to mourn the loss of Sol's dignity as well."

Úna pictured a second wicker coffin being lowered slowly into the dirt.

They hadn't seen Mrs. P much since that awful day—her mam's new job left no free time for organising visits—so Úna was glad when the widow showed up at the house this afternoon. Then she saw the ache in the widow's eyes and she wasn't glad at all. She took the plastic bag from her and peeked inside. The shop-bought Victoria sponge was cracked down the middle, great jagged lines that would surely never heal.

By the time all seven men were in, the house felt crammed to bursting. Úna's mam had stuffed bunches of flowers everywhere. She didn't say if they were free or if Helen would dock them from her wages. Úna glanced out at the garden, which was scraggier than ever—her mam was just too busy these days to take proper care. Úna supposed a gardener was another thing she could do or be.

They served the lunch, then left the men to it and retired to the sitting room. Luckily, a new distraction had been put in place to diffuse the awkwardness. Úna's mam had purchased the television for her husband's birthday; had shown him how to plug it in and use the remote control. This time he had been the one to force a smile he clearly didn't feel.

So now they all focused on the screen where a man in a pinstripe suit had just appeared. Úna remembered the portrait from Civics class. "Eoin Goldsmith," she said. "That's him—that's the Bull." He was being led out of a car by a Garda while all around him lights flashed and cameras strobed. Sometimes the glare caught a glint of metal from the handcuffs that poked from underneath his sleeves.

"It is." When Mrs. P spoke, Úna realised they were the first words she had uttered since her arrival. "He's been arrested for all sorts—scamming contracts, dodging taxes. They also think it might have been him making and selling the MBM that caused the Irish cows to get sick. Thanks to him, a lot of men have lost their livelihoods."

When the camera panned out, Úna saw there were indeed a lot of men, only these ones weren't in suits; they were in fleece jackets and caps. They were penned in behind metal barriers, shouting their faces off and carrying homemade signs:

BSE BULL!

JUSTICE 4 FARMERS!

GOLDSMITH ONLY CARES 4 GOLD!

As Úna watched the chaos brewing, the photographers clambering over one another to get the best version of the very same shot, she thought about men losing their livelihoods and their dignity; about people losing their faith and their identity. She wondered if there was a special place these things went when they were lost and if they could ever be found again. She felt her stomach give another flutter. Maybe her butterflies had come crawling back after all.

"I need water." She had made it only as far as the door when she heard the two women gasp. She assumed it was something shocking on the tele—a man climbing over the barrier; a violent fist slamming into Goldsmith's chiselled jaw. But when she turned, the women had abandoned the TV to stare at the stain on the couch. Next they stared towards Úna's trousers, so she contorted her body until she could see the damp proof for herself.

She thought of the spill on her bedroom floor from her very first mouse.

She thought of a rusty hook piercing an old man's frail foot.

She thought of a red line trickling down Car McGrath's neck.

She ran up the stairs and straight into the bathroom where she sat on the toilet lid. She clutched her head in her hands so she didn't see her mother appear; didn't see anything except the floor and her trousers peeled gently away; the white contraption produced from her mam's bottom drawer.

She heard a surge of laughter—men's laughter—from the kitchen below. She knew she was definitely going to be sick.

"Love, can you hear me?" After a while, she heard her mother trying to talk to her, or at least, to this creature she had apparently become.

Her mother offered her a bath.

Her mother offered her the lake.

Her mother offered her an explanation she didn't recognise. "This is it, love, you are a woman now."

I'm Scary.

I'm Sporty.

I'm a woman now.

But just when Úna was about to scream, her mother placed eight fingers on her skin and offered two final things. The first sounded like this: "They forget we know more about death precisely because we can give life." This time, Úna didn't need to ask who she meant by "they." And then her mother offered the second thing—the one Úna liked the most; the one that made her stomach, just for a minute, settle down: "I tell you, love, we know more about blood than they ever will."

When she finally descended, the cushion had been flipped around. Mrs. P whispered "congratulations," the tiniest glimmer back in her eye. But then she stood up and said it was time to go and her eyes were agony once more. "They are sacred things." As she walked away, her voice croaked. "Our bodies, I mean. I just . . ." She shook her head. "I cannot understand how someone could possibly think otherwise."

Watching her shuffle into the hallway, her whole being cowered, Úna thought again of the small scissors, or better yet, the large serrated chopping knife. She vowed that if she ever discovered who had done those things to Sol—who had caused this gorgeous woman so much pain—she would hurt them every possible way she could.

The farmer was standing out on the front doorstep as if he had been waiting there all along. In his hand was a rope and on the end of the rope was a black-and-white cow. Úna noticed her udders were swollen as huge as a head. She noticed, when he spoke, the man's accent wasn't local. "I'm looking for the Butchers."

Her mam stepped forward and smiled the way Úna suspected she did for her customers. "Just a moment," she said, "I'll go and fetch my husband."

Hovering in the doorway, Úna noticed a smell, a faint must, though she couldn't decide whether it belonged to the heifer or to her.

When her father arrived, his cheeks were blotched pink from the heat and the wine and the bitter-sweetness of reunion. The farmer hadn't said another word. "I'm looking for the Butchers," he repeated. The cow exhaled loudly through her nose.

"Mr. Fitzgerald, isn't it?" Her father wiped his hand and held it out. "Lovely to see you, sir—it's been a while. But you mustn't have heard, we—the Butchers, I mean—I'm afraid we have been forced to . . . *retire*." Here he paused. The reality still hadn't got any easier to admit, no matter what words he used. "It was no longer safe. And what with the new legislation on animal tracing, it makes it impossible—"

"My wife is after giving birth."

If her father hesitated, it was only for a second. "Congratulations!" His smile matched his own wife's perfectly. "But we still can't help, I'm very sorry. There aren't even eight of—"

"I want my daughter to be a believer too."

Úna thought she saw her father's eyes flicker in her direction. Her mother had missed a patch of hair on the back of his neck. There was no sound except the heifer swishing her dressing-gown tail.

Soon enough, the silence bred more men—first Wyn, followed by Farley and Con—until the whole doorway was stuffed to the brink. Úna's mam led her and Mrs. P back through to the sitting room where the tele was showing the very same clip of the Bull being dragged in his handcuffs from a car. Or maybe, Úna wondered, the footage was actually live and he was just being made to re-walk that gauntlet endlessly—a fitting punishment set by a canny judge. Because that way the farmers could shout at him and spit their anger over and over; could make sure he never forgot all the heartache his greed had caused.

Úna assumed the scene was somewhere down in Dublin, which made her think again of her cousin. She promised she would finally reply to his letter tonight; would finally admit she used to know all about herself, but that she didn't any more. She would also admit she hadn't heard the myth about the Minotaur—could he explain it?—but that she did have a favourite myth of her own. It was called "The Curse of the Farmer's Widow," and even though it wasn't very famous, it was probably just as ancient as his. It was about a woman who lost her husband and seven sons in a war, so she placed a curse that said no man was allowed to slaughter cattle alone. Instead, seven others had to be there to preserve the memory of her grief, otherwise it would come back and poison the land. So for hundreds of years the people of Ireland heeded her words and made sure to follow the proper protocol when killing their beasts. Then a group of men travelled around to do the killing for them; to make it easier to keep the old ways alive. But eventually they gave up and, sure enough, the land turned diseased and all the animals started going mad. Then the people started going mad too—some tried to blame it on England; some tried to blame it on the animals' food. And some tried to escape to America, but America wouldn't let them in for fear the madness was infectious, so apart from the wealthy beef barons who managed to smuggle themselves out, they all began to die and soon the country turned rotten until eventually it wasn't even a country any more, just a shrivelled sod of earth that used to appear in some silly old stories. But even the stories became infectious, so people stopped telling them too, until no trace of the madness remained.

When she walked out to the hallway, the chattering fell quiet.

"I'll do it."

All the eyes were aimed in her direction. In the silence she could feel it—the same feeling that had come over her in the playground with Car McGrath. And she knew she finally had the answer to her cousin's request.

Tell me all about yourself . . .

My name is Úna and I am a Butcher.

"Úna, we've talked—"

"The myth only says no *man* can slaughter alone." She threw a half glance over her shoulder. "It doesn't say anything about women." She saw Mrs. P, whose husband had been mutilated and who would never be told why or by whom. She saw her mam who gave the tiniest nod.

They forget we know more about death precisely because we can give life.

Úna stepped past the bodies into the night. "Why don't you lads make Mr. Fitzgerald a cup of tea while he's waiting?" She took the rope from the farmer's hand. "We won't be long."

The cow looked at her and followed at once.

We know more about blood than they ever will.

CHAPTER SIXTEEN
Fionn

Dublin, December 1996

All around him, the reek of the place was a totally different reek to that of O'Connell's—more alkaline than acid, if he had to say, though it was no less unpleasant. Beneath him, the envelope was tucked snug in the right arse of his jeans. Fionn thought of a hen squatting warm on an egg.

He almost laughed, already gone on the farce of him being sat here on some wonky stool in some unfamiliar corner of some unfamiliar Dublin pub. On the walls and around the windows, there was a general smattering of festive tat. He noticed the decorations were more of the Santa than the saintly variety. He had also noticed the lack of television. He glanced from the clock to the door and back. He had nursed a pint of Coke and sucked the lemon to the rind. He still couldn't get over the price.

He was wearing a shirt even though he had packed only three to last him the entire trip. He had combed his hair, then got annoyed, scuffed it up, then combed it back again. On the table to his right, two lads were chatting about cricket or some other West Brit sport. Fionn had a hankering for a bag of crisps. He clinked his ice around his empty glass.

He checked the clock and the door, but still there was nothing—no sign and no saints and no television screen. Fionn sighed. There was no trace of his only son.

He could still remember his first ever trip to Dublin when he was twelve years of age. Ireland were playing the Spaniards in a World Cup qualifier and his daddy had managed to get some black market tickets off a tout. They had taken the train with Martin Fahey and his father; had packed ham sandwiches and a plastic bag of cans, which meant the older men were legless by the time Heuston Station stumbled into view, the two boys just as giddy; just as pink.

There had been hours to kill before kick-off, so they had set about strolling the capital's streets, Fionn's daddy spinning stories of the 1916 Rising as they went along. They visited the GPO with its bullet holes, Kilmainham Gaol where the rebellion leaders were executed. More than once, Fionn thought he spotted a tear in his daddy's eye. But later they had been turning on to the North Quays when they spotted the cattle penned in makeshift droves. Fionn had stopped, confused. There wasn't a blade of grass in sight. Apparently the Liverpool boat had broken down so now the herd wouldn't be loaded that day after all. Fionn's father had noticed his mouth agog and laughed his arse off. *Catch yourself on—you'd think you'd never seen livestock in your life!*

Of course, there would be none of that any more—the Dublin cattle mart shut down back in 1973. These days the capital felt further from muck and shite than ever. Fionn had forgotten it was the Faheys they were with that afternoon. He could remember him and Martin sharing a 99 ice cream;

could remember feeling relieved when Ireland won because it meant his daddy's temper wouldn't be so bad.

Davey had boarded a train of his own just two weeks after the funeral. Another week and he had phoned from his halls to say he had arrived in one piece. After that, the silence on the farm was so complete Fionn felt like the last man on earth—even the swallows had buggered off early this year. But then the lawyer had written regarding the Bull's investigation, so straight away Fionn had booked his ticket; had phoned Davey and told him to choose an evening and a pub. It gave him six weeks to get everything in order and put into action the plan he had already been deliberating. It had nearly killed him, but finally he and his envelope were here.

And yet, when he checked the time again it seemed everything might not be in order after all. The clock's face was wrapped in a tinsel headlock—deck the halls and the pubs and the timepieces. Fionn thought of the Millennium Clock and how the River Liffey kept wrecking the mechanics. The Council had finally decided to shut it down for good—two hundred and fifty grand down the toilet and all the way out to sea.

Speaking of toilets, Fionn needed a go—the Coke had found its way straight through. He decided if there was no sign by the time he got back, he would return to his hotel. But as soon as he stood, the door flew open and the draught it brought was an icy mare.

"Were you giving up on me just as easily as that?"

The hinges slammed shut and the draught was gone. Fionn felt the warmth spread straight through his chest. "I was just getting in another round."

Davey uncoiled his scarf from his neck. "A G and T. And a packet of nuts if you're feeling flush."

Fionn had to turn very quickly to hide his smile.

As he waited at the bar, he banished his bladder and forced himself not to be looking back—not to be checking where his son sat awaiting, not standing him up or letting him down. It was less than three months, but already Davey looked older. Finer. Though also, truthfully, a bit gaunter—he had always had cheekbones, but Jesus those were a vicious pair of yokes.

Fionn ordered the drinks from a lad in reindeer horns. A packet of nuts. "Actually, make it two." He had eaten earlier, but he was still famished after the day of interviews in windowless rooms. He watched the Coke spit brown from the tap and barely wished it was something stronger.

Still the envelope sat curved against his cheek.

He carried the pint glass in one hand and the tumbler in the other with the little bottle wedged between the fourth and baby finger, because two trips were for country eejits who couldn't manage or keep up with the pace. The nuts were in his left-hand pocket, one batch salted and one dry-roasted, because who ever knew the difference, really?

A radio started up with some tinny cheer. God rest ye merry gentlemen reunited from dismay.

Davey added the tonic to the glass, then swirled it all around with the little black stop-sign stick. Fionn set to the packets. The foil kept slipping through his hands, until eventually it popped and a few strays went flying. He blushed pink as a boy; felt the glances from the men to his right and wanted to tell them to shove their cricket bats up their arses.

"Good luck." Davey's glass was raised. Above his cheekbones, black circles traced beneath his eyes.

"Your good health." They nodded at one another, though their rims didn't actually clink. Fionn only felt like the second last man on earth.

Their chat began, not easy but not particularly tough either. "They've put me up in Jury's for the week." Fionn cocked his head to the left, though the hotel could have been any direction from here. "Mind you, they warned me yesterday it might be longer. On account of all the new charges that keep emerging." The Coke was flat. He hadn't been given a lemon this time. "The MBM production is the main one, obviously, but then there's tax evasion, bribes to vets. Modern Ireland—land of saints and scholars and agricultural scams!" Fionn's laughter startled the neighbours again, but this time he didn't mind. He wondered if they had ever seen a tractor before in their lives.

He was still struggling to get over the farce of some of the things he had heard about this week—splattering blood on counterfeit documents just to make them look real; using fake Islamic stamps to sell meat to the Pakis that wasn't Halal in the slightest. Fionn had answered a few questions about the border runs; about the use of false tags. He had answered more than a few questions about the role of Fergus Hynes. He had been cautious at first, but soon he realised how little energy he had left for the silence and the covering up—God knows, there had been enough of that in this country to last a lifetime. Plus, the lad doing the witness-interviews seemed a decent sort, even if he was from Dublin. He kept saying the word "tribunal" like it was meant to make an impression. He kept saying the Bull would be taken right the way down.

Fionn was wary, though—not of broken legs or of phone calls warning him to keep his gob shut—oh no, he was expecting those at the very least. What made him wary were alibis; convenient scapegoats that were already starting to emerge. Some said the Bull was claiming total ignorance. Others said he was leaning on his powerful friends. He had contacts in the Dáil who were pulling all the right strings.

Fionn went for his Coke. A splatter of fucking blood.

And Fionn had assumed the Butchers would have come up in conversation by now. The prosecutors had asked about the abandoned cold store; had mentioned a particular interest in the *irregular*. Then again, maybe the lack of mention was fitting since, according to the rumours, the group had broken up—the end of an era. Some said they had emigrated; some mentioned the Aran Islands. Fionn tried to picture it—the remaining seven stuck on the arse end of Inisheer, knitting Christmas *geansaí* out of boredom and the tail-ends of history. He remembered Sol saying he had a wife, so now Fionn imagined writing her a letter to say that he was grieving too. He remembered Sol saying he had no children, so now Fionn looked across the table at his son. Greedily, he opened the second packet of nuts. "And tell me, Davey, how're you getting on with the course?"

Davey brightened to the topic, reciting words like "essays" and "tutes"; fancy phrases like "intellectual rigour" and "philosophical enquiry." He said he had his first lot of exams right after Christmas, which meant he would probably just stay in halls over the break.

Fionn nodded; felt the pressure of the envelope. He didn't tell his son there would be nowhere else to go.

"It's not easy, though." Here Davey's brightness seemed to wane. He put down his glass, then found his hand redundant so placed it between his knees. "I'm finding it . . . It's a big leap from the Leaving Cert, you know?" He stared around the room towards the bar. The man behind it was staring back. He had acquired a red flashing reindeer nose.

Fionn nodded, though of course he didn't really know. Instead he found himself thinking, as he so often did, about the day of Davey's Leaving results. By the time Fionn had returned from the shops, the Fiesta was already gone. He knew straight away—realised she must have driven down to collect her son; to enact their old ritual one last time. The car was found mangled in a ditch a half-mile from the school. Fionn told Davey her seizure had happened at home. It wasn't easy, but Fionn was determined to spare the lad that. He knew guilt could sometimes be even more vicious than grief.

It took him until the next round to finally produce the envelope. He saw that he had written his son's full name across the front: *Davey McCready*. Even though the whole point was that the McCready bit didn't matter any more. Fionn had learned, at last, that taking care of family sometimes meant letting them go.

"What's this?" Davey returned from the bar with his gin and Fionn's final Coke. He would be awake all night with the pissing as much as anything.

Fionn waited for his son to sit, then reach across the table. The cheque looked so flimsy in his hands.

"I got rid of everything."

And though it might not have been clear, Davey seemed to understand straight away. "But that land belonged to your father. And to your grandfather before that. And—"

"I know."

Behind them now, the radio was playing "Fairytale of New York." Fionn half smiled. They've got rivers of gold, all right.

Davey wasn't finished. "What about the girls? Surely you didn't sell them as well?"

Fionn's chest rushed with joy hearing him use that word. It wasn't "herd" or "cattle"; it wasn't even "animals." He had taught him something at least.

But then the rush was over as Fionn thought of them; of what, in the end, he had done. He hung his head. The runaway nuts lay crushed by his feet, looking like little grains of meal.

It was years since he had been down to the National Ploughing Championships. This one was an even bigger affair than usual. There were flags everywhere: "IRISH BEEF IS BETTER BEEF." Any illegal feed had been destroyed. They said the industry might just be OK after all. But Fionn wasn't paying attention to any of that, was only searching for the black market scumbags he had heard about from the rumour mill. In the end, they gave him a decent deal; gave him a plastic box filled with a liquid grey and thick. Fionn had stashed it in his glove compartment and sped all the way home through the lashing rain. Modern Ireland—land of saints and scholars and agricultural scams.

He knew only one girl had to test positive for him to qualify for the government compensation scheme, but he also knew, somehow, that it had to be her. He suspected it was to do with sacrifice, or maybe it was just so that he could do the honours—otherwise it would be some stranger in some sterile slaughterhouse where all the infected animals were sent.

Fionn had tried his best not to breathe when he opened the plastic box, but even the trace he caught was diabolical. Glassy's eyes rolled back in her head as if she could see the stuff the needle was injecting—the pulp of plaques from other, weaker brains. Fionn hadn't cried at Eileen's funeral—had only stared at the Virgin Mary and the green-eyed woman who slipped in down the back. That night, he had curled up sobbing in the empty byre. By morning the roof had finally caved in.

"What will you do next?"

Here in the pub, his eyes were dry. He licked the salt from his fingertips. "Maybe a bit of travel. Your mother always talked about Los Angeles. You never know—I might send you a post-card of me sitting in the *O* of the Hollywood sign." He stopped. The pain of mentioning Eileen ran through his bones and locked his jaw.

But he saw Davey's mouth smiling: "Thank you, Fionn." So Fionn forced a reply: "It was the very least I could do."

•

Eventually, final orders came and went, and soon after that the bright lights faded up. Fionn considered making a joke about city folk having no stamina, but secretly he was more than a bit relieved.

Davey left for the loo and Fionn remembered his own burning desire, but there was no chance of a tandem trip. Instead he waited outside, buttoning the jacket he hadn't actually taken off—such a waste of a decent shirt. The yellow glow of the taxis blurred with the festive halogen. The cranes above had been decked with twinkles too. The poster on the bus stop was for a new Liam Neeson film called *Michael Collins*. It seemed even Hollywood wanted a piece of rebel history these days.

Fionn would stroll back to the hotel and make a cup of tea with a thimbleful of UHT milk. The lawyers wanted him in tomorrow at nine, although that just meant more sitting and waiting around—the Irish knack for inefficiency and the tribunal prep only getting under way. He was certain they would extend his stay; would rope him in for other lines of questioning. He tried to remember the face of the Protestant lad who had met them on the border. He wondered if Mossy and Briain were playing dumb. He wondered if he would have to go to Penneys for another shirt.

But in truth, it didn't matter how long it all dragged on—how many nights he spent on those synthetic pillows—how many times he scoffed those ginger biscuits that were always replenished by some invisible, benevolent hand. Because what did he have after this? What else would fill his days? Only an emptiness stretching blank like a darkness rolling over a border and far away until it meets the sea.

"Here you are."

Fionn turned to his son, who was holding a cigarette he had rolled himself.

"Will I walk—"

"I'm going—"

They both stopped. Neither of them went again. Instead they stood, their breaths mingling up to a sky that was a bit smoggier than back home, but even still there was no denying the stars.

"You know the way I always told you about Glas Ghaibhleann. Giving milk, like, to the multitudes? Well, there are other versions of the story too. I've been . . . They've been at me a bit this week."

Next to him, Davey didn't answer, but he didn't walk away either. By now, Fionn could more than settle for that.

"Obviously some greedy chancers wanted to take advantage of the cow's abundance. To harness her powers, like, and turn a profit. Up in Donegal a group of lads decided to pen the poor thing in. But she soon got restless and levitated herself into the air and eventually disappeared into the sky. And since then they say there has never been any free milk on the island of Ireland."

Behind them now there was a bang, which made them both jump. The barman bolted the door. He had shed his horns and his nose. He looked from one man to the other, then gave Davey a wink. "Hope I'll see you in here again soon." Fionn willed his son to wink back.

"But they also say you can still see her milk spread out across the sky. That's why the Irish for Milky Way is *Bealach Bó Fionne*." Fionn paused before he translated. "The Way of the White Cow."

"She loved you very much."

293

Fionn tried not to jump again. "She loved you too." Then he laughed. "We had that in common at least."

"We did."

And as he watched his son walk away for the very last time, Fionn tried to spot some other shared trait; some feature or genetic link that had been passed down. When he found nothing, he closed his eyes and smiled, already tasting tomorrow's fry. There would be rashers and sausages and crispy hash browns. He would make sure to ask for extra pudding. He had always preferred the black to the white, even though he knew that it was bad; even though he knew it was mostly to do with blood.

EPILOGUE

New York, January 2018

"Drink?" He is reaching for the cabinet even before he has asked the question because he knows his own answer anyway. He places the Jameson on the counter while she finally removes her duvet coat. He hadn't noticed her boots before. She keeps them on.

She barely stopped talking all afternoon, yet in the cab she was oddly quiet. Even when the driver tried to ask about her visit, she only mumbled something about a cousin living with his partner upstate, journalists both. Ronan realises he hasn't actually asked what it is she does for a living. He kicks the roll of bubble wrap out of his way and moves towards the elevator-sized fridge. The dispenser summons ice all the way up from its toes.

She takes the whiskey from him without a word of thanks, too busy staring out the industrial windows. The giant grid splices the sleetscape into a series of images like a black-and-white contact sheet. He downs his glass, then refills it. "OK," he concedes. "OK, it's through here."

Inside his makeshift darkroom, he clicks the safelight on. The low buzz kicks in straight away, the colour a dim and headachy red. He plugs in the timer and the enlarger while she hovers by the door. She still hasn't said a word. On the line

295

hang a couple of prints he took recently as part of a commission for the National Portrait Collection. The first is Senator Mitchell, the American lad who helped negotiate the Good Friday Agreement. This year will be two decades of Northern Irish peace. His overbite is a slice of peroxide white.

Ronan mixes his developer, his stop bath, his fixer. He doesn't usually allow himself to drink in here, but tonight is quite the exception.

The second photo on the line is of Eoin Goldsmith—or "the Bull," as he is still sometimes known. It was taken shortly after the award ceremony in Dublin for the Freedom of the City. Ronan had never seen a standing ovation that lasted so long or sounded so loud. He has never seen so much coldness in one face.

He puts down his glass and rifles through the drawer, digging deep for the negative strip. He knows he has buried it in the very darkest corner.

In his speech, the mayor praised Goldsmith's integral role in the formation of "Modern Ireland." He quoted some figures to illustrate Goldsmith's ongoing contribution to the nation's economy. He didn't mention the three-year tribunal nor the controversy when the judge somehow let the charges drop.

When Ronan finally finds it, he cleans it and loads, twisting to get the focus right. He removes the paper, but before he puts it in the developer he takes one last look at her. He could still stop; could still tell her she has it wrong and he doesn't have a clue what she is talking about.

He could pop a few pills and make the whole thing go away.

But something is propelling him forward—the prospect of finally sharing the secret that has festered all these years. He places the paper in the tray. There is science here and there is magic, every time. He rocks it back and forth like a baby in a cradle saying *hush hush* and *lullaby*, while she begins to crane her neck, curious as if there were indeed some infant splashing in the puddle below.

In the darkness, there is only the sound of his thudding heart. There is only a second left to turn back.

When Sol arrives, Ronan removes his hand from the developing tray, though still the liquid laps back and forth; still Úna cranes and still Goldsmith's portrait watches down from on high. Ronan wonders if, from up there, the Bull can recognise his premises in the photograph. Ronan wonders how much about the incident he ever really knew.

The angle of the fall looks awkward in the picture, but there is no trace of blood or even bruise. Sol's heart must have failed slowly enough for him to lower himself very carefully to the cold-store step. The eyes are not cold, they are just wide; the eyes of a man who saw through death all his life. The boots on his feet are sturdy and in desperate need of a polish.

The laces were a nightmare to get off; three knots each for two manic hands.

"I stumbled across him just after dawn." Between the closeness of the four walls, Ronan's voice comes out far too loud. Some photographers listen to music in the darkroom. He has always been superstitious about silence. "I hadn't slept—I was so wired after the fight in O'Connell's, so I took something to calm me down. And then something else to bring me back up." The details are coming through, rising out of the liquid. The wisp of a grey eyebrow. The sag of a tired and doughy jaw. Ronan wants to reach in and rinse the picture off, but of course by now he cannot possibly move. "I was in a pretty fucked-up place back then. The project wasn't working—I still hadn't found my stand-out image. I photographed him like this, but I knew I could do so much better. Then I had an idea." He inhales, ready to say the same lines he has been saying for over two decades. He wonders how sick of them the darkness must be. "He was already dead. I didn't . . . I checked his pulse, but he was definitely already dead." He looks at her to make sure she believes. She only has eyes for the photograph. "I dragged him inside and lowered the ropes. It wasn't easy. It wasn't personal. It was just . . ." The last words are as pathetic as they are crucial. "It was just art."

When he is finally finished, he takes a step back and instantly she fills the space. She bends over the tray to get the best view. The hum of the light turns her shoulders scarlet. While he waits for her to speak, Ronan looks again at the picture of Goldsmith; thinks of the tribunal that decided he had done nothing wrong—no MBM production, no tax fraud, no elaborate scams. Ronan has never realised it before, but the pair of them have something in common—two men carrying around a lifetime of sin.

After another minute, she still hasn't spoken; hasn't even acknowledged his confession. So he decides to try one final thing. He really does have nothing left to lose. "I've never shown the picture before—not to anyone. I figured that way they couldn't figure out what I had done. But tell me, Úna, how did you know?"

At last she stands up straight and rolls her red shoulders back. Her hair is still tied in a ponytail. Her voice is not too loud; it is perfect. "My mother once told me that women know more about blood than men ever will."

He nods, though he doesn't have a clue what she means. Instead he waits, knowing there will be more, but when she moves again it is back out the door into the living room where the spotlights seem staggering by comparison.

"Where are you going?" He sees her reach for her coat on the back of the couch. "You have to stay," he blurts. "We have . . . There is so much to discuss." He can hear the desperation creeping in, but by now he cannot help it. "Please—another drink? Tell me about yourself. You never said what it is you do for a living?" It is a stupid question—as if they are back to small talk instead of the biggest talk of his life. Or at least, it would be the biggest if she would only engage; would only acknowledge the burden he has just unloaded.

"For a living?" And yet, strangely, this is the thing that stops her. "The same as you," she says.

He doesn't know if the fact makes any more or less sense. "You're a photographer?"

She laughs. "No, I mean I also do the thing I always wanted to do. I also managed to prove my parents wrong."

As he swallows the information he wonders how on earth he could have been so stupid not to suspect it from the start. "I thought the Butchers disbanded back in '96?"

"They did." She starts to approach. Her steps are heavy from the weight of her boots. "But I didn't. You see . . ." Her eyes meet his. They are greener than ever. "It was personal."

Only when she is close, very close, does he notice she still isn't wearing her coat. Instead she is holding something she must have just fished from its pocket. He watches as she turns it, very slowly; then she does it again, a little quicker; and then a third time in the direction of her heart.

By dawn the worst of the snow has melted and the world is dripping again. The sun over the Hudson glows a clear and pallid green. A heron stands poised, patiently, then spears through the surface in a single flash, the scales of her prey catching the light like a newly minted coin.

ACKNOWLEDGMENTS

Thanks first and foremost to Tipperary's finest storyteller, Donal Comerford, who sparked the beginnings of *The Butchers' Blessing* during a bank holiday road trip many years ago; to Anthony Good and Daniel Bennett for early feedback, and the wonderful Margaret Stead for delicious lunches and so much more. Thanks to Grace O'Connell for medical chats, John Connell for cow chats, Garett Carr for border chats, Gerry Blake for photography chats, Sinéad Brady and family for farm chats and visits; to the many researchers whose works I consulted, especially Maxime Schwartz, Christopher Booker and Fintan O'Toole.

Thanks to my agent, Sophie Lambert, for being so incredibly warm and determined; to James Roxburgh and Masie Cochran for the insanely intelligent edits; to Karen and the gang at Atlantic, and Molly and the gang at Tin House. Thanks to Luke Kennard and my wonderful colleagues at the University of Birmingham; to everyone at MacDowell and the Tyrone Guthrie Centre at Annaghmakerrig for weeks of inspirational solitude and glutinous cookery.

Thanks to my brother, David, for always providing the soundtrack; to my parents for getting even better with age; thanks to the Lovets for keeping me sane and, of course, to Debbie for keeping me close even though we are far apart.

Final thanks to Alex for key Euro '96 advice—I cannot imagine what this book, or my life, would be without your spectacular football knowledge or your spectacular soul.